"Broaddus delivers in a voice that both whispers and roars and cannot be ignored."

Bram Stoker & International Horror Guild Award-winner Gary A. Braunbeck

"A wild, imaginative journey grounded in a gritty reality so compelling that you'll swear these characters must live in your own city. Put this on your must-read list!"

Brandon Massey, award-winning author of Cornered

"Deft characterization, authentic dialogue, exciting plot. Add a highly original premise: the Arthurian Legend magically springing up in the 'hood, including the return of the King, Merlin, the Knights of the Round Table, and even a dab of chivalry. Maurice Broaddus has definitely brought his A-game to this urban joust."

Gene O'Neill

"Maurice Broaddus' writing creates a dangerous and authentic mood. The language is fierce and evokes the gritty realism of life on the streets. When the supernatural elements are introduced, they drift through the novel like smoke, leaving the reader gradually horrified as the end game is reached..."

Fantasyliterature.com

D0273189

ALSO BY MAURICE BROADDUS

The Knights of Breton Court Series
King Maker
King's Justice

Orgy of Souls
(novella, with Wrath James White)
Devil's Marionette
(novella)
Dark Faith
(editor)

MAURICE BROADDUS

King's War

THE KNIGHTS OF BRETON COURT
VOL. III

ANGRY
ROBOT

ANGRY ROBOT

A member of the Osprey Group
Midland House, West Way
Botley, Oxford
OX2 0HP
UK

www.angryrobotbooks.com
Dragonfall

An Angry Robot paperback original 2011
1

A catalogue record for this book is available
from the British Library.

ISBN: 978-0-85766-129-6
EBook ISBN: 978-0-85766-131-9

Set in Meridien by Argh! Nottingham.

Printed and bound by CPI Group (UK) Ltd, Croydon, CR0 4YY

For Mom

"Fairy tales do not tell children that dragons exist. Children already know that dragons exist. Fairy tales tell children that dragons can be killed."

G K CHESTERTON

THE PLAYERS

The Crews

Breton Crew Folks (Traize)

Lonzo "Black" Perez

Benito Torres

La Payasa

Phoenix Apartment People

Dred

Garlan

Bo "The Boars" Little

Naptown Red

Broyn DeForest

Mulysa (Rondell Cheldric)

Nine

The Clients

Preston "Prez"
Wilcox

Fathead

Isabel "Iz" Cornwall

The Police

Capt. Octavia
Burke

Det. Lee McCarrell

Det. Cantrell Williams

The Rogues

Omarosa

Baylon

Rhianna Perkins

The Knights

King James White

Lott Carey

Wayne Orkney

Merle

Lady G (Vere)

Tristan Drust

Percy

PROLOGUE
The Glein/River Incident

All stories ended in death.

Lost in the white noise of the engine, that was the first thing that popped into King James White's mind as he idled down 16th Street. Sitting tall and straight in the car seat, he shifted uncomfortably, visibly muscled, but not with the dieseled appearance of prison weight. A head full of regal twists fit for a crown, he had the complexion of burnt cocoa, and a fresh crop of razor bumps ran along his neck. The thin trace of a goatee framed his mouth. He scanned the streets with a heavy gaze, both decisive and sure. He hated driving and doing so put him in a foul mood. Not a gearhead by any measure, he neither had oil in his blood nor an overwhelming need to be under a hood. For that matter, he didn't have any love for huge rides, trues and vogues, ostentatious rims, booming systems, or any of the other nonsense which seemed to accompany a love of cars. A ride was just a ride. He much preferred walking, to have the earth solidly under his feet.

His ace, Lott, who rode silently beside him, simply believed him to be cheap, not wanting to pay the nearly $3 per gallon unless he absolutely had to. Lott always seemed a week past getting his low-cut fade tightened up. His large brown eyes took in the passing scenery. His FedEx uniform – a thick sweatshirt over blue slacks; his name badge, "Lott Carey" with a picture featuring his grill-revealing smile, wrapped around his arm – girded him like a suit of armor. Lott drummed casually to himself, caught up in the melodies in his head.

Scrunching down in his seat again to check the skyline – as if maybe the creature might fly by in the open skyline by day – King turned at the sound of a beat being pounded out on the dashboard.

"What?" Lott paused mid-stroke under the weight of King's eyes on him.

"What you doing?"

"Nothing." Lott grinned his sheepish "been caught" smile, both beguiling and devilish. A row of faux gold caps grilled his teeth.

"We supposed to be looking for this thing."

"We don't even know what this *thing* is."

"What kind of man would I be if I ignored that?" King asked.

"A man. An ordinary man." Lott began drumming again. "Ain't nothing wrong with that."

For days King had trailed a beast strictly on the say-so of a mother's plea. Not even a year ago, he'd have dismissed the tale as another barber shop story told to pass the time, little more than a campfire story in the hood. The only monsters who prowled about in the dark were strictly of the two-legged variety. That was before he found himself caught up in a new story. One filled with magic, trolls, elementals, and dragons. The shadow world, an invisible world, once seen couldn't be unseen. Now the world of demons and creatures was far too real. All he knew, all he had sworn, was that nothing would prey upon the weak and defenseless in his neighborhood.

Descriptions of the creature changed with the teller of the tale. Sometimes it had wings. Sometimes the body of a lion. Sometimes it had the body of a snake. Sometimes claws. King feared he might be dealing with more than one creature, which was equally as bad an alternative to facing one creature with all of those characteristics. Even in a concrete jungle, life belonged to the swift, the strong, the smartest. King stalked among it, the latest generation of street princes. And heavy was the head that wore the crown.

"We heading over to Glein?" Lott asked in his lazy drawl, obviously pleased with himself. He loved accompanying King on his little missions.

"That where the Harding Street bridge folk ended up?"

"As long as the problem is swept under someone else's rug, the mess is considered clean."

"I think so. Been hearing reports about it. Been wanting to check out this 'tent city'." For his part, King was energized by Lott. It was like there was nothing he couldn't accomplish with Lott by his side. The pressure piled on King more these days. Everyone seemed to turn to him for answers. To solve their problems. The streets were becoming his even more so than they were his father's, except he hated the sheer… responsibility of it all.

Lott rolled with it all. The FedEx gig was working out.

The company would be promoting him soon and he'd
get a better shift. His story, too, had changed much in
only a few months. Gone were the days of living in an
abandoned house. He had a job with a future. And, for
the first time he could remember, he had a friend who'd
walk through fire for him, one for whom he'd do the
same. Lott wasn't one to swear oaths of allegiance to
anyone, but once he called someone friend, he was loyal
to the end. And King was his boy.

King wasn't the type to make friends easily. Investing in
people wasn't worth the effort: in the end, they all abandoned him. A melancholy cloud had settled on King over
the last few months, but it wasn't anything either felt the
need to talk about. Not every little feeling had to be talked
through. Sometimes it was better to just let folks be.

They continued west on 16th Street passing Martin
Luther King Jr Boulevard, Methodist Hospital, and the
Indiana State Forensics Laboratory. On Aqueduct Street,
they pulled into a gravel lot. Signs pointed toward the
Water Company, but they were more interested in the
park across the street. Calm and resolute, King stood motionless, taking in the tranquility. His tall and regal
bearing was swathed in a trenchcoat, matching his black
jeans and black Chuck Taylors. The wind caught his open
coat ever so slightly, the brief flutter the only movement,
revealing the portrait of Medgar Evers on his T-shirt. And
the butt of his Caliburn tucked into his waist. He never
looked more lonely.

Only a few nights ago, they had cleared a corner. It was
one of those little runs King didn't tell Wayne Orkney –

the other member of their triumvirate, who was also on staff at a homeless teen ministry called Outreach Inc – nor his mentor, Pastor Ecktor Winburn, about. The grumbles of their disapproval of his off-the-book runs would echo in his ears for weeks.

But Lott would be all in.

For all of his bravado and certainty whenever he went about his business, King needed someone to watch his back. To Lott, he wasn't Robin to King's Batman, but rather Batman to King's Superman. He rather reveled in that image.

Dred, though east side, hadn't been heard from; Night, once king of the west side, had been dropped by King (so the story went). The Eagle Terrace apartments bordered but were a respectful distance from Breton Court, King's undisputed dominion. A couple of non-descript fools, in baggy T-shirts and baggier pants who couldn't have been more than fourteen years old, not even a hard fourteen. Lott could practically smell their mother's milk on their breath. The first one leaned toward tall, a little bulk about the shoulders but with thin legs, like a basketball player growing into his body. A threat from the waist up, it was a dead giveaway that he'd found a set of weights and concentrated on his arms and never worked his legs. The other was short, stocky, with brown eyes too big for his head. Too quick to show his teeth, he cracked endless jokes about doing the other's girls heedless of the fact that he was on the clock. And then two brothers who meant business stepped to them from the shadows.

"You gonna have to move on," King said with no play in his voice.

"This is our spot. Who gonna move us?" the tall one said. His head had been filled with how good he was, the tone of entitlement in his voice.

"I am."

"I know you?"

"Name's King. Don't make me tell you again."

He'd said it and he meant it. King wasn't much older than either of them, but he had the hard and tested body of a man. As it was, it wasn't a fair fight. Lott hung back, mostly to enjoy the show and guard for the unexpected. But these two boys? King had this.

The lanky one turned as if to walk away, but King read the positioning of his feet and the shifting of his weight to know that the fool planned to swing on him. When the boy pivoted to throw his punch in "surprise", King jabbed him in the kidneys, grabbed him by the throat, and slammed him onto the hood of a parked car. King had a way of blazing in and dropping fools before they knew what hit them.

A grin had broken and froze on the face of the other boy. He reached under his shirt tail. King drew his Caliburn and trained it on the boy. Whenever he pulled out the Caliburn, folks knew what was up.

"You got something you want to show me?"

"No." The boy slowly dropped his hand to his side.

"Good, cause I'm only saying this once. This here was a friendly warning. Our neighborhood is tired of this mess. So why don't you give it a rest. We cool?"

"We cool."

Lott reached into the boy's waistband and removed the Colt. He emptied it of its bullets and tossed the weapon into the bushes. "I didn't want any surprises should he scrape together some courage with our backs turned."

King and Lott walked down the alley of the apartments nodding but not smiling to the folks they recognized. The respect left Lott so swoll, more so than any workout; respect born out of the work, of doing right by the neighborhood.

"You a good man."

King trained himself to keep full rein on his emotions. Prided himself on his ability to compartmentalize, remain objective, and disciplined. Some mistook it for aloof or indifferent, as if he didn't care, but Lott knew he cared too much.

With the Caliburn tucked into his dip, King adjusted his stride. He rolled his shoulders slightly, like a boxer entering a ring. Though the gun fit in his hand with a natural ease, as if he was always meant to wield it, he was still getting used to it.

"You need that?" King asked as Lott retrieved a bat from the back seat.

"Ain't all of us got weapons tucked in their shorts."

"Don't be jealous. It's not the size."

"When that thing busts a cap all premature, don't come limping to me."

A hill rolled down from the street leading into an impenetrable tract of trees, a scenic backdrop to the park. Lott tugged at his shirt front as if preparing to get into character. With an exaggerated bounce to his steps, he strutted for an unseen audience. But he had his game face on, a mask of unflinching stone etched into flesh. In his cool stare was a flicker of warning and a hint of hostility. He may have despised battle, but he never ran from one. And too often he sought them out with the determination of a man trying to get into the drawers of a woman he knew was no good for him. Resigned to his old way of thinking – the only way he knew – a lifestyle that ended in being locked up or in an early grave.

Despite his carefully contrived appearance, there was no way to ease down the hill and maintain any sense of street cool. They could take only a few awkward steps at a time, down the steep incline, as rocks littered the grass and made it difficult to maintain their balance and sure-footing. Down, down, down they went and it was as if they left one world and entered another. It didn't take long for the sounds of traffic overhead to fade against the steady thrum of the rushing White River. The currents roiled; the water climbed high up its banks due to the melted snow and recent heavy rains. The greenish water appeared brackish with up tilled silt, not that the White River was the healthiest of waterways to begin with.

Scattered among the thin brown weeds passed for grass was rebar and smashed concrete. A red and white umbrella canted against a tree. A bed of large white stones formed a channel leading from a pipe to the river. The bridge loomed above them, dwarfing them. It never seemed this large whenever they drove over it. The slate gray arches gleamed, only a few years old since the city remembered this side of town. The arches created an echo chamber as the water rushed under it.

"Some nice work." Lott nodded toward the groups of

tags along the base of the bridge. The spray-painted figure of a life-sized, 1950s-era wind-up robot with the head of a kangaroo. Two sets of names in so stylized a script, the letters were indistinguishable. The final figure was of a Latino boy with his cap turned to one side with an expression reminiscent of Edvard Munch's "The Scream".

"Too bad you can't tell what they're saying." King squatted in front of the formation of rocks on the opposite side. Half-rotted textbooks, newspapers, and Mountain Dew bottles littered the ground in between. Sweatshirts, pants, the occasional blanket, coats, and towels piled between two rows of stacked rocks. Another circle of stones, all charred, had a grill top resting on them.

"Odd place to lay out your stuff," Lott said.

"It's a mattress."

Lott stared at the arrangement again and pointed to the blackened rocks. "Yeah, I see it now. That's his stove. We in someone's squat."

"Someone not a part of tent city."

"Means we on the right track."

"You ought to wipe your feet before entering a man's abode. It's just plain rude."

At the sound of the voice, King and Lott turned. Merle's slate-gray eyes peered at them. His craggy auburn beard matched what wisps remained around his huge bald spot. Aluminum foil formed a chrome cap, which didn't quite fit atop his head. A black raincoat draped about him like a cloak.

"You stay here?" Lott asked.

"It's one place I stay, wayward knight, though not my secret place. You don't think I only spend my time with you lot. Sir Rupert craves the outdoors." A washcloth popped up, causing King to jump back. A squirrel peered left and then right, then dashed from beneath the cloth and scampered past his legs.

Lott could never shake the feeling that Merle never quite trusted him, like they shared a best-forgotten secret only the crazy old man knew. He would chide himself for caring what the bum thought of him, though part of him feared it might be jealousy as Merle seemed to have King's ear in a way he didn't.

"Don't mean to bust your roll or nothing," King said, "but we on a mission."

"Oh? A quest? Is it that time already? Mayhaps we'll encounter a questing beast." Merle danced in a circle around King, hands spreading from his face in jazz hands wiggles as he cried out. "'A star appearing in the sky, its head like a dragon from whose mouth two beams came at an angle.' An egg-shaped keystone, mayhaps a tower. A keystone illumination on the winter solstice. A sacred geometry. A date carved in stone. No wait, a stone unearthed from under a poplar tree, archaic names scribed into it along with strange symbols. A silver chalice, the Chalice of Antioch."

With that, Merle curtsied.

"You done?" King asked.

"It is finished," Merle said.

"Come on, we're checking in on Glein."

"So shut up and stay down," Lott said.

"Aren't you people supposed to be sassy?" Merle said.

"Wayne would say something sassy."

They tromped through the woods. The smell of car exhaust from overhead gave way to the trill of budding flowers and furtive spring. Merle occasionally muttered about the state of his shoes or the ubiquity of mud in the tract of land. Undistracted, King charged forward. Glein, the tent city, was the name of this ad hoc ministry. Rumors spread about how a church sponsored the site. They collected men from their various squats and put them up here. The men had their own assortment of stories. Vets, businessmen, and Ph.Ds alike among their number. Some found themselves without homes after the housing market crashed, or after layoffs. Some had simply dropped out of society, not wishing to live by anyone else's rules. Some were simply sick. The church had a regimen for the men and if they worked it, they were moved to some apartments the church owned. The whole setup had an odd vibe to it. Wayne said that Outreach Inc, was investigating, but if the site dealt strictly with older men – most of whom had already checked out of society – it was out of their purview.

"I feel like I've been here before," King said.

"Déjà vu is the word," Merle said. "God's way of telling you that you're exactly where you're supposed to be."

"So I'm right in line with my own destiny."

They wound along the river's edge. Branches snapped underfoot and leaves crunched as their inexperience as woodsmen betrayed them. The scent of campfire swept through the trees. Still early spring, the blues and yellows of the tents popped against the bleak landscape, easily spotted against the brown background of bare trees and dead leaves. Easily spotted once one chose to look for them.

A lone figure leaned against a thin tree, using a long wooden spoon to stir within a large metal saucepan. A University of Miami jacket, blue jeans, socks pulled up over the cuff. A thick beard, gray-streaked hair. A thick skim of gray to his face, as if caked in ash. A black bag slung over his shoulder. A foot shorter than King, but he barely glanced up at their approach.

"Who that is?" the man asked.

"King."

"You say that like it's supposed to mean something."

He had. It did. It meant the weight of responsibility. It meant the consciousness of leadership. It meant the burden of his people. "I'm here to help."

"Anyone ask for your help?" the man asked.

"Methinks, young liege," Merle said, "that perhaps this situation bears further investigation."

"What? You rule these here parts… King? You got a crown tucked away in that mess of hair of yours? Maybe you just got a cape under that jacket or something."

"There are things out here." The heft of the Caliburn became acute in King's waistband.

"And what you gonna do?" The man took a bite of his macaroni and cheese. His face upturned and, with a shrug, took a heaping spoonful. Bits of food flew from his mouth as he spoke. "You ain't nothing but a punk with a gun. We know what's out here. And we got our own protection."

King didn't notice any movement, but he sensed something was amiss. It was as if now that his eyes had been opened to the story he found himself in, he could

see it all around him. His eyes widened as he caught sight
of the shadow. Perched on a thick limb, hidden in gloom
among the tangle of branches, the creature's granite gaze
narrowed to grim slits studying King. Now that King
spotted it, he recognized the silhouette of such beasts
from atop cathedrals and lining many buildings downtown. A gargoyle. Industrial magic come to life.
Obviously the great beast which haunted his streets. A
supreme grotesquerie, a disturbing ornamentation to the
camp. Its concrete body transmogrified to flesh, stone to
color – gray, like shark hide – newly awakened; cracks
and dents gave way to barely healed wounds. Scars.

Knees bent, ready to flex, its corded muscles tensed
with the patience to squat immobile for decades. Nails,
which could drive into a skull with the ease of digging
into overripe cantaloupe, gripped and re-gripped the
branch. Lids over lizard eyes, the beast frowned, a fool
grimace of slobber and bared fangs, leering down at
them. In its eyes, King saw brooding nightmares invested
with the lusts, hatreds, and angers of its creators.

King pulled out the Caliburn with the ease of reflex.
As he assumed a battle posture, Lott fell to his flank,
preparing to guard it as well as stand by his friend. Another reflex. The creature became a mass of snarling lips,
murderous eyes, claws, gothic wings, and clenching
talons. King fired a shot, hitting it center mass.

"No!" the man and Merle screamed in unison.

Their piercing cry shattered King from his battle fervor.
The gargoyle spread its bat-like wings, fibrous and leath-
ery, flapping them to stir the camp. The creature
skimmed skyward.

Lott ducked as the gargoyle dove in and swooped low, barely dodging as its talons grasped at empty air. Wind whooshed as it passed him. Off balance, he didn't have a chance to reposition himself and swing his bat. The beast, however, grabbed its intended target.

Talons dug into King's shoulder, tearing deeply before it flung him into a tree. Mid-swoon, the world spinning. The beast was a series of half-caught images. Yellow orbs. Huge teeth gleaming. Gaping jaw. The creature towered over him, swaddled in shadows, feral eyes gleaming down at him. Atonal chittering gave way to a blast of the beast's fetid breath. Sick with pain, King raised the Caliburn again and took aim.

"King, stop," Merle cried out. "You are the intruder here."

"But it attacked us." King paused, half-turning toward Merle but not wanting to take his eyes from the beast.

"Only after you so carelessly brandished your Caliburn. Were all those years with Pastor Ecktor wasted? Didn't he teach you how to think? You can't fight every battle with guns. Jesus didn't arm his disciples and start taking out Roman soldiers."

"I'm not Jesus."

"Believe me, I know. You would've early on called out Judas as 'a trick ass bitch' or some such." Merle reached for the pointed snout of the gargoyle, holding his hand out as if letting it catch his scent. Blood trailed down the beast's bulbous belly. "Oh dear, the wound is serious. It will take much to heal it."

King searched the beast's eyes again. Truly seeing it this time for what it was, he saw the soul in its eyes, the passion of devotion, awakened to yet another new age from its long sleep. Gentle. Protective. In a lot of ways, it reminded him of Percy, the young boy who so often followed them around. Large, awkward, yet ferocious when those he cared about were threatened. Only then did it occur to him that he might as well hunt a unicorn.

"Thanks for looking out for us, O King. We are much safer without our protector in play," the man said.

"I didn't know."

"You don't know much." The man stroked the back of the gargoyle with the affection of a boy and his dog.

Merle sidled alongside King. "It's okay, King. We are all ignorant about something or another at one time or another. The question is, are you willing to learn?"

"And you know things?" King asked without sarcasm.

"I know your real name. I know your father. I know the magic. I know your call."

"Anything else?"

"I know your glorious doom." Merle turned from him.

"And you'll stand by me through all of it?"

"I will be by your side until I'm not."

There is no guarantee with friendships, Lott thought to himself. It was easy to make promises. The true test was if the person would be around when times got tough. Friendships were forged in fire.

Looking back, they would consider this to be the good days.

CHAPTER ONE

It was a long and lawless time after Luther's death and before King first calmed the streets. Many feared it was only a matter of time before the eye passed and the storm raged again. For a time, things had settled down. King and his crew locked things down. Folks began to call this time King's justice, the young prince having come into his own. All felt it. And it was as if the neighborhood was tied to him. The community had been wounded. Rage and suspicion marked the injury. Everyone knew the treachery, cut to the quick by betrayal, a bloated pustule on their soul waiting to be lanced.

Lyonessa Maurila Ramona Perez clutched a blonde doll clad in a pink dress to her chest. Her grandmomma had attempted to buy her any of a number of darker-skinned dolls but Lyonessa would have none of it. She fussed with the doll's hair, never quite satisfied with the lilt of its curls, and dreamed of doing something with her own long, boring black hair one day. She held her doll up for her momma to kiss, which she did after gently chiding her daughter that she was getting too old for such games.

The Los Compadres Food Mart smelled of earth, a vegetable musk thick with the cloying scent of spices. Trailing her through the aisles of the store, Lyonessa loved going grocery shopping with her grandmomma. She didn't even mind the dull, fluorescent light which cast everything in its pallid glare. She tugged at her ill-fitting soccer shorts, hating the way they hung on her and gave her the figure of a boy. A smile curled on her lips at the memory of the note from a boy in her class. She lifted up the back of her doll's dress to check on the folded piece of paper tucked in there.

Dear Lyonessa,
  Will you date me? You are very cute. I like how you wear your hair. I love you. Do you like to play with me. Do you love me?
  Reese

Scrawled on a piece of paper that had red hearts along its border, she had the note memorized. Reese had given it to her at recess. Lyonessa suspected that he might've tried to kiss her if the teachers weren't hovering nearby. She blushed at their all-too-audible "aw"s and didn't give him an immediate reply. She smiled – a wistful, unsure thing – and folded the note. Reese left, grinning ear-to-ear.

Such was the tumultuous love life of a seven year-old.

Not that she could share any of this with Grand-momma. If she had, she'd have received an earful about being too young. And he was Anglo. Her brother, Lonzo, was just crazy enough to go up to the school and threaten Reese.

"Can we go now?" she said in her native tongue.

"One minute, baby."

"We're going to be late." She brushed her hair behind her ear at the thought of Reese. Though she hated soccer practice, it kept her out of the house. Away from bodies pressed in so tightly together that she had to step over three to go to the bathroom at night. On the field, she could run free. It felt like flying.

Garlan played with his ring. Like a wedding band he never got used to, he was always aware of it. It fit snugly on his fingers most days, but sometimes it had enough give to it to allow him to slip it over his knuckle. And back again. Over his knuckle. And back again. With the ring came responsibilities, duties, and obligations. With the ring came times where he had to do things he wasn't quite down with.

The teal-colored PT Cruiser with black-tinted windows circled the lot, a slow-cruising shark lured by the chum of innocents. The speakers of the truck boomed from half a block away. Its forty-inch rims, like the vehicle itself, paid for in cash, knowing the attention such a purchase would bring. Sometimes Garlan wanted to be seen.

The Van Dyke he sported accentuated his sharp, angular face and the triangle shape of his face. Small twists crowned his head, marking the beginnings of a thick mop of braids on top. The color of cooked honey, his eyes contained a practiced hardness. He wasn't a dumb man.

At the ripe old age of seventeen, he'd accumulated quite
the resume. A bid in juvey for grand theft. Several assault
charges. Possession with intent (plea-bargained down).
He was good with his hands – the fresh scars over the
knuckles of his right hand attested to that – but he got
by on his wits. Knowing when the risk was too high.
Knowing when to cut his losses. Knowing when to pay
attention to his gut.

His gut screamed now.

A thick plume of endo smoke filled the cabin of his
truck. Garlan wished that Dred had sent Mulysa on this
little mission as this was certainly more up his crazy-ass
alley. No, instead Dred sent him and he could only guess
at why since Dred never played anything straight... especially how he went after his enemies.

Garlan took another deep hit then passed the joint
back to the knuckleheads in the back seat. Colvin was
yet another in the line of would-be princes of the street
put down like the mad dog that he was by King. What
was left of his splintered crew was immediately scooped
up by and consolidated under Dred. Noles was a slack-
jawed plate of hot mess who only sprang to work when
he knew someone in charge of his wallet was around.
One of Colvin's white boys, with hair in a Caesar cut, a
razor-thin goatee with and a random growth of a beard
only over his Adam's apple. With his ill-fitting dress shirt
only sometimes tucked into jeans, and a jacket he always
wore when on the corner no matter how hot it got, he
dressed like a redneck business executive.

Melle had become one of Colvin's top earners, the little
man due to be promoted. A young hothead in a wife

beater and baggy blue jean shorts, with the scarecrow build of a krumper. He had shaved off his wild, unchecked Afro because Five-O could identify him from blocks away. Both jacked up, wild-eyed, and too eager to make a rep for themselves, they were the latest in a seeming endless procession of would-be soldiers. Like much of their crew, these two had run in a leaderless direction, in desperate need of an anchor. Squatting from building to building, as random movement made it hard for the police to track them, they lived strictly day-to-day. Sure, they could work a corner, run off a wayward, crew sling whatever product they could get their hands on, and generally take care of what business they knew about, but they, like many other rootless boys, waited for someone to step up and take the reins. Garlan considered starting a franchise called Rent-a-Thug. Maybe Hoodrats 'R Us.

The PT Cruiser circled the parking lot again.

Lyonessa bounded after her grandmomma. A half-dozen people mingled at the entrance door as she pushed her way through. Grandmomma stopped to chat. Again. Lyonessa swatted the air before her nose, brushing the cigarette smoke from her face. The gangly man in the plaid shirt and white hat nodded and backed away before tamping it out against a brick column. Tipping his hat to her, he then crushed the remains under his boot heel. That made her grin.

The bright-colored, slow-moving car caught her eye. It was the second time she'd seen it pass. She liked those kind of cars because they looked old-timey.

Lyonessa tugged at her grandmomma's dress.

"Let's go, Grandmomma." There was a hint of whine to her voice. If they didn't leave soon, they'd be late for soccer practice. They still had to load and unload the groceries into the car and lug them into the house. Maybe if Lonzo had stopped by things would go faster. Or he could take her himself. But he rarely seemed around much these days.

Her tongue ran to the gap in her teeth. The third tooth lost this month. No tales of tooth fairies were spun around her house, though she often heard her classmates ridicule each other about believing in fairies. Reese once was the victim of such barbs, but he smiled his two-missing-teeth smile and pulled out five dollars and said "I believe in this." He reminded her of Lonzo when he did that. She'd go to soccer practice, maybe see Reese, maybe smile at him. It would be a good day.

"Come on, Grandmomma."

"Madre Dios," her grandmomma said with feigned exasperation. She smiled at her granddaughter, understanding the secret language of girls and confident that she had raised a good girl with a good heart. Not a fast one like some of the other girls in the neighborhood, even at such an age.

The PT Cruiser circled again.

This time the man in the plaid shirt took notice and stood up straight against the brick column. Everyone seemed suddenly attentive and oddly tensed, as if an electric current passed through them all. Lyonessa clutched her doll to her chest.

The tinted back window of the car rolled down. The next thing Lyonessa knew, a body slammed into her, knocking her to the ground. The report of thunder boomed, followed by loud pops, louder than any firecracker. The man in the plaid shirt reached into his belt and then his body jerked three times, invisible strings tugging at him like a toy on the fritz, before he collapsed. Lyonessa hated the way his hat tumbled from his head.

"You do one of ours, we do one of yours!" a voice cried from the van. The words had an ugly tone to them made worse by the slightest trace of a southern drawl.

Not sure what he meant, Lyonessa kept her head down. People scattered in a torrent of screams and more bangs, but two bodies had her pinned. She dropped her doll but tried to remain as still as Grandmomma. Her fright made it hard to breathe. Why wasn't Grandmomma moving? Why wasn't she coming after her and scooping her up and holding her close like she did whenever she was scared?

A pair of rough hands grabbed her and pull her to her feet. Lyonessa lashed out in frenzied struggle, slapping at the grip the man had on her wrist. The men smelled of sweat and bad smoke, eyes half-shut as if bored. They shoved her into the van.

"You tell Lonzo," the first one stood in the open rear passenger door shouted to no one in particular. He sort of reminded her of her pastor, the way he shouted and paused as if waiting for a response.

They knew her brother, but they sounded so angry. Lonzo would calm them down and make everything all right. He had that way with people. The white one put his hand on her knee. At first she thought it was to get her to settle down. But the way he stroked his fingers up and down her leg made her more scared. The man in the front seat looked sad, disgusted, as if he had a plate of food he didn't like but was forced to eat.

The old-timey car pulled off.

Lonzo Perez insisted his crew call him "Black," not "El Negro". Hazel eyes, glassy and expressionless, a snake's eyes, stared at nothing in particular. Though sporting a Boston Celtics jersey, he had no love for the team. The green and white, however, were his crew's colors and its sleevelessness showed off his arms. Along his thick bicep and forearm was a tattoo of his humerus and ulna. A disconcerting effect against his honey-complected skin. The tattoo of his skeleton ran over his ribs and legs also, like an X-ray in a black ink. What gave him pause was the thought of doing his face, just the right half. Regardless of his decision, he knew he couldn't do his hand as it remained sheathed within its glove.

There was an art to being alone and he was the consummate artist. The name, the insisted English, separated him. It carved him out into an even more specialized niche, as if his people didn't already fear and respect him. In that order: fear then respect. Which was fine because he, too, feared them. He feared connection, found the burdens of relationship odd and heavy. Other than Lyonessa and his grandmomma – with his older brothers out of play, one dead, one in prison – he had no stability. No center. Nothing which weighed him down or left him vulnerable. Weak. Exposed. His life was a broken center and he was adrift, going whichever direction he pleased. The price of connection was often too steep.

The front room was the largest room, a mismatched couch and love seat ringing the enclosed space around the television. Grandmomma wrapped her arms around a tattered couch cushion. A picture of a needlepoint flower was stitched onto its front half. She had picked it up at a garage sale for a nickel and hugged it as if it were a talisman that was her only hope to hold back the evil spirits. The television was on, but no one watched it, though it helped drown out the noise of his men. Whiling away the hours in endless chatter about sex, money, and power, not truly knowing what to do with any of them. Sitting in the center of the room, all activity orbited Black.

Black hated this place. It reeked of poverty and shame. A dozen members of his family crammed into a tiny apartment. Barely enough room to sleep in peace. Broken old men, stoop-shouldered and thick-armed, killing themselves as day laborers, doing the scut work to fuel other's versions of the American dream. All scared and anxious. Black lived on the other side of town. Eagle Terrace, close as it was to Breton Court, and even though it was not controlled by a rival gang, often proved problematic. But there was no place he feared going into. Even his cholos gave him wide berth, standing around in their over-sized white T-shirts, gold chains, baggy shorts, and white knee socks, recognizing the electric tension of the room. His people scoured the block, the neighborhood, the city, searching for any trace of Lyonessa. Dred had gone too far. He'd been bucking for a war for a long time. He was about to reap one.

Every crew in their set had two leaders. Black was *primera palabra*, the first word. The *segunda palabra*, the second word, the leader when Black wasn't around, was La Payasa. She possessed a lithe physique and walked with a lilt; her body in constant twitch, as if she was constantly ready to burst into a dance, moving to the rhythms of life that only she heard. Blonde hair with black roots exposed to three inches. Black and gold, her colors, set against her butterscotch complexion which some might have been called "high yella" back in the day. A crease, an old scar truth be told, etched the side of her face.

La Payasa stood at the back of the room, hating the idea of being touched. She was loath to interrupt him. She knew it was bad this time. In her mind, gangs lived by a code and certain things were just off limits. Children especially. The rules of the game had changed, if indeed there were rules. She too was afraid. Not for herself, mind you. She'd programmed herself to not be afraid. It came with always having to prove that she was down for whatever. Half black, half Hispanic, she always had to prove herself. But her soul already knew the night would not end well. And her heart steeled itself for the inevitable blood that needed to answer blood.

Someone rapped at the door. Black nodded and one of his boys opened it. Two police detectives identified themselves. Their eyes told the story long before their lips did. They had found Lyonessa's body. Grandmomma's mouth opened, wordless. A tear pooled in her rheumy eyes. The screams would come later. Without a word spoken, La Payasa knew she was to rally the soldiers because the streets would soon feel Black's rage. She knew Black's instinctive thought.

"Someone burns for this."

CHAPTER TWO

The Marion County Coroner's Office was a non-descript brick building west of Methodist Hospital, just outside of downtown Indianapolis. The name Doctor Dennis T Nicholas was engraved on a plaque as if to say "the doctor is in". Ghosts in blue scrubs and blue gloves and blue masks, behind plastic face shields, the pathologist on duty was elbow deep in another body while a lab tech took photos of bodies as if for a thug fashion shoot. Posters of human anatomy hung on refrigerators like a child's drawing. Specs of the victims filled a dry-erase board.

Cantrell Williams stood over the body of a child and his heart mourned that the world was not the way it was meant to be. Right now, this portrait of an angel at rest had no name. There was no trace of the horrors she must've endured during her final hours frozen onto her face, only the face of a doll, a smooth brown framed by dark hair. Wearing a yellow gown over his suit, like an apron as if he prepared to barbecue, Cantrell hovered about the body. He hated the rustle of his mask every time he took a breath.

He almost didn't notice the cameras.

Some of the other detectives enjoyed their minor celebrity status. A three-man crew followed him down to the coroner's office as they filmed another episode of *The Squad*. They shadowed several of the detectives, hoping that maybe something they were working might turn into something more. Cantrell considered them a pain in the ass, more intrusive and a hindrance to real investigative work. Captain Octavia Burke thought it a shrewd public relations move, perhaps shining a bit of light on their dark corner of the universe. Maybe with more attention, the department might get a budget increase.

His partner, Detective Lee McCarrell, couldn't be bothered to be here. Action junkies hated the waiting and paperwork of the job. At best he would glance at a report or let Cantrell give him the highlights later.

Cantrell flipped through pages of the report. Diagrams of the head and body, though to his eye, the drawings were too Caucasian. The report was a litany of brutality. Details of vaginal and anal tearings. Wound tracks measured. He fumed to himself that he had to do this on his own. "She got a name yet?"

"Lyonessa Maurila Ramona Perez," the first blue ghost said. He cocked his head to the camera, affecting the pose of grief mixed with pensiveness.

"Guess that makes her official. We got ourselves a bona fide homicide." Cantrell wanted to call bullshit on the doctors, but his own words sounded crafted for effect.

"When will we have the official report?"

"Tomorrow. End of the week at the latest. We're getting backed up."

"Things are heating up. What's the unofficial word?"

"Someone brutalized this child. Her last hours were filled with pain and terror." The pathologist attempted to pay little attention to the camera, yet carried herself as if on stage delivering lines she'd expect to hear on one of those prime-time cop shows. Cantrell waited for her to deliver a bad pun and dramatically don some sunglasses. "Scrapes along her forearms, a cross-hatched scar across her neck. Skin under her fingernails from where she fought her attackers."

Good girl, he thought.

X-rays lined one of the walls, body parts in close up. Shoulders. Arms. Feet. Ribs. Legs. Head. A pastiche of anatomy, no longer recognizable as human. The X-rays showed where the merciful bullet entered and the direction of it. Bruises and welts along her right thigh smeared into a blue-maroon blotch. A scratch mark ran across her shoulder. A red smear like poorly applied blush on her cheek.

She was twelve years old.

"Abrasions on her neck, possibly from a stranglehold. A contusion possibly followed with a temporary loss of consciousness."

"What happened here?"

"Those marks are several hours old. From tape. Adhesive in the tracks. Looks like she was restrained during the assault. She tried pretty hard to get free."

"She was a fighter," he whispered in respect and sadness, a mix of mourning and pride.

"As best she could. We have carpet burns on her legs like she was forced onto..."

"I get the picture."

"How much more do you want to know?"

"How much more do you have?"

"Significant trauma and tearing to her vagina and anus."

"I've got enough." Cantrell turned to the camera hoping the disgust on his face didn't play as unconcern.

For the last year or so, other than the occasional hiccup, the streets had been calm. King and his Youth Solidarity organization, unorthodox methods and all, had been an effective rule. But things on the streets had heated up. It started small, a match or a tussle here and there as if testing the waters. Then an attack. Then a rape. Rumor had it that the Latinos had raped a black woman. Not that any such crime had been reported, but the rumor had life and power of its own. Now bodies were dropping. With this many bodies falling, it would only be a matter of time before the Feds came in with RICO and the Patriot Act behind them. Too much talk of drug wars and gangs put a rarified scent into the air – cutting through even their terrorist mandate – and the Feebs would come in like it was mating season ready to hump anything that moved. Federal indictments had a way of driving people mad. Cantrell hoped to put the cases down before things got any further out of control.

The squad room was little more than a sanctuary of desks. Three long rows of them, overgrown and strewn with paper and stacked folders. Brown folders lined up on them under a fluorescent glare. Every now and then, slips of pink paper sprang up beneath wayward piles in response to the constant bleet of the phones. Every bit of open space was an opportunity for another file to land on a desk. Mismatched file cabinets stood like soldiers at attention. A stereo rested on top one of them; an American flag magnet clung to another.

"What do we have?" Captain Octavia Burke cut an imposing figure despite barely passing the height requirement to join the force. A full-figured woman in a gray business suit, she wore her glasses low on her nose in a tacit declaration that she was smarter than whoever she deigned to talk to, detective or chief alike. Before her promotion, she'd been Lee McCarrell's partner also, so perhaps working with him was a fast track to promotion. Like the mayor's detail, if the mayor was a mediocre redneck detective who had managed to not be fired.

"Suspicious vehicle driving real slow in the parking lot. Opened fire. Folks scattered. Scooped up the girl."

"A kidnapping?"

"Can't tell if it was intentional or she was an easy opportunity. Then the shit jumped off." Cantrell turned to the cameras. "Can I say shit? Anyway, they went up High School Road."

"Where's Lee?"

"Checking in with one of his CIs." Cantrell handed her his report and studied her desk. He hated lying to the captain, but he needed to cover his partner's back. His confidential informant was actually off the books and was too plugged into the streets to not be into some dirt herself. And his partner was sleeping with her.

"Let's start at the beginning." Octavia did that thing with the glasses again. Most days she still missed the rush of being a detective. She missed the opportunity to read people. She missed unraveling mysteries. Like the bullshit story Cantrell handed her about his partner. Lee McCarrell might have been a good cop at one point, but he often succumbed to the need for short cuts. Not necessarily lazy, but he often made poor decisions. And his partners were often the ones left holding his bag of shit.

"Lyonessa Maurila Ramona Perez. Went to Jonathan Jennings Public School 109. From the amount of bruises, she went through hell in her last hours."

"What about the family?"

"Hispanic. Grandmother worked nights as a maid at the Speedway Lodge. Mother and father both deceased. There's an older brother. Lonzo 'Black' Perez. He's in the system."

"Gang?"

"And drugs."

"This related?" Octavia paced behind the desk reading the report.

"Things have been heating up. King's been out of play…"

"Let's not confuse a community activist with someone doing police work." The mention of King James White caused her to bristle. Whenever his name came up, bodies fell and the police were left with more questions than answers. A whole lot of mystery – and things she didn't *want* explanations for – and open cases. She hated the paperwork and going before the bosses with a plate full of "I don't know".

"He runs a program. Gets gang members off the streets. Finds them work. Does after-school tutoring."

"Riiiiiiiiight. Well, the community is under siege and we're stretched thin running around after something has jumped off in order to get ahead of the problem." Octavia pushed the glasses high on her nose with a sigh. "What about the vehicle?"

"Robbery investigation unit informed me that they recovered a car matching the description in my report." For a brief, beautiful moment, he broke his own rule. He had hope. But he soon paid the price and was dashed against the rocks of reality. "The car was a burnt husk. Torched in order to hide any evidence. They got it over at Zore's Towing. Even the VIN was totally gone. A hot burn, probably gasoline used as an accelerant. The forensic team was called in and they found a hidden VIN. It traced back to one Garlan Pellam... who had reported it stolen a day earlier."

"I know that look, detective. What is it?"

"The owner, Mr Pellam. He's not in the system, but he is on the radar of the Gang Task Force. Known associate of many of Dred's crew."

"And the report that it was stolen..."

"... feels a little too convenient."

"Might be worth a conversation. Anything on Dred? DOB? Photo? Sheet?"

"We got nothing. A name. A nickname probably, unless you believe his momma took one look at her beautiful baby boy and decided to call his bald ass 'Dred'."

"Keep your ears open just in case. What's your next step?"

"Got some witnesses coming in to give descriptions of

the shooters. Looks like two perps. Black. Working on ID-ing them."

"See if you can speed up the DNA tests from the fluids on the body. And keep your partner in line. A lot of eyes are on him."

As lead detective on the Perez homicide, Cantrell needed to make sense of the chaotic crime scene as well as the players. On one side, he had one Lonzo "Black" Perez, head of a Hispanic crew, local franchise of some national set, whose activities had been slowly amping up as their gang pushed into new territories imposing its will. And whose baby sister was raped and murdered. If something like that was to happen to Cantrell's baby sister, badge or no badge, there'd be hell to pay. On the other side was the mysterious Dred, who'd been a shadowy figure for years, more rumor than anything else until King came on the scene. Suddenly Dred became more active. There were several open cases tied to him – and for that matter, King – that went down with the Colvin affair. No one wanted to look too hard at that as Colvin went down and bodies quit dropping. But the mayor's office, whipped up by the media, pressured the captain on this one. A little girl was dead. An innocent caught in the middle of two junkyard dogs yanking on their junk to prove their manhood. That wasn't going to stand. Hopefully his esteemed partner had something.

"You dig up anything on our case?"

"Like what?" Lee McCarrell sauntered to his desk, a head nod to the filming crew. The crew leapt to readiness, if for no other reason than because Lee made for great commentary, most of which the brass would rather

have left on the editing room floor. Still, any opportunity
to jam a thumb into their eye he'd take.

"Like motive? Hell, anything."

"Motive? Money, dope, or pussy. That's always the
motive."

Cantrell cut a furtive glance at the cameras, but Lee
only winked at him, enjoying the bully pulpit they afforded him a little too much. Words had a way of
catching up with folks. And Cantrell, over conscious of
the cameras, parsed his with care. "Looks like it may
have some gang connections."

"That's what I'm saying. Sell the shit and walk away.
People will always have their vices. Smokes. Porn.
Booze. Prostitutes. Pussy and drugs in one way or an-
other. And someone around to make money off them.
Porn does billions on the internet. You don't see bodies
dropping over it."

"Well, maybe of AIDS."

"Why you want to go there?"

"I'm just saying…"

"Man wants to enjoy rubbing one out. He don't want
to have to think about junkie tracks or AIDS."

"Not to mention all of the exploited girls in the sex
trade."

"There you go again. Enough to kill a good hard-on.
Well, yours, maybe."

"You can think on AIDS and underage girls and still
do that?"

"I can compartmentalize."

"Come here." Cantrell led him out of taping distance
of the cameras. Lee had his minute in the spotlight, but

Cantrell had some personal things to discuss. "You all right?"

"What do you mean?" Lee's self-pleased grin still contorted his face.

"You've been moody. Distracted."

"You make it sound like I got Detective's PMS."

"I wish you did. A few days from now you'd be fine. But this has been going on for weeks."

"Thought better of making a slumpbuster joke."

"You get that situation with your CI straightened out?"

"I got it handled."

"If IA starts sniffing around..."

"My job on the line?" Suddenly Lee came to attention.

"I'm just saying, I ain't lying to cover your ass. You need to close cases. Without incident. Period."

CHAPTER THREE

Wayne Orkney scratched the scar on the back of his neck. His keloid itched constantly these days, to the point where he considered going to the doctor to see what he could do to get it removed. A hard-faced man, he had the build of a defensive linesman, stocky and chiseled, with the swinging step of someone who knew how to use their size should the necessity warrant. Passing the Indianapolis Colts training complex, he slowed to a brisk walk along the sidewalk of the West 56th Street corridor of Eagle Creek Park. His early morning amble counted as his aerobic exercise for the day. Despite the fact that he felt twice as good, twice as strong, in the morning, he often carried an old walking stick he'd picked up on a short-term mission trip to Jamaica some ten plus years ago. This morning he clutched his new collapsible baton in a fist. From the six inches which fit into his hand like a roll of quarters, it extended out to sixteen inches of balanced bludgeon. It was his peace of mind, something to keep whatever predators prowled the early morning at bay.

It seemed that nowhere was safe anymore. It wasn't too long ago they had to haul a body out of the park. Merle and his crazy ass ran across a body. That Walters boy. Lamont "Rok" Walters. A good boy. Well, relatively good. A wannabe roughneck with more attitude than sense, he got involved in some foolishness. What either of them were doing in the weeds was beyond him. If it wasn't a family reunion or barbecue, because nothing brought a fool out like free food or… he couldn't begin to speculate what motivated Merle. It seemed almost criminal for youth to be squandered on the young. From the way the story laid out, Wayne knew King had to be involved somehow, but no one had seen him in weeks. But that was the way things went around here. No, Wayne couldn't hazard much of a guess about much that went on in his world these days.

The front entrance of Eagle Creek Park was a lush lawn of overgrown grass and trees in full bloom. The wind snatched at him, an odd brisk chill. Though late in the season for such a cool morning, he appreciated it for his jogs. Wayne maintained a peculiar pace, somewhere between a stroll and a speed walk, his arms nearly flapping alongside him. He wasn't much for scenery. On some mornings he might spy an errant deer since they ran about like squirrels out here. The smell of rotting meat hit him as soon as he rounded the bend. Wiping his nose, he twisted up his face as if that would cut the smell. A dead raccoon stretched out along the median of 56th Street. Its tongue lolled out of its mouth though its eyes were missing and its belly had been split open.

Vultures circled up ahead, just inside the entrance,

with macabre intent. Wayne slowed. The calculations of curiosity stilled his steps – a feeling more than anything else. The sight of the birds, so many of them, circling and settled in the trees like a jury taking in evidence.

Wayne veered off the path.

Rush-hour traffic hadn't begun in earnest, barely a trickle with only the occasional car looking to get on I-465 south. The chain link fence cordoning the park quaked as he tested it with his weight. In a less than graceful scrabble, he made it over and stopped to smooth out his jogging suit once he was on the other side. His breath frosted the air. His stomach both hungry and nauseous.

Wayne had barely waded through the first wall of trees and into a clearing when he saw the body. The skeleton splayed at awkward angles, twisted in brush and leaves. Insects made a home in the remains of his face. Clothes with chunks torn from them as animals had gnawed past them to get to the cool flesh. His shoes were missing. The rent torso laid empty of lungs, kidneys, intestines, and liver; the ribs snatched free. A few fingers had been chewed off.

"Aw… damn." Young dude. Couldn't be but fourteen or fifteen. From what Wayne could see, he'd caught a couple shots in the chest after taking a beating. Yup, these days it was almost a crime to be so young out here. Even as he reached for his cell phone to call the police, another feeling seized him. "Damn it, King. What have you done started?"

The area around 34th Street and Georgetown Road was knows as Eagledale. Back in the 1950s there was such a demand for housing it was one of the planned communities constructed. Little pre-fab, all-aluminum exterior, sidewalks, and concrete streets from $10,000. The boom lasted into the 1960s with schools and churches and the Eagledale Shopping Center constructed.

The nearby village of Flackville – 30th Street and Lafayette Road – which had been around since 1900, was annexed by Indianapolis in 1961. Overshadowed by the expanse of the Eagledale suburb. That was then. The only remainder of Flackville was the eponymous abandoned school building. It was rumored that a group of Haitians owned the building but a church owned the property. With the two groups at odds, the building stood boarded up. Ripe for squatting though no one did. The words "No Trespassing. Especially trucks" spray-painted along its driveway acted as a near-mystic rune, warding off most would-be squatters.

Lady G recognized the pair of legs dangling out of the trash bin of the neighboring restaurant.

"Get out of my trash." A short man, with skin as dark as wrought iron, scrambled back and forth waving a broom, to little avail as the object of the threatening spectacle had the top half of his body buried in the trash bin.

"What do you care?" The voice echoed from within the bin. "Were you going to eat it?"

"It's trespassing."

"You have some control issues. If any of this meant so much to you, you shouldn't have thrown it away."

The legs danced about as the owner swatted him with the broom. Merle tumbled out, an arm full of containers clutched to his chest with dirty fingernails. A black rain-coat draped about him like a cloak. Unwinking, Merle had a way of looking about at the world with the cu-riosity of a child inspecting a new toy. His craggily auburn beard came out at all angles. A bird's nest of hair retreated from his bald spot, capped by his aluminum foil hat. His slate gray eyes – big and round, yet knowing and without innocence – cast about, but without spying Lady G.

"Go on!" the owner yelled, as if to a pestful cat.

Not that Lady G much blamed the man for chasing Merle out of his trash bin. She once knew a meth head who went through people's garbage searching for can-celed checks. Or she snatched bills out of people's mailboxes. She would wash the checks and then make them out to herself for hundreds of dollars.

"I eat here twice a week. It's a good time, right before the garbage truck comes. My best luck is right after the lunch rush. You can't deny a man his fried chicken. Chicken!" Merle waved a chicken leg in the air in mad triumph, other boxes tucked under his other arm. Merle cocked his head at her, quizzical, like an owl befuddled by the sight before him, then wandered off, distracted by whatever internal song that called him.

Despite the warming temperatures, Lady G dressed in layers. A thermal shirt under a T-shirt, swathed in a black hoody. Nothing form fitting as to hide her shape. She chewed on her index finger, which protruded from her fingerless gloves. Acne bumps flared along her forehead, red and swollen against her toffee-colored skin. Lady G's stomach fluttered with unease. She couldn't quite catch her breath. She didn't know what kind of reception to expect from him. And she didn't want to admit her sheer terror. Isolating herself, she rarely left the confines of her room at Big Momma's, the woman who took her in when she was homeless. Lady G rarely met her eyes these days. All of her old haunts filled her with sadness. Her life was a maelstrom of hurt. And shame. Grief flayed her. She searched, hoped, for someone to confide in, who could make things clear for her, but King was no longer there.

Lady G barely kept pace with Merle's crazed lope, following him past the Flackville building to the small stretch of woods behind it. The stand of trees grew at odd angles, a small pool of shadows signaling the entrance. A sign caught her attention: "Warning: No Trespasing! This is Merle's camp. Anounce yurself."

"I see my prayer for noble weather has not been answered." Merle hunched over a Styrofoam container of tossed-out barbecue tips.

"I have a surprise for you."

"My dear, I don't think I can survive another one of your surprises. You are a chimp with a nuke."

"I…" Lady G held out a box of caramel-filled ice cream drumsticks. Part of her hoped Merle might be able to see past the hurt she caused and realize she'd been hurt, too. Even a self-inflicted wound was still a wound. Her friends abandoned her. They shunned her and she accepted her banishment. Profound loneliness, that punishing isolation, flensed her soul. Not knowing where to turn, praying for a safe place of refuge, she sought out Merle.

"It's always important to carry a towel." Merle didn't glance up from his rib tips.

"What?"

"The world isn't a safe place."

"We're coming apart. The family." She grieved the loss of something precious. She cried because she had no self, only her own mood and whim. Self-indulgent, selfish, she had no center, and had no thought at all of causing another pain. She was shadow. Wrapping herself in sheets of innocence and victimhood, her instinct was to blame. Her naïveté, she was a hapless plaything in the hands of more powerful personalities. She loved King, she really did. She longed to please him: read the books he liked, went to the places he did, learned as much about him as she could, wore her hair the way that pleased him. He read the poems she wrote, the rough sentences and poorly formed images and ill-constructed rhythms, and praised her. He stared into the shadows of her soul, all of the gray and ugly bits, and loved her. Ill prepared for the possessiveness, the jealousy, she knew the totality of his love, and it broke her. "I'm doing surprisingly well for a pariah."

"That's the thing. Times like these, you find out who your friends are."

"And I have none."

"Ah, the melodrama of youth. Blind to the obvious. Complaining about being alone… to someone. Your instinct for female recklessness stalls your maturing. That and the false, hollow bravado you feel compelled to perform."

Big Momma had told her the same thing. How a teenage girl trying to get out of trouble will roll on any-

one, including the very people she both loved and hurt.
Big Momma's voice always had an undertone of concern, like she wanted to impart something to her. Like
she was warning Lady G of her power. That she had a
smile about her, trusting and innocent. And had her own
strength of personality, a beguiling innocence that
sucked people into her orbit. A disarming charm that
caused people in her world to want to protect her. Because inside the fragility which seemed to seep from her,
she truly was a bird with a fractured wing.

"Some ladies don't prize what they can have. But you
have a lifetime to repair the damage. What do you have
to say?"

"I have no words." Out of fear – fear of King, fear of
the burdens of responsibility, fear of love and being loved
– she did unbelievable things. Hurting herself to protect
herself, she dragged Lott into her maelstrom of self-de-
struction. She loved him, too, and would know him
intimately in ways she never knew King. But the men
who defined her were no longer around to protect her.
When it came to important decisions, she was incapable
of making them, reacting emotionally and leaving it to
others to clean up her mess. She wasn't the person they
believed her to be, however, she didn't need anyone to
catalog her list of sins. She knew her terrible acts. In her
heart she feared she couldn't be forgiven. That some
cracked trusts couldn't be mended. "I'm so sorry."

"Brave deeds. Honorable actions. Be the woman you
know you were created to be. Let your life show your
repentance. Even misery doesn't last forever. In the
meantime, there's no pain like the present."

Merle sucked loudly on his ice cream drumstick. They shared a commiserating glance. Not nearly as alone as she would have believed. Both living in the crater left, the fallout of her choices. Hers. All the minds of her friends seemed now closed to her, sticking her in a story she knew she'd have to live with. Lady G could never have their lives, so she would have to forge her own.

The window latch clicked slightly as the glass slid up. An exhalation of a breeze jostled the curtains. The window screen had been easily dislodged, little more than decoration the way it was attached to the window. Many of the first-floor windows of the apartment complex had bars on them, an out-of-pocket expense for the tenants which the landlord mentioned when they signed their rental agreements. The bars gave the appearance of coming home to a nicely decorated prison. But in this neighborhood, safety was a precious commodity. Better to feel safe in one's castle than worry about the many predators in the night.

He slipped in noiselessly. Despite his build he moved with the grace of a thief, light of foot and touch. The sleeping girl's mother certainly didn't lack for imagination. She wanted her daughter to have a magical, sheltered childhood. The little girl's room enchanted him. A white picket fence served as the bed's headboard and footboard. A clothesline hung between the bedposts with her old baby clothes pinned to the line (including the ones she wore home from the hospital). An unfinished toy trunk had been painted apple green, with the quilt her grandmother made for her resting on top of it.

A sunshine-yellow, three-drawer wood chest had large cartoony ladybugs stenciled onto it. Stuffed animals took their seats around the small wooden table set for tea.

Whenever his emotions wore him down, he drove by the place. It made him feel better knowing he was near even if he couldn't talk to her. Touch her. Lately, he had to be closer to her. Let her know he was still a part of her life, even if he couldn't be there the way he liked.

She snuggled into a thick pink blanket and pillow. For a moment he stood over her, just watching her sleep. He covered her mouth and eased onto the bed next to her. Her eyes sprang open, large with panic. Her balled little fists slammed into him, then slowly ceased as recognition filled her eyes. He removed his hand.

"Daddy!" she whispered with enthusiasm, sitting up to give him a hug.

"Nakia," King said.

"I didn't think you'd come back."

"I'm not supposed to, you know that."

"But I wanted to see you."

"I know. That's why I'm here."

"Tell me a story." Nakia sat fully up and pulled her sheets up around her, making a tent with her knees. King loved her so much in that instant he took a moment to catch his breath.

"There once was a king. He was a lonely man because all the people he loved left him. But he had his kingdom and he had people he wanted to keep safe. This gave him purpose and mission, but in his heart he still wanted a queen. So he searched high and low throughout his kingdom, because you never know where a queen might be.

"One day he walked into a tavern…"

"What's a tavern?" Nakia interrupted.

"It's… a liquor store. With tables."

"Oh." She huffed a mild disappointment, expecting something far more exotic.

"One day he walked into a tavern and took a seat near the back so that he wouldn't be recognized by his people. Then he saw her. The most beautiful woman he'd ever seen. He could tell by the way she moved that she didn't know that she was a lady of great beauty… which made her even more beautiful."

"Am I beautiful?" Nakia fished for the compliment she knew would be lavished on her. It was almost a game the two of them played. She knew her father was busy doing important things and that her mother was mad at him. So between the two, he couldn't be around much. And she had the sense that him staying away was him protecting her because there were bad men who sought to hurt King by hurting her.

"You are *so* beautiful. And you are loved. And if you hold that love in you, it's like a seed. And you will grow up to be even more beautiful."

"Like the queen?"

"Don't jump ahead. Let me tell you my story. The king definitely thought he'd found the one. But he didn't want to scare her off so he decided to wait until the time was right."

"Boys are so silly. He shouldn've asked her out then. He don't know she'll be around later. She might be too busy for him."

"Girl, you're gonna be fierce one day."

"That good?"

"That's great. You'll be a princess who won't need saving."

"So did he ask her out?"

"The king had his duty to attend to. One day a terrible dragon entered the kingdom. It scared the king's people, devouring them slowly, and seemed to be everywhere at once. It wasn't too long till people began falling under the dragon's power and fighting alongside the beast against their own people. Now it was the king's duty to battle the dragon. Everywhere the dragon went the king was there to fight it."

"Did he kill the dragon?"

"The dragon was so huge and so powerful, but the king didn't realize he couldn't fight it alone. So he continued to fight the power of the dragon."

"The king was brave."

"Or stupid. Or too proud. Or all of the above. One day the beautiful lady got caught up in their battle. The dragon kidnapped her and held her captive. The king grew even more relentless and chased the dragon to the ends of his kingdom. There was no place it could hide from him. Finally, fearing the king's wrath, the dragon released the lady and went into hiding."

"Was she the one?"

"He thought she was. He was prepared to make a life with her, offer her his kingdom or even set it aside for her... but then another took her away. The king was alone again."

"That's not true. The king still had his people. And maybe there will be another queen."

"I think the king realized he already had a princess he needed to take better care of. Keep her safe from his many enemies."

"That why the king doesn't come around very often?"

"To keep her safe. He should probably go."

"I'd rather not be safe."

"What do you mean?"

"If it means I'd get to see you more, I'd rather not be safe."

King leaned in and kissed her forehead. He never wanted to be that kind of a father. Absent. The kind who put his work, no matter how important he thought it, above his family. And now the choice had been taken from him. He'd made too many enemies in the game. Families, not even little girls, were no longer off limits. He needed to put an end to the foolishness and get out. Maybe start over. That was what he wanted most: the chance to do things over again. Make different decisions. Maybe choose different people to surround himself with.

King walked toward the rear of the Breton Court condominiums. In the gloom of night, the overgrown branches stretched like tentacles ready to snatch him away, and the sad stretch of creek was reduced to a trickle as it hadn't rained in a while. He stopped at the bridge along High School Road, the site of his betrayal. Closing his eyes, letting the pain of the memory of seeing Lott and Lady G together stab him anew. No matter how much he wished it, the darkness wouldn't swallow him. No all-consuming shadow reached out to snatch him into its ebon haze. Only the oppressive weight of anguish – the squeezing on his chest, his very being – reminded him that he was still alive. Memories replayed in his head. What didn't he see? The way they sat near. The furtive glances. Lott even sat in between King and Lady G on occasion and no one thought twice because they were all friends. Family. When did it start? What did he do wrong? Questions he never thought to ask. And why should he have? Lott was his ace. Lady G was his girl. He trusted them with his life. He wished he'd never seen the Caliburn at all.

His condo faced Big Momma's and he didn't want to chance seeing or being seen by Lady G. He simply wasn't ready. The image of her haunted him. He thought he saw her everywhere he went, in crowds, at coffeeshops, passing him on the sidewalk. The ghost of her lingered everywhere. So he had taken to entering and leaving his place through the rear.

A cement block pressed the back patio door shut; the trick was letting it fall into place when he left (though many times he simply scaled the walls). Either way, it was a lot of effort for "security" as all anyone had to do was push the door open.

Like Pastor Ecktor Winburn had done.

"What are you doing here?"

"A good shepherd goes after his lost sheep." A low-cut Afro with gray streaks drew back from his forehead, lengthening the appearance of his face. Like a scarecrow funeral director, his black suit hung from him, his tie too thin. He hunched his shoulders close and bridged his spider-like long fingers, his suspicious eyes taking the measure of King. "Figured I'd given you enough time to lick your wounds in your cave."

"I didn't ask you to come." The words came out in an angry rush. King balled his fist and released it, then pushed past Pastor Winburn to the unlocked backdoor. There was a time when he'd hung on the man's every word, but these days King could barely stand to listen to him. Somewhere along the lines things had changed, like somehow the pastor should have been there for him, been more solidly in his corner. Instead he felt like he'd washed his hands of him, distancing himself ("giving you time to lick your wounds" crap), and now doing just enough to cover his ass for when folks asked him about King.

"I'm here now." Pastor Winburn followed him inside. Better to give him something, any distraction to keep him from exploring any further down this dark path. Sometimes the best way to get over a problem was to get involved in someone else's. To take his eyes off of himself and his tiny corner of the world. "And you've still got a job to do. We're losing our men to the streets. To drugs. Hell, to their couches. There's nothing like comfort to make folks feel like they can get through life on their own. But no matter how good they have it, they're never content. Start getting that itch and feeling the need to scratch it. Wherever and with whomever they can."

"I been thinking a lot about my father." King reached to pull the Caliburn from his hip, his reflex ritual upon returning home. After all this time, he still forgot that he no longer had it.

"Yeah?"

"Wondering if we're all meant to be our fathers' sons."

Heavy, intense eyes rested on him. People loved putting folks on pedestals almost as much as they loved knocking them back down to earth. Hollywood stars. Pastors. Parents. Life was a set-up game which you couldn't let go to your head. "You know what I've always thought? The story of the prodigal son could have easily been called the prodigal father, at least to the son that stayed faithful."

"What do you mean?"

"Here you have two sons. One is faithful to his father, being the best son he can be. The other is selfish, self-focused, out for himself and his own good time. The faithful son stays with his father, continues his work, while the prodigal goes his own way and squanders his life. The faithful son sees his father bend over backwards to reward the wayward son. It can be a tough thing to swallow, seeing your father behave in ways you don't understand, yet love him anyway. Luckily for them both, they were still around to talk things through."

"My dad's no longer here."

"You are a hurt and angry child."

"What did you say to me?" King hated this. He wanted to punch something. Someone. And Pastor Winburn… he hated the man to see him like this. So weak. Pathetic. He wanted to prove himself to the man. To be the man Pastor Winburn saw in him. To even be better than him. Such was the way of fathers and sons.

"You were a… knight. A hero. Now you acting like some simp who's been played by a girl."

"You have no idea what it's like to think you know someone, to love them, and realize it's nothing but lies."

"Nope. Because love is strictly the provenance of the young. I was never young, never hooked up with anyone, and never got hurt by anyone. You're the only one who has ever been through something like this. In the history of mankind."

"You're not helping." King's face remained inscrutable. He kept his face a pallid mask, unmoved even by his own pain.

"It's all right to be angry with Lott. Lady G. Both of them. This whole situation. It sucks."

"I should be beyond that."

"Why? You still a man."

"And I don't want to put you in the middle."

"What middle? They did wrong. I'm pissed at both of them. Love them, but I'm pissed at them."

"They were laughing at me."

"Who?"

"Both of them. I did this for them as much as anyone else. To be a hero to Lady G. To be worthy of Lott's friendship."

"To prove yourself to them. I'm sorry if I don't seem real sympathetic. I'm not going to pretend to know what draws a silly country girl's heart. I'm not trying to minimize the dull shock of sorrow you want to wallow in. I'm really not. My heart hurts for you. I wish you could just remember the good times you had with them and hold on to the love you have for them. But I also know you can't just yet. Right now all you can do is think of the pain. All you can do is re-visit each memory through the lens of that pain and question everything."

"I just want to make all the hurting stop."

"I know you do. I know how hard it is to open up and reveal yourself, only to be rejected. That's the big fear of relationships." Pastor Winburn drew up his sleeves and revealed a scar line of old track marks. "The world is a painful place, full of things and people that will hurt you. And I know the temptation to numb yourself from it and do whatever it takes to keep us from dealing with life and what's going on. That's an easy path to walk down. You're no different than any other addict out here, you just used a relationship to numb yourself. Living life on your own strength, within your own fears."

"That's easy to say."

"What you've been doing hasn't been working." Pastor Winburn rolled his sleeves back down. "How about you listen to someone else other than yourself? You want to run away from folks and be all alone, that's on you. But you'll have no one speaking into your life except you. You don't want to be alone with your demons unattended. They are so many and it gets awfully noisy with all of those competing voices in your head."

"Everything just seems so... It's too much. Too loud. It's confusing."

"I wish I were one of those quick-to-forgive people. How when I feel dishonored, disrespected, or disavowed, or otherwise holding on to memories of someone's mistreatment of me, I can just go 'I forgive you' and all of the hurt and ill will just vanishes. It's like we feel this tacit pressure from other Christians. They hear our struggles with the pain of our situations – the anger, the hurt, the sheer pain of it – and confuse that with not being able to forgive. Almost as if we aren't forgiving on their timetable or that a good Christian would have forgiven by now. Or faster. Or better. On-the-spot forgiveness works with smaller slights, but deeper wounds require more, especially if they tap into a familiar one. Sometimes we have to ask if part of what has wounded us is us carrying something else with us from the past that we are connecting to this present person or circumstance. That's part of what forgiveness is about, freedom from the things which hold on to us. A hardened heart can't feel the love nor the forgiveness a faithful and just God has to offer, it has walled itself off. Pursuing forgiveness is agreeing with God that there needs to be healing and trusting Him to heal us through the process. And sometimes it's a hard, long, messy process. But what's broken can be redeemed. And there's a real you that you have yet to find."

King leaned against his kitchen counter. "Help me understand how to do that. How to get to the real me."

"You're always asking 'what do I need to do to make this work?' because you operate out of a need to control. Faith and control don't exist well together. When you are moving from a place of faith, you're asking 'God, what are You going to do to make this work and how do I get involved with that?'"

"I want to be that man."

"Look, King... I've seen how you've carried yourself. How you've fought. There's always going to be someone stronger. Everyone loses some time. It's what you do. In defeat, that defines you. You can become broken and bitter, just like in victory, you could become petty and small. Victory is a matter of spirit, not might. You have a mighty sword by your side, but you do not have to draw it. To wield it is to draw blood. Real love risks and offers redemption."

"Where do I start?"

"Go back and clean up what you messed up." Pastor Winburn put a tentative hand on King's shoulder, not wanting to crowd him if he wasn't ready. But King neither flinched nor pulled away.

"You always have a lesson for me. Just like a father."

"King, I... I was never your father. Though I'd have been proud to call you my son."

"There's more to being a father than blood. How about you listen to someone else other than yourself."

Lott dribbled the basketball three times, took aim, bounced it three more times, held his pose for a moment, then released his shot. The ball arced through the net-less rim without sound. Putting on a limp pimp roll strut to chase down his own rebound, he pretended to evade a couple of defenders before laying back with a fade-away jumper. The game was easier this way.

The other day he was in a pickup game with folks he knew from around the way. And he was every bit as alone. No one on the court chatted with him. No girls flirted with him from the sidelines. No one met his eyes. No one passed him the ball. Getting a rebound resulted in elbows to his gut or face. Too aware of their scrutiny, their wariness, he retreated. He knew what to expect, but the pain of the reality was nearly too much. Maybe underneath it all he wasn't this awful person – the villain in everyone's story – maybe he was still the caring, loving little boy his grandmother tried to raise. But it seemed, he could sense it in his heart like stomachs turned in his presence. He just wanted to get away. To retreat.

Lott's disheveled hair needed tightening up, a week overdue. His large brown eyes checked for anyone who neared him. His tongue traced where his row of faux gold caps once grilled his teeth. A scraggly beard scrawled along his face in tufts like a child's cotton ball art project. Lott had lost his job at FedEx. It was the job Wayne had helped him get through Outreach Inc which took him out of the streets, and he'd been there for a couple years. He'd been doing well. They were even talking about promoting him again.

Then the stuff with King and Lady G went down. He loved them both. He'd hurt them both. It was selfish of him to get with Lady G no matter the love he believed he had for her. She was King's girl. He was King's ace. And he betrayed them and it grieved him. He carried the weight of the pain he caused to work with him. The shame ground him down, affected his performance. His supervisor said he'd become bored and spiteful at work, not all the young man he thought he was giving a second chance to. And definitely not living up to the potential he thought he saw. Then that was that. Lott didn't disagree with his boss's assessment and would've fired him his own self. But the part that hurt was the fact that even during the firing, his boss had a sting of pain in his eyes, as if begging Lott to find the words to keep him from doing what he had to do. As if it hurt him to be adding to Lott's pain. Lott welcomed the firing. He welcomed the punishment. He knew he had to suffer for what he'd done and just wished everyone would stop giving a damn about him so he could throw his life away in peace.

"Why'd they have to do him like that? He was a good kid."

"He was into some dirt."

"No more than anyone else. And he was trying to put it behind him. Folks wouldn't let him."

So the whispers about him went. But he knew how they saw him. This unfeeling monster. Beyond tears. Beyond redemption. Sometimes a body had to move on, get away from a place. Run from the memories, history of hurts and betrayals, otherwise they became trapped by a story. A tale told by others and believed by more. Such was his story. A story that would define him in such a way that he began to believe it himself. One that wouldn't allow him to grow out of it. He had to break his routine, his habits, shake up his world and paradigm.

The ball swished through the net. But there was no roar of a crowd. Nor any elation in his heart. Only the dull ache of moving when he didn't want to. He ran down his own shot then dribbled out for another.

Lott could never figure out why he wanted, needed, to block it out, to kill off the person he was. Because he hurt. The pain bobbed and ebbed, varying in intensity, but always there, and he simply never wanted to hurt again. Pain drove people mad and the self-loathing he felt was a raging fire fed by bits of his soul. One he'd do anything to quench. His life in drugs was no different than how he treated women, they were both attempts

for his selfish need to come first and allow him brief moments of escape. What he hated was how he was
powerless to make any of the changes he knew he had
to make. His life was a runaway train, one he tried his
best to ride out because to change, to stop, meant he'd
risk losing Lady G or his friends and that he couldn't
bear.

Instead, he lost everything.

The scorched earth of his life left him with a profound
regret at having taken himself away from the people
who loved him. Whom he loved. Pangs of guilt gnawed
at him whenever he went by their old spot, overwhelmed by a sense that home was forever lost to him.
No one wanted any part of him, they all turned their
backs on him so that he could move on. And perhaps
they could escape the chaos he brought with him. He
didn't blame them. He hated himself probably more than
they did. He had no idea what real betrayal was, what
depths he was capable of sinking to.

"I am not a man," he thought.

He always had this vision of the kind of man he
wanted to be. Noble, but a bit of a roughneck. Honorable.
Honest. True. Trustworthy. A hoodrat knight. He didn't
want to be the kind of man his father was. Quick to dive
into any bit of pussy that strayed across his path. No matter whose woman she was or whether Lott's mother was
in the picture, Lott's father was a ghost in his childhood
and absent in his adulthood.

Lott lined up his next shot. Dribbled again. Let it fly. It
clanged off the rim and off to the side toward a group of
fellas.

"Li'l help," he said, nodding toward the ball that rested in the grass by them. The men cut him a sideways glance, one sucked his teeth, and kept playing. Lott picked up his backpack and walked off, not wanting to feel their judgment or their pity.

Off 52nd Street and Georgetown, along a windy bend, was a tiny church, Bethel United Methodist, behind which was a cemetery. The last few weeks he'd called the spot home. All the drama in his world sucked up all the emotional energy, and he had nothing left to care about anything else. Not his job. Not where he lived, which was a good thing since he lost his room at the Speedway Lodge, formerly a Howard Johnson's, soon after losing his job. And the graveyard matched how he felt. Dead inside.

Lott knew too many bodies buried in this yard.

There was a spot under a tree out of view of most of the cemetery and far from the street where he stayed. The closest thing nearby was the utility shed of the apartment complex. Three men chatted up a girl. Lott's wary gaze followed them. He'd seen the "hey, you girl" routine often enough. Brothers pushing up on a girl, trying to talk to her. He didn't like their predatory leer nor how they crowded the girl. A pack moving to cut off her escape routes. A feral gleam leapt to the eyes of the tallest of them. With the hint of a nod, the man behind her grabbed her while the other scanned the deserted lot and unlocked the storage shed. They dragged her in with the tallest man being the last to enter the shed.

"Careful. Don't jump if you can't see bottom," Lott heard an internal voice say, but he was to his feet and half-running toward the shed before his mind caught up to things. The latch on the shed had been torn out at the hinges and the rust on the nails indicated that it hadn't been secure in a while. Pressing his ear to the door, he heard the sounds of struggle and muffled cries. His blood heated up. The door slammed open behind the force of his kick.

A vegetable odor filled the room, the smell of spent seed seeped into the woods. They turned and froze at Lott's entrance. Two of the men held the girl down, each one clamping down on an arm, though one attempted to cup her breast. The third, the tall one, pulled at her panties. Spitting into his hand, he slowly began to stroke himself. The more she fought, the more excited he got. Despite Lott's unexpected entrance, he kept touching himself.

"What the hell are you doing?" Lott yelled.

"What it look like, money?" The first one looked up from the struggling girl.

"You want in on this train?" the tall one asked.

The girl locked eyes with Lott. A few acne bumps dotted her forehead, red and swollen against her toffee-colored skin. For a moment, all he saw was Lady G. Then she came more into focus as the girl she was. A little thinner and lighter skinned, though still in need of having her honor defended. Lott took two steps in and planted his foot into the crotch of the first boy. The other two scrambled to their feet, but not before he put his full weight behind a punch that dropped one to the floor.

"Get out!" Lott yelled to her.

The girl tore out without hesitation. The third man leapt at Lott, grappling him about the middle. Lott kicked backwards, slamming them both into the wall, taking the wind out of the assailant. Then the ground fell away from under him. All he could think of was all the friends he'd hurt, the trust he'd betrayed. The life he'd fucked up. Panting, the tallest one noted the fight leaving Lott and began to punch him. Lott took the blows to the ribs and the stomach, but not in the face though, as he wrapped up and collapsed into a ball. Sirens snapped the men out of their rage fugue, the tallest administering another kick before cutting out.

"The hero got his ass wa-za-za-zah-whooppedzz!" the tall one shouted on the way out. Then, in case he was a snitch, too, he warned, "Keep your mouth shut."

Lott stayed on the floor, with the pain as comforting as any blanket.

CHAPTER FOUR

Near the intersection of Sussex Avenue and Faygate, two streets over from Martin Luther King Jr Boulevard, the houses on the block were piled on one another. With barely a few feet between them and their small, fenced-in yards, each was close enough that everyone could hear everyone else's business. However, most people neither saw nor heard anything, especially at the two-story home on the corner. Bound to his wheelchair after his wounds suffered at King's hands, Dred remembered being confined to the house. Many nights he retreated to his chamber, bereft of any furniture, more cavern than room. Its steep shadows gave the illusion of it being deeper than it was. Bay windows faced the moon, yet the light never seemed to penetrate much beyond being a dim glow about the window. He found a certain comfort to his cave. Despite owning several stash houses, money houses, pea shake houses – none in his name, of course – he needed a place to lay his head. A place to call his own.

The muscle memory, or lack thereof, of the wheelchair faded as he now walked down the stairs, into the hall in front of the living room. The clack-clack-clack of paws on hardwood floors echoed behind him as Baylon's dog trotted past the open doorway. Baylon manned the doorway, allowing entry to Naptown Red.

"What you no good?" Naptown Red's uneven skin tone gave him the appearance of a high yella Rorschach test. His bulbous eyes, yellowed and bloodshot, were framed by black moles. His auburn hair had once been straightened, but now came back in natural, though no comb had touched it in a while. Whiskey seared his breath and seeped from his pores. The man tugged at his privates before reaching out for a hand clasp.

"Ballin'. Shot callin'." Dred took his hand and bumped shoulders with him, unaffected by the gesture. He nodded toward the next room where the others had gathered. Of course Red had been the last to arrive. He thought it proved that he was the man, that everyone waited on him. But as far as Dred was concerned, every now and then you got a fool. Naptown Red was so far behind and always sleeping on the game – a mistake his mom should've corrected before he was born.

Dred tired of a life of inconvenience and neglect. Every off-center smile was a threat; every unturned eye a challenge; every undeferred step disrespect, so easily insulted because "respect" was what defined them. Look at them, his foot soldiers. Naptown Red, scheming-ass nigga, not fooling anyone; Baylon, a tragic, perpetual fuckup; Garlan, so insecure in his role as muscle, certainly no Mulysa, but he'd have to do; and Nine, who insinuated herself into the group with promises of handling a particularly meddlesome problem for him. Something about being in her presence made you want to trust her. Love her. Shaped by rage, formed by scorn, molded by uninterest, Mulysa was a magnificent hatred. Now he sat at court waiting on a judge to let him know if he could sleep in his own bed tonight.

Eyes half-closed in on-setting ennui, Baylon stood on the fringes as the others gathered. His body reeked with the stench of death. From its sockets, pale yellow, bulbous, unnatural eyes – eyes which had seen so much, like staring into the sun – were dulled to lifelessness. His clothes seemed to cling tightly to his body like seaweed to a sunken ship. Baylon took a few uncertain steps. The grave called, but he continued to resist it. The air, stale and musty, swirled about to embrace his lithe form. Melancholia and weariness enveloped him, though his horrid body hid a certain nobility. The silence was tangible around him, as if taking one last peek at his gravesite, longing for his disturbed peace. He knew that folks considered him soft. He used to be, but now he'd been through a lot. Lost a lot. Being in the life changed you. You didn't get to just throw on a suit and enter the square world. You were boxed in and down for life. Little more than a dog gone savage from pain.

"You remember me? I was part of Rellik's crew." Garlan sidled up to him with a practiced hardness. He lightly fingered his ring.

"Want something to drink? I think I got some scotch." His voice little more than a croak. Baylon's mouth opened and closed. His breath reeked of a swamp bed.

"This shit's getting deep."

"What you mean?"

"You can't feel it? Like a noose closing in on us."

"Bout time."

Garlan glanced at him, made a mental note correcting whatever assumption he had made about the man, and started to move toward his spot on the couch.

"It's like a convention of unfuckables in here." Nine pushed past them. She took the unoccupied chair off to the side of the group, a regal pose to her bearing.

Naptown Red had the gift of assessing threats. He could take the temperature of a room with a glance and know who the true players were and who were the busters. Dred called the shots cause he was the man with a plan and the resources. Not because anyone especially feared him. There was an insecurity to him that Red knew he could exploit to roll him if need be. Garlan was straight-up soft. How he became an enforcer was further testimony to Dred's weakness. Dred didn't want anyone he deemed too great a threat at the table. Mulysa was buck. Even the new boys, Melle and Noles, he insulated himself from through Garlan. Baylon was spent meat, a used-up husk of a soldier. He was fierce in his day though. Which left the sister. Nine. She was a potential problem.

"Let me holler at you for a minute, baby."

"How you gonna try and push up on me? Your chest looks like Treebeard mated with a sad manatee." Nine's skin was the color of scorched oak, her face both passionate and cruel, her eyes vaguely Asian. She spread her finely manicured fingers as a stop sign. Her nails glinted like talons decorated for a kill.

"How'd you earn a place at the table? I've never heard of you."

"Oh the breadth and depth of what you've never heard of. You never needed to hear of me. I play the game at a whole different level. The fact that you've heard of me now means that *you* are now at a new level. Me, I've always been here. Right under your nose."

"I don't trust you. I get the feeling I'm supposed to. Some weak-ass glamour?"

"What do you want?" Nine arched an eyebrow, the only giveaway that he said something which surprised her.

"Just want to know who I'm dealing with."

"*You* don't. I deal with Dred, not his lapdogs."

"Where's Mulysa?" Naptown Red called out, already angling to take his seat. Naptown Red was faux-rage, wearing anger like a fashion accessory, more motivated by power and opportunity. Keeping his head above water exhausted him, yet hope sprang eternal with the latest scheme, the constant grind to line his pockets with Benjamins. His chest puffed in a slow waddle as if the meeting revolved around him.

"Got a court date," Dred said.

"You post on Mulysa?" Garlan asked.

"Had to. For one, we got to show loyalty to the crew. For two, we don't need to make no enemy out of one of our own." Dred was bored. The power was his, yet he was still somewhat dissatisfied. He always needed a mountain to climb, had to have a next objective, a next level. When in doubt, he built a mountain. Alexander may have wept when he realized he'd conquered the world, Dred only realized that his world was too small.

Of the remains, any who showed any game was put on. Naptown Red. Mulysa. Garlan. Nine. Baylon was still around, but Garlan was the new number one. Having Baylon around was a grim reminder of the past and what it took to step up.

"We could use him." A coy smile crossed Nine's mouth. "Specially if we gearing up for war."

"What makes you say we gearing up for war?"

"Whispers."

Dred turned to Garlan. Garlan oversaw a lot of the pee wees and wannabes. All those ten to eighteen year-old knuckleheads had to be put to the test to see if they had heart. It was more Mulysa's side of the street, but Garlan had to learn to walk it sooner or later. He might as well step up if he were testing others to see if they were ready. "How them boys work out?"

"We gonna promote little dude. Not sold on the white boy yet. They both down for whatever, though. Straight-up hoodiculous." Garlan grew anxious and down, his head all turned around as he thought about stuff he wasn't ready to think about or deal with.

"He from our set. And where we from, we take care of our own."

Dred shifted in his seat, taking in the room. He had moved to his aunt's house when he was nine. His aunt already had three kids of her own: a boy, a girl, and a toddler. The house was crammed, but she and her husband – the father of the toddler – took him in. Dred slept on the bottom of a bunk bed set with his cousin, foot to head. His female cousin got the top bunk to herself.

Every so often, he'd get a phone call from Morgana.

"Mom, when are you coming home? I miss you." His mother paused. He winced regret, knowing he'd been caught in a lie.

"You're a liar. But you go through the motions well. You're probably already fooling your aunt." Her voice sounded like pinpricks jammed into the meaty part of an infant's thigh, delighting in the pain she inflicted. It wasn't a memory as much as a recalled sensation. Remembrances of pain past.

"I want to come home, Mom."

Dred found himself looking around the room as if his mother's voice made him uncertain of his own reality. She always had that effect on him. "Who's there with you?"

"My cousins."

"Yeah. How old is she now? Eleven? Twelve?"

"Twelve."

"Yeah. She probably is already wearing a bra. You sneak peeks at your cousin while she's getting ready for bed? You think about her at night while lying next to her brother? You probably don't know what to do with yourself. Dick getting all hard, her brother jammed up next to you. All these feelings hitting you at once."

"Mom..."

"You're weak. Pathetic. You let things happen to you. You are life's perpetual plaything. Always the victim."

"But..."

"Let me speak to your auntie. The sound of your voice is making me ill. To think that something so weak came out of me."

He showed no weakness now. The Latinos would know the height of his strength and cruelty. And no one would think twice about flexing his way. To dare think on it, he'd take out their momma, sister, or daughter.

He'd left no such weakness in his life. From there he would move forward, thinking large, none of the pussy-ass dreams of these short-sighted fools. He took on the Mexicans head-on in a bid to expand his network to go national. The play was simple. Most of the crews were weak, decimated by being put on charges. Most of the rest, they hollered at. The ones that gave him any beef, he put Mulysa on. Or Melle and Noles. Those two were bloodthirsty. He'd send his young'uns into the military. Maybe provide scholarships to send them to school. That would bolster his public image as a community leader – fuck King, study your opponent, learn his moves, do them better – plus he'd own lawyers, doctors, maybe even a few police along the way. Yeah, fuck King. Dred knew him better than he knew himself; what he was going to do before he did it. All Dred had to do was wait for that moment. Or let the situation provide.

"How's our spot at the Phoenix?" Dred asked.

"Sending four birds of dope down there," Garlan said.

"Black is a more pressing matter. That refried bean eatin' motherfucker needs to get got."

"That's what I been saying," Naptown Red interjected. He hated to go too long without hearing his own voice.

"We barely up and running and you want to take on the Mexicans?" Garlan knew better than to press a challenge. He walked a fine line between checking Dred's thinking and obedience. But he wasn't doing his job if he didn't press Dred some. Respectfully.

"Folks need to know we here for real. We hold off, we can't maintain."

"So instead of stepping back, you stepping up," Nine said.

"Now you feel me. Next go round, I want product so strong it drops fiends two counties over. Look at the pieces on the table. Most of the city was divvied up between me and Night."

"Then King came along and fucked things up." Naptown Red swirled his empty glass in Nine's direction, expecting her to get him another drink. She glared at him as if he'd lost his damned mind then flipped him off. With both hands for good measure.

"King provided an opportunity. See, I stepped back, let everyone think I was out the game, every wannabe shotcaller stepped into the light. Colvin, Rellik, all them fools got taken out... *after* they built up networks, supply lines, and connects. Did my work for me."

"Only leaves one player. The Mexicans. And they shit is locked down," Garlan said.

"Don't even know how all this shit started. But they take down one of ours, we take down ten of theirs. Let's see how they like that math."

Dred knew. He'd played this game before with a girl named Michelle Lalard. He manipulated the situation to cause Baylon to have to kill her, driving a permanent wedge between him and King. And by being there for Baylon in his moment of darkness and loneliness, welcoming him with the embrace of a friend, he earned Baylon's loyalty. People never forget who was there for them when things were bleakest. Those were the people they knew they could count on when things got hot. And Dred was going to keep turning up the heat.

"Profits are up. Our control is just about absolute."
Dred peered at Baylon and Garlan with something approximating pride. "We have to work hard and stay vigilant. Done made ourselves our share of enemies."

"Do dirt, get dirty," Garlan said. Garlan's mouth tightened as he studied the cracks in the floor tiles. It meant something to be treated with respect, to be treated like a man. Dred and his crew relieved him of that isolation, but only he knew the intimacies of his pain, how it bricked him up inside. How the desperation of loneliness and feeling unimportant added this level of crazy intensity to the people you reach out to when you're alone. The game was spinning out of control. The drama they were talking about was already too costly and there was no end in sight. He needed to slow it down or get out.

"Everyone at this table has got respect. Earned it."

"No disrespect," Naptown Red began, "but what have you done?" The air seemed to have been sucked out the room. The players all but physically moved away from Red, carefully distancing themselves in case he didn't check himself. "I mean, this is your show, no doubt. No doubt. But how long we gonna put up with King?"

"King," Dred began in a slow, halting tone beset with threat, "is out of play."

"Why not finish him?"

"He's suffering."

"I'm just saying, you don't want to appear soft. To the Mexicans."

Dred had climbed the mountaintop and controlled everything. But no one knew. King had been defeated, had become despondent, and was out of the game. The cops barely knew who he was. He was so far behind the scenes, his name didn't ring out the way he wanted. Or that others would respect. He had the power of position, by way of title, but too many thought it was handed to him. That his crown was unearned. "That how you all feel?"

"Just saying, if King had been a thorn in my side," Naptown Red's bravado becoming bolder, "even if he's hurting now, I'd go ahead and put that dog down. But it's your show."

"Bloodless ascents," Nine said with a hint of a smirk, "blood carried out in your name but not by your hands."

"You think too small. There's a whole world beyond the hood. Got to think big. Like businessmen. Expand the trade in ways we haven't thought about. Time to finish our hostile takeover." Dred read the room. Confident in his overall strategy, he accepted that he'd have to put in a more personal touch in order to hold the center. "Red, you and Baylon handle the Black problem. I'll take care of King."

"We all have our part to play," Nine said.

CHAPTER FIVE

Wayne ripped the first pair of rubber gloves he tried to put on. Making a mental note to have a conversation with their volunteer coordinator, who also ordered supplies, that not everyone had "medium" sized hands, he slipped another pair on. The gloves were so tight-fitting they restricted his movement, but better ill-fitting gloves than no gloves at all. Now he was ready for the task at hand.

Isabel "Iz" Cornwall had been admitted to the hospital. Complications from drug withdrawal on her hopelessly over-taxed immune system. The doctors administered high doses of antibiotics while observing her for a few more days. Tristan Drust, her girlfriend, dropped off her things to the Outreach Inc. house, then disappeared mysteriously yet again. Wayne recognized the restlessness on Tristan's face, the caged beast waiting to go on the hunt. Revenge seethed in her eyes. That kind of anger had a way of consuming a person, but she wasn't in a place to talk. Instead, she dropped off trash bags full of Iz's stuff.

"The glamour leave yet?" Wayne passed a trash bag to Esther Baron.

"What glamour?" Esther pulled on her gloves with ease, but stared at the bags with mild distrust. She hated the way she looked and was always at war with her body, from one diet to the next, counting calories and miles walked in a day. She considered herself too short (which she could do nothing about) and too dumpy (which she was determined to change). Esther was one of those people easily overlooked in a room. Not the center of attention, not quick to speak, and without the presence or immediate kind of beauty people gravitated to, she simply went about her business. Her actions spoke for her as she dove into life at Outreach Inc with both feet. She had been volunteering with Outreach Inc for over a year now because she wanted to be a part of the hope the organization represented.

"You know, the idea of helping homeless teens. Most folks figure it's just handing out food, water, and socks, and calling it a day."

"No, I'm in it for the long haul." Esther hid behind the belief that she would always be seen as the outsider. The rich white girl who lived in Fishers who occasionally slummed with the poor folks to make herself feel better. White liberal guilt as a fashion accessory. Whatever. People could think what they wanted, she couldn't control that. She focused on doing what she knew she ought to be doing. "Now quit."

"Quit what?"

"I feel like you're always testing me. Pushing me away to see if I'll leave."

He had been. Sort of. He didn't want anyone around the kids who couldn't commit to being in their lives for months. They needed to see that folks would be there and be consistent and not simply abandon them when things got tough. They'd seen enough of that. "Well, if you say so, dig in."

Esther opened up her bag, took a whiff, and shut it again. It smelled of moldy cellars and damp closets. "What are we doing?"

"These are the worldly belongings of Miss Isabel Cornwall."

"Iz?"

"The one and the same."

"They're soaked."

"Yeah. Probably sat outside for a day or two."

"Or a month." Esther tentatively opened the bag again and peeled back a layer of jeans. She hated the sticky sound they made as she pulled them apart.

"We need to go through her things. Look for any ID or prescriptions that can help us."

"Help us do what?"

"Verify parts of her story. Establish who she is so that we can help her get whatever ID, papers, assistance we can. Any meds so that doctors know what she's on."

"So we need to…"

"… go through all her pockets."

Esther stretched the pair of damp jean out along the floor and reached into a pocket. Something jabbed her finger and she dropped the jeans as if she'd been bit. Visions of junkie needles and a future living with Hep C or AIDS flashed through her head. Gingerly, she opened the pant pocket. It was a hair clip. "Oh."

"You okay over there?"

"Yeah. just surprised by all the random things I'm finding."

"Me too." Wayne opened a pink purse. Inside was
nothing but damp panties. He tossed them onto the pile
of them he'd found in purses, pockets, and packages. "I
have never seen a larger collection of panties in my life."

"A girl's got to have drawers. Found some over here,
too." Esther rifled through another purse. "She's fond of
leopard prints."

"Found a prescription." Wayne turned a coat pocket
inside out. "Abilify."

"Found another one." Esther smiled at keeping pace
with Wayne's finds. Having two older brothers, the blood
rush of competition reared its head. "And..."

Wayne paused with his hands full of bras and a bewildered look on his face. The sight caused Esther to burst
out laughing. "What?"

"Here." She handed him a social security card.

"Bam!" Wayne exclaimed. "That the biggie. This
should make getting her some assistance much easier."

"It's almost time for drop. Should I throw those in the
wash?"

"Yeah. Only cause she's in the hospital and we don't
know when Tristan will be back."

"Or if."

"Right. But, as much as you may want to, don't get
into the habit of doing that kind of stuff. I know it may
seem like you're helping, but you wouldn't be. We're not
their personal assistants. We don't do for them what they
can do for themselves."

"Got it. I'll take care of this. Someone's already here."

Esther toted the two trash bags, waving off Wayne's initial move to assist her. Wayne peeked out the window. Rhianna carried her newborn, swaddled in two layers of blankets. Normally, he'd let her wait outside until it was time for drop, as it was important that the kids learned and respected boundaries. But he wasn't going to leave her outside with the little one.

"Good evening, Rhianna." Wayne bowed before her and waved her in.

"You so silly." Her hair flared, interlocked lockets in need of re-twisting. She carried herself with a fierce sexiness. Upon closer inspection, her worn, bruised skin added a hint of purple to her sepia complexion. Her half-jacket, with nothing underneath, exposed her pierced belly button and tattoo on the small of her back. Over blue jeans. She had the sour tang of unwashed ass.

"How's the little man?" Wayne teased the blankets away from his face to get a better look.

"Good."

"What's his name?"

"Haven't made up my mind yet."

"So what do you call him?"

"Baby."

"Girl, you a trip. Let me hold him." Baby struggled as if he wanted to crawl back into her womb and wait for a better world. Wayne hoisted "Baby" with ease and noted the brief grimace of worry on Rhianna's face, and it reassured him in an odd way. Her attachment to the newborn.

The child was all Rhianna would know of love. She'd spent too much of her teen years going to parties or hooking up. Too worried about food to dream of a future. She had no room for baby thoughts or baby dreams. And a still, quiet voice within her hoped his thoughts and dreams would rub off on her. From the moment she found out she was pregnant, she knew she didn't have a choice but to be with him. She'd have this baby. Have someone to love. Things would be different this time.

Rhianna's mother once crossed a set. She had the rep for sleeping around, not caring which block they came from or what set they claimed. And she had a knack for choosing the precise wrong ones. Word on the street for those who listened, had it that she once dumped Geno for Speedbump, two up-and-coming young princes of the streets. The two men exchanged words. The argument was heard by Speedbump's brother, who came down to get his brother out. Bama, who was country crazy and only needed an excuse, saw the brewing fight and got his weapon. When Bama came out, all he saw was Geno and Speedbump's brother after Speedbump. He didn't realize or care that Speedbump had broken away from his pursuing brother – who only wanted to keep his brother safe. Geno caught three bullets to the back. He survived, but he was never the same. Dropped out of the game.

The streets buzzed with the news, the blame quickly traced back to Rhianna's mom, who was set to get a retaliatory beat down. Possibly take a bullet herself when the female members of the crew caught up with her. They caught up with her at her aunt's crib. She called the police even before she heard them bang at the door. Rhianna couldn't have been older than four. Her mother beat her, slamming her face into the bathroom sink,

and when Five-O showed up, she blamed the girls. The confu-
sion bought her mother time. That evening, she was gone.

"You alone?" Wayne asked.

"With my boyfriend."

"Where'd he go? Or does 'boyfriend' imply much more of a commitment to the relationship than he's ready for?"

"He didn't even leave a tip."

"Chivalry is dead."

"Said he was coming through though."

"You see Lady G lately?"

"Nah, I ain't trying to hang with her no more."

"Thought she was your girl."

"She was. Till she did King like she did."

"Everyone makes mistakes."

"You hang with Lott?" Rhianna asked.

"No, but he's been on the creep tip. No one knows where he's at."

"Cause he know, too. You don't just do your boy like that."

"We supposed to be family. Family can work through problems together, no matter how hard, because at the end of the day, we still blood."

"I ain't trying to hear that."

"If we can't find a way to forgive and..."

"Ain't. Trying."

Someone pounded on the front door then – either impatient with the lack of immediate response or just noticing the doorbell – rang the doorbell five times in a row. Wayne passed Baby back to Rhianna, his mood spoiling with each additional ring.

"Hey, my dude." The young, white, red-headed boy had a heroin thinness to him and the disposition of someone who would sell out his dying mother for his next fix or to avoid prison. A patch covered one of his eyes, the surrounding area of his face webbed with healed-over scars.

"What's up?" Wayne said. "You here for drop?"

"My breezy said I could swing through. And I'm all about the free swing, you feel me?" He raised his fist for a bump. Wayne let it hang there.

"I'm Wayne."

"My people call me Fathead."

"Where you stay at?"

"Used to stay with this one dude. Partner had a cat. One day the cat turns up missing and he blamed me. Said I let it out and shit. So he kicked me out."

"Did you?"

"I ain't trying to keep track of no pussy that walks on four legs. Shit. Dude still owes me so I took his bike and pants."

"You took his pants?"

"Wasn't like they were his no way."

This was the kind of introduction that made his job both frustrating and exhilarating. Wayne had met many "Fathead"s over the years. Nothing was ever their fault and trouble just seemed to always – completely randomly – follow them about. Still, they had their quirky charm about them – so genuine in their utter bullshit – that he couldn't help but be drawn to them. Every Fathead was an opportunity to show God's love and mercy.

Wayne stepped out of the doorway to let Fathead in. Rhianna rushed up to him as if they were long-lost friends reunited at long last, and hugged him for several moments.

"We'll be having dinner in a few minutes." Wayne put his hand on Fathead's shoulder, nudging them apart.

"Hey man, do you have any points?"

"We don't do needle exchanges here."

"Oh my bad."

Esther walked into the dining room carrying a large bowl of salad as one of the other volunteers for the night toiled away in the kitchen. She hesitated when she saw Fathead, then not wanting to stare at his eye patch, arranged the array of salad dressing.

"No worries, baby. I ain't self-conscious of this shit. My pops put a cigarette out in my eye when I was a baby. Had a glass one, but I lost that shit. Got a marble I use sometimes. You want to see it?"

"No, that's all right."

"Not 'Baby'." Wayne glanced over at Rhianna and smiled at the irony. "Her name's Ms Esther."

Percy wandered out of the kitchen. Tipping nearly three bills, he had a darker knot above his left eyebrow in the shape of a crescent moon. His downcast eyes rarely met people in the eye. Carrying a tray of cinnamon graham crackers and milk, he liked to pretend that he'd made them from his secret recipe. They were the last addition to the food set out for that evening's drop night. Wayne stood at the dining room table and gestured for them to join him. He took Esther's hand as they all clasped hands.

"Percy, you want to bless the food?"

"God is great, God is good. Let us thank Him for our food," Percy said. "By His hands we all are fed. Thank You, Lord, for our daily bread."

"Amen." Wayne clapped Percy on the back. He'd come a long way from the shy boy too spooked by his own shadow to speak. And there were still untapped pools of potential they hadn't begun to reach. Percy radiated a peace about him, a simplicity many confused with him being simple.

"Has anyone seen Prez?" Percy asked.

"Prez ain't right." Rhianna sprawled down low in a wooden dinette chair which only matched three others pulled around the table.

"What you mean?" Wayne passed a bowl of mashed potatoes.

"He stays up in his crib. Avoids us."

"You know why?"

"Cause of… how things went down. You know how tight he was with King."

"Yeah. I keep meaning to check in on him," Wayne said.

"Someone ought to. He up in his room all day."

"He back with Big Momma?"

"Naw, he on his own." Rhianna piled salad on her plate. "He's just sort of… lost… without King."

King's personal mission, Prez, had come far, too. He'd fallen into drugs, but King walked with him through his addiction to the other side. Addicts could always find one another, like they had a radar for that weakness.

Despite the familiar sickness in his stomach, Fathead

still chased after his high. Though he remembered the first time he got high with crystal clarity – a memory driven home by the fact that he had sex for the first time while high – the rest of that summer he could barely recall. Not feeling whole, he doubted himself. But when he smoked marijuana, it was like aspirin for the soul and fixed the ache for a while. The shameful things he had to do to earn only gave him more of a reason to get that high. Shooting up was the next obvious progression. The first time he shot up, he shot his load straight into his muscle. It burned so badly, he didn't think he'd walk again. Luckily, he had internet access and taught himself how to properly shoot up. Setting up his rig, he located a vein on his wrist and got off. The high was perfection. Effortless. For the first time, he knew wholeness. All his hopes, dreams, and worries faded; fear no longer consumed him. Life suddenly worked. A few hours later, it was over and he was scared again. After that, it was a short trip to the land of an addict's broken promises and second/third/fourth chances: snorting crystals up his nose, drunk on Stoli, stoned on Ambien stolen from rehab, breaking into his parents' house, and writing checks to himself.

Fathead plopped down on the couch in what passed for a living room in the Outreach Inc house. He shifted without purpose, not quite knowing what to do with himself. His family didn't exactly sit around discussing the day's events with one another, so he withdrew from the dining room table, unsure what to do with himself. His hands found a pencil next to a notepad on the coffee table beside him. Without asking whose pad it was, he began to doodle his name on the pad. An ornate "F" as if he sketched what a tag of his name might look like.

"Man, look at you. You about as uncomfortable as a fat man adjusting his thong." Wayne walked over to him. "Want me to hook up the games?"

"I don't even recognize that gaming system. This shit should be in a museum." Fathead covered his mouth in a "my bad" gesture for cussing.

"It's free. It's here. And your alternative is sitting on the couch staring at nothing."

Their Nintendo 64 couldn't exactly compete with the latest game system, but it had been donated to the house, in that way rich folks gave away their "old" things when they got the latest model. Part of him chided himself for being so constantly cynical. It wasn't as if he wasn't called to love the wealthy also, but somehow it was so much harder for him. He hated the waste, the excess, the sense of entitlement. Life was simple and was to be lived simply. Plus, he grew up with this game system, so he could beat any of the kids on the games.

Fathead picked out a hunting game that came with guns that plugged directly into the television. Spreading his legs shoulder-length apart, he relaxed his knees to squat low. He pulled his bandana up over his mouth and turned his gun sideways. He twisted his right and then left, popping the joints in his neck, then nodded to Wayne.

Wayne did a sly double-take, staring at the boy like he was a damn fool. "Does the mask help?"

"I'm more into it." Fathead raised the mask. "You know they call me 'Wolf', right."

"Thought they called you 'Fathead'."

"That too. See, I used to raise timber wolves on my uncle's property. One day, when we were out hunting on his property – man must have a thousand acres – we found a litter. The mother had been shot dead. So we decided to raise the litter. Sold all of them but one off. My uncle decided to keep that one for himself. Probably how I got such a good sense of smell."

"What do you mean?"

"This one time I was standing downtown on the circle, I turned to my friends and was like 'Dude, I can smell Noles from here. He's on his way.' Now Noles stay down on Washington and Lynhurst, and sure enough, two and a half hours later, he came walking up. I smelled him just as he was leaving the house."

"You use the truth interesting ways." Wayne hit start on the game.

During the course of the next hour, Fathead claimed to be a trained martial artist and having died and been brought back five times in one night. What Wayne had been able to glean from the endless stream of BS that flew out of his mouth was that Fathead sold weed and hung out with a rougher set than he intended, who attacked him a few times. And trouble always followed him.

Percy, hanging a few steps away from everyone else, hid on the couch. Where the spread of light from the lamps failed to blanket. He loved many of the people in this room, Rhianna, Wayne, and Esther especially, but he sat on the fringe of them as if an invisible wedge separated him. A recurring dream troubled him in ways he didn't understand and couldn't articulate. At first he thought about how his friends all seemed beset by disturbing dreams which set them on edge. But his dream came from a different place. The images stayed with him during the day. No one noticed his odd posture, shoulders pulled in, a large man tucking his body within itself if possible.

A ruined church, a place of hope reduced to a darkened chamber. Overturned pews and a broken altar, the hall lit by the suffuse light of dimming candles. A boy came in holding a white gun – a pearl-white hand grip, white shaft – on a velvet pillow. He passed in front of a fire. Two boys each carried stands of ten candles. A young girl, in his heart he wanted her to be Rhianna, came in holding a cup. The cup was pure gold inlaid with precious stones. Percy knelt before the cup, ready to drink. The liquid burned like fire and tasted of ash. Then he'd wake up.

The familiar sickness rose in Fathead's stomach and threw his game off. Eating probably wasn't the best idea, but he didn't know when he'd next have a proper meal. He hoped that something sweet would take the edge off his pain. As if she knew, Rhianna brought him a plate with two pieces of pie on it. He was struck by how sweet his fellow users were. That was, when they weren't scheming to take each other off. Unlike Rhianna, who had her baby to give her a reason, he was afraid to come off the drugs. Bad as things got, despite the terrible things he had to do to earn, the only times he truly felt worthless were when he didn't have a girlfriend. He'd go home when he ran out of options. Then it occurred to him that he had no idea what movies were out, what television shows were on or if a new war had broken out. That world didn't matter.

A coiled threat waiting to spring, Tristan waited beside Iz's bed, her knee bouncing with its own energy as she ground her teeth. The room door remained closed as she waited for a doctor to make her appearance. This was not how she wanted to spend another evening. She missed the days of sitting on the floor between Iz's too-skinny, white-girl legs, Iz's fingers scraping the jar of hair-braiding oil, foraging for it to give up the last of its contents. Not that Iz was all that skilled at braiding hair, but her touch was intimate and knowing, her very presence reassuring.

Tristan shifted in the uncomfortable green vinyl chair, which had no give to it so she never found a sweet spot she could rest in. Her black hoodie covered her crest of mauve-dyed braids and shadowed most of her face. She filled the seat with her big-boned frame, though she didn't have a trace of fat. Amber eyes with gold flecks took in the features of her beloved while she slept.

"You about to jump out of your skin." Iz toted an IV stand behind her as she baby-stepped from the bathroom to her bed. A tattoo of a dragon on the base of her back on full display within the flimsy hospital robe. The fabric of the sheets scraped against her thin skin and she winced. Tristan flinched in her seat, ready to bound to help, but Iz waved her off.

"Just anxious is all."

"It'll be all right. I'll be all right."

"Look at you. A good breeze could bowl you over."

"Doctors said I'd be fitten to get out of here in a day."

"Shouldn't have been here in the first place."

"I said I was sorry."

"Shit. No, baby," Tristan slipped onto the edge of Iz's bed with a tenderness that belied her stocky frame, more built for fighting than nursing. "I wasn't blaming you. I was thinking of Mulysa. He did this to you."

He did other things, too. Maybe. It was all such a haze to Iz. Her head pounded and her vision blurred.

Though always on the scrawny side, Iz's body had shrunk down to a prisoner-of-war thinness. Her sunken cheekbones framed her face, a long nose embedded with a stud appeared more so against the hollow pits of her eyes. The dye of her black hair slowly faded revealing her natural brown hair. Picking at her skin, she caught sight of Tristan's disapproving gaze and tried to find something else to do with her hands. And not think about the terrible burrowing beneath her skin. She wondered if Tristan understood her shame, as she spent so much time in the bathroom picking pellets out of her ass because her body was no longer producing stool.

The first time she smoked pot, she was nine. In the fugue state of her relapse into drug use, she accidently shot up the piece of cotton drawn into her needle. The ride felt like she'd fallen head first onto the sidewalk from five stories up. She remembered throwing up until she blacked out. And Mulysa's hands exploring her. The room spun.

Without warning, Iz sprang out of bed with no trace of recognition in her eyes, and she lunged at Tristan. The first swipe caught the meat of Tristan's cheek, the scratch drawing blood. Tristan cocked a ready fist to defend herself, a survival reflex, but caught herself. This wasn't the first time Iz had flipped out, a kind of psychotic break. Tristan backed away, hands held out as non-threatening as possible.

"Iz, baby, this isn't you. It's me, Trys. I love you, baby."

Iz chased after her, a glare somewhere between fury and pain, biting at her and arms flailing. Tristan grabbed her arms and wrapped around her as best she could.

"Come back to me. It's okay."

Exhausting her spindly frame rapidly, Iz heard her, the light of familiarity filling her eyes again, and they collapsed onto the floor.

"What'd you do to yourself, girl?" Tristan whispered, closing her eyes to press back the tears.

Her dad had died from years of alcohol abuse when his liver gave out. Or maybe it was the pills. Iz was too little to remember, and her mother never had a good memory to share of him. Destruction was in Iz's nature. She once took a pair of scissors and tore up all the clothes in her babysitter's closet. This made it hard to find babysitters, not that it stopped her mother from going out. Her mother once abandoned her for two days. It was the first time Child Protective Services was called for her. Mother always left her to go somewhere to cop the best drugs, and she was only about the best. She strung together boyfriends based on who dealt the best stuff. When the school needed to get a hold of her, Iz gave them the cell phone number of her mother's dealer. And when she was out of money and her body was used up, she sold one of her other daughters. That was the last time CPS was called on her mother.

Iz remembered her first stint at rehab. She wasn't ready yet but the court mandated a stint at the Beacon House. When they found her, she had a spray can pressed to her face as she huffed in the janitorial closet. She ran away soon after. When Tristan found her in the alley, a prostitute beaten and left for dead, but still dragging herself along the gravel by her fingers toward her dealer, then she had bottomed out. Tristan sat beside her during the worst of it then. Tristan sent her to school and kept anyone who might distract her from her dreams at bay. And it was Tristan whose anger burned so hot her embrace was like a cauldron.

"Someone has to give Mulysa what he deserves."

CHAPTER SIX

Not one for existential considerations, Lee McCarrell hated the vague ache in his chest, as if he'd been hollowed out, as he pulled into the abandoned bank parking lot. A piece of hot tail reduced him to his high school days of bad poetry and rubbing his joint by moonlight, pining away for cheerleaders who didn't notice him. Every fiber in him called him the damned fool, the played-out simp, obsessing over a girl. A girl. An errant piece of pussy had him all twisted up inside and chasing after even the hope of catching a glimpse of her. Though, truth be told, it was a fine line between being led by his heart and being led by his dick. For the last few nights he'd made it part of his routine to pass the empty building as often as possible, no better than going by the cheerleader's locker after every class. If a body dropped or he had a run, if he had a lunch break or simply took lost time, he drove by. Across from the Phoenix Apartments, it was a known haunt for prostitutes, but there was only one working girl he was interested in.

Omarosa.

An atrophied brick husk of a building, the drive-through an easy shelter from the rain, the alcove an easy place to ditch one's works, the overgrown bushes a place to store a change of clothes, and the front exposed to a full view of 38th Street and the Phoenix Apartments. The bank building fell into disrepair once the branch had been sold from one big-name bank to another. And the "another" decided a branch across from the Phoenix Apartments, in such a high-crime, high-risk, high-insurance area, wasn't very profitable.

A lone woman paced the sidewalk like a panther trapped in a too-confining cage. Sleek, angry, muscles coiled and ready to pounce, only the slightest lock of her head betrayed that she knew he was near. He slammed the car into park and stepped out as coolly as his anxious heart allowed. He stopped to light a cigarette to force him to wait or at least not immediately dash over like a strung-out school boy. Crossing the lot with a determined stride, he marched with a rapid pace undercutting his air of cool control. His gaze looked on hers, neither flush nor anxious, oblivious to being the only white boy out walking the streets, marking him as either cop, fiend, or fool.

"Been a minute," Omarosa said with an aristocratic air despite her black halter top over a blue jean skirt, which had a set of handcuffs dangling between two loops. A blade clung to her inner thigh, a deucy deucy in her purse, and a shotgun in the bushes, all within easy reach. Lee's usefulness had about come to an end and she prepared to discard him the way this age discarded magic.

"I ain't see you around, thought I'd chance swinging by one of your spots."

"You were lucky I didn't mind being found." A nest of fine braids, not a hair out of place, lined her head. Skin the color of overcreamed coffee, she possessed high cheekbones and a long, aquiline nose. Her eyes had a winsome slant to them. However, her pointed ears betrayed the fact that the blood of the fey ran through her veins. She brushed close to him, perfectly aware of the effect her presence had on him. Her musk intoxicated him and she stepped nearer to allow him to feel the heat of her proximity.

"What are you up to?"

"Hunting."

"Hunting what?" Lee tired of her games, though not to the point where he would risk having her leave his bed. She was his ears and eyes to the streets. All gained through whispers between his sheets. She read things and had a view not even the most seasoned cop could. Her intel and insight made him a god in the gang task force. Too on-point, he determined, to not be mixed up in it somehow. But he pursued a "don't ask, don't tell" policy as her info led to busts which kept him too useful to fire. Still, even the best runs came to an eventual end. As she lost interest in him, reading the streets became like him fumbling over Braille. And Omarosa could easily go too far.

"Who."

"Hunting who?"

"The slayer of my brother, Colvin," Her voice was husky and feminine, sultry with a hint of threat.

"You looking for Baylon?" It was the name she uttered the last time she'd spurned his advances. "Word has it that he's holed up with Dred. Ain't left the man's side like he's a newborn after some tit. Or else he knows you out here waiting for him. So why not lay low" *(with me)* "and wait for him to pop his head up when he thinks it's safe?"

"You don't understand our ways. My brother needed to be put down like the rabid beast he'd become. But honor demanded it be by someone whose hand was worthy."

"Like King?"

"As you say. Not the dog of a scoundrel."

"Like Dred." Lee struggled to connect the players in this puzzle. Unlike Cantrell, he wasn't that kind of cop. He needed a door to crash through or a head to bust. "I don't know why you're so worked up. It's not like you had any love for him."

"Love isn't the point. He was of the fey. That motherfucker Baylon needs to get got. The longer I have to wait, the worse it will be for him."

"I don't give a fuck who he was of. You don't get to 'hunt' on my watch."

Omarosa's eyes narrowed. That was the only warning Lee had, not that it did any good. Gone were the moments of a cat toying with a wounded bird, which was the normal thrill of her encounters with him. Gone were the ideas of using him to misdirect police attentions or gleaning information about police investigations. Gone was any of the cool numbness which passed for affection from her. All she had was rage. She stabbed her elbow into the side of his neck, then administered a double-palm heel blow to both ears. His arms lashed about, stunned and grabbing the air for purchase. Omarosa grabbed two fistfuls of his shirt and drew him near.

"Who are you to judge the ways of the fey? You do not realize your place in the scheme of things. Should you or your brethren get between me and Baylon, you will learn what Baylon will suffer firsthand, what true fey rage is capable of."

At the release of his shirt, he dropped to the ground. His instinct was to grab for his weapon and haul her ass in. But he knew two things: one, he'd have a hell of a time explaining the nature of their relationship; and two, if his hand had touched a weapon, she'd have killed him three different ways before he had the chance to draw it.

Merle poured enough ketchup next to his cheeseburger to make his makeshift plate of cardboard look like a congealed crime scene. He dipped his cheeseburger into the red pool then took loud, wet bites. Reaching for a nearby straw, he dragged it through his ketchup pool. Something in the blood-like smear drew his attention. He poured more ketchup on his plate and plunged his straw into the mess. His eyes glazed over with sights privy only to him. Tracing patterns into the sludge, spreading the goo like a Neanderthal along a cave wall, his hands sped up in a manic fashion. Part of him dreaded this meet, being caught up in things beyond his (no, their) control. Tormented by unwanted persistent thoughts of her. Of them. He marveled at his ability to hold two sets of contradictory thoughts at once.

"Hold on, hold on," he muttered, both non-committed and diffident. "Think of it as the principles of geomancy mixed with automatic writing. Ketchupmancy."

Merle didn't have the heart to tell King the truth, not the complete truth anyway. The complete truth was too large to handle, like staring into time, past, present, and future at the same time, seeing all of the possibilities and connections and not going a little bit mad in the explanations of it all. So a simple-sounding question like "How could they do this?" asked by King might have gotten the response "you mean 'again' or 'why not avoid it next time'?" Would that have been any better an answer than "They are bound by the echoes of the story. Just as you are."

Merle tore pieces of bread and scattered it on the ground before him. A brown and black squirrel with a gray streak along its back scampered back and forth between lobbed pieces.

"What say you, Sir Rupert? How do you say he was chosen? Chosen by the story. There was once a man like any other man. At times brave. At times selfish. At times bold. At times troubled. He had a call, but often ignored it. Fought it. Even ran from it. Sorrow without top, sorrow without bottom."

The squirrel reared up on its hind legs and chewed in greedy rapid bites.

"Yes, yes. He stirred something in them and they dared to hope. They lived for a dream long denied.

King's uncertainty broke the circle. His doubt. Once again, it's all at risk. What had been a place, a community, was now separate houses threatening to be razed."

The squirrel froze. Its nose twitched. Once. Twice.

"Sir Rupert! That's no way for a gentleman to speak of a lady."

It scurried up a nearby tree across a limb and onto the roof top.

"You're back," Merle said to the figure emerging from the shadows.

"Did you think I wouldn't return?" Nine circled him.

"No, I feared you would. I know who you are." It was as if he poured himself into her or her into him. Like using the dragon's breath, giving herself to him, yet holding part of herself back. She refused him her person, letting his unrequited passion bind him to her. The most ancient of magics: lust. A silly girl's power to besot foolish old men. His heart longed for her and doted on her.

"Didn't I fool you for a minute?" Her confidence working up to where she wanted to go, slithering in the dark. She traced the letter "M" in the air, green iridescent sparkles shimmered in her wake.

Yes, he knew who she was. She unnerved him. His mouth ran dry. "You're acquainted with my mother, Mab, the queen of the fairies? They are the oldest of all. Like all creatures of old, they came to this new world and slept. Or blended into the background when it wasn't their time. They know things. Their kind was particularly fond of glamours. Some were necromancers and wielded death magic. Some used the power of both and could assume any shape. Recreate themselves. A useful skill when one needed to bide their time. Or was driven underground."

"Does this form please you, mage?" Nine danced near and ran her finger along Merle's chest. The flattering attention from youth to fill an old man's sails. She delighted in bending men to her will. Beauty and enchantment. Hers was the weapon of jealousy. Trapped, she was doubly dangerous.

"Does it come with a story?"

"It does. I was home-schooled for my entire childhood. Cloistered away in a familial nunnery of sorts. My parents were afraid of outside influences. But while they clung to one image of their little girl, other people could sense my dark side. Other home-school families shunned us and encouraged their kids to do the same. They hated me. The other women didn't trust me around their husbands even as a young teenager. Made sure to read me the story of the adulterous woman whenever they had a Sunday School lesson to impart. They constantly harped on my clothing: my skirts too short, my tops too revealing. Always striving to make me insecure about how I looked. Do you think my top is too revealing?" Nine leaned over to allow a full, teasing view.

"That's a good story."

"I thought so. Enough to make you feel rather sympathetic toward me."

Nine was a clever story but a simple one. There was another story Nine could have told. About a little girl long ago, overlooked in her family. Their little girl, all but ignored by the brighter lights in her family. Older siblings. Cousins. No one noticed her or her gifts. Except for an uncle. He crept into her bed late at night. His breath on her neck, light kisses on her back, lost in her dreams. Next thing she knew, a weight pressed on her chest. Some folks called it witch riding: when you think you're awake but can't move anything. You wanted to move and you know something bad was going to happen. If you could move anything, wiggle a finger or something, you snapped out of it. But it wasn't a witch sitting on her chest. She awoke to him on top of her. Then he was in her and her virginity was taken from her. That was the last time anything was taken from her. The world taught her that it was out to fuck her so she had made up her mind that she was going to fuck it first. The next night, he had the nerve to once again crawl into bed with her as if he had done her a pleasurable service the night before. She slit his throat from ear to ear and was sent away.

"You have not perfected your faults. Does your son know who you are?"

"He'd kill me if he knew. He's already tried once."

"You nestled the serpent too close to that poisoned sac you call your bosom for too long. You need to punch him in the throat like a space ninja."

"Oh, mad mage. You know who I am, yet you wanted to see me again."

"Because you are my end," Merle said.

"And you come willingly into my arms?"

"That's the story that has been written."

"Show me your magic. Teach me the ways of the dragon."

"My final lesson?"

"Yes."

"When King needs me at his side most?"

"That's the story that has been written." At the mention of King's name, she stepped back in pause. The final battle loomed and those too near were liable to fall.

"And what do I get in return?"

"I offer you the pain you inflict on others."

"I fear Sir Rupert will never let me hear the end of this."

La Payasa had no time for foolishness.

Black wanted his power to be felt, his name to ring out. He'd fought too hard to reach his spot for him to be pushed aside. He wouldn't be punked. The streets would know his rage and acknowledge his presence. For La Payasa, it meant making sure his own house was in order.

Black's mother's home was holy ground. No one neared it without facing La Payasa. Not any chavalas. Not the police. Not even broken down old men repairing cars in the parking lot. She approached with a lilting step, at first glance no one to take notice of. Her yellow hair had black roots. Black and gold, the colors of her crew, and her way of proudly displaying their colors.

"You go to move this shit." Menace filled her eyes.

"I got to earn, too. You ain't the only one who needs to get over," said an old man with a head too small for his body, from beneath the hood of a car. Revealing a teak complexion, and gray goatee, when he fully stepped from behind the car, he fumbled inside his shirt pocket for a pair of thick, black-framed glasses as if dou-ble-checking a vision.

"I said you gots to go, old man." La Payasa repeated. She hated repeating herself as it lowered her in the eyes of her men. And she'd worked damn hard to rise to her rank.

"That's some bullshit, girl," the old man said in front of her men. "It ain't fair."

"You just don't listen, do you? Got to make this harder on yourself. I got something for you."

A wall of vatos in white wife beaters and baggy shorts crowded around, blocking the scene from prying eyes. La Payasa couldn't let challenge to her authority go unanswered. Especially openly. The five-point crown was peace. Violent only when necessary. She raised the cross that dangled from her neck, kissed it, then tucked it into her shirt. She went to a different place when she had to put in work. A place of raised voices, when a raised voice meant violence soon followed like lightning to the storm's thunder. The place of the lie. When the words "Hija de la gran puta, desgraciada no sirves para nada!" may as well have been her name. To be con-demned as a disgraceful daughter of a bitch, good for nothing, then beaten with whatever she could get her hands on. Extension cords. Brooms. Belts. Shoes. All were fair game. All were layers of gasoline and timber, ready fuel for the fire she would have to unleash. Even on herself. Fed up, one day she snatched the belt from mother's hands. "This is how you spank someone," she shouted, then beat herself so bad she bled. Her mother left her alone after that. She no longer lived in the flinch, that state of readiness, of expectation of the raised voice. She *was* the raised voice.

Punched in the face, stomach, and kidneys until he dropped, the old man didn't resist as he was hauled away. Swatting their hands, he crawled off. "Fuck you," he spat out a drool of blood.

"Se la sale como agua," she said to herself.

An unmarked berry idled slowly toward the scene, the siren chirping once for them to disperse. At that, Detective Cantrell Williams stepped out of the car and marched toward La Payasa. His partner Lee McCarrell lingered closer to their car.

"La Payasa." The detective introduced them in Spanish. Cantrell had taken Spanish in high school more because Amanda Fisher took it and he was a thrall to his teenage crushes, though he never did work up the nerve to ask her out. Lee spoke English and demanded that the world, or at least its representatives that crossed his borders, spoke it also. Lee made scowling faces, the international language of increasing displeasure.

"Detective." La Payasa sucked at something stuck in her teeth.

"You ain't afraid to let your people see you chatting with me?" Cantrell had ducked out on the cameras, claiming a personal errand. He had been working on building up relationships within the Hispanic gangs. He figured if he were more of a presence, not just the face of police to lock folks up, he could get more cooperation.

La Payasa he knew from her numerous run-ins with the police, from all kinds of petty drug stuff to attacking her mother.

"What's to see?"

"That old man looks like he had a rough day." Cantrell nodded in the direction the old man stumbled off to.

"You need to talk to him about that. Find some witnesses and build you a case."

"Still, wasn't no need to fuck him up like that."

"I know. It's the cost out here. It's the message. You can't show no weakness."

"Cost is too high. Taking a piece of your soul every time." La Payasa was a bright girl, the kind that both gave Cantrell hope and broke his heart. She had so much leadership potential that went wasted on the streets.

Her hands danced in a frenetic dance, her hands twisting in odd contortions as she spelled out the name of her crew. Inverting her arms to nail down some of the more intricate finger placements – her pointer finger under her middle, curving thumb to make an "S", crossing her ring finger and then spreading her other three fingers – each hand pose was a point of pride as she stacked their clique.

"You done?" Cantrell took mental notes.

"You know how we do?"

"Yeah. But I'm here about her." Cantrell flashed a picture of Lyonessa. He painted a picture of a girl in the wrong place at the wrong time. Caught up in the foolishness of an older brother and those meant to watch out for her. And that perhaps she was cute enough that despite her not being blonde and blue-eyed, her image might get some play on the evening news.

"Nobody cares."

"We do." Cantrell said with a touch too much earnestness in his voice.

"You wouldn't even be here if it wasn't for them." La Payasa picked up a newspaper. "A few Mexicans get killed too publicly and no one can sweep them under the rug.

"Look, we're still collecting information, but so far, no witnesses have come forward."

"Around here bullets go off like car alarms and folks ignore them just the same. And folks're so scared to be thought of as snitches, gave them the case of the mutes for their own health."

"No one wants to admit that they think of a little brown girl being killed as neighborhood beautification."

"You're right. Lyonessa was invisible. To us, to most folks because staying below the radar was part of her job. Doesn't mean she was any less important."

"What do you want?"

"I want the violence to stop. No more bodies to drop while we have a chance to get into this. We know where to look."

"Then look."

"We need Black to back off. He made bad choices, but she was a good person."

"I know."

"Whoever killed her should pay for what they did."

"I know."

La Payasa didn't go the sexed-in route to the gang: she was jumped in. By men. Time had not erased the memory of the pain. She braced herself for the rain of fists and knew no mercy would be shown. Time crawled. Every punch landed with fury on any exposed body part. Ears. Ribs. Kidneys. Kicks were the worst. When she got up, her fingertips tingled and her arms shook. The cholos were all smiles like they weren't the ones who just beat her. It was all strictly business. Black first to embrace her.

"What do you say?"

"Do you think you're some kind of hero?"

"No, I don't."

"You lie. To me, if not to yourself." La Payasa turned back to her men. "I'll talk to Black. But blood... it pours out like water."

The other day, La Payasa cried.

She had a nightmare about a man climbing through her window and skulking over to her bed while she slept. He loomed over her sleeping and powerless form, at first content to just watch her. Then he reached down, slowly and deliberately, to touch her.

The number 13 had been emblazoned on her shoulder. Black roots sprang from her blonde hair, a regal crown that finished her look. She was her gang through and through, no questions, no doubts. It was like little magics ran in her blood. Loyalty was a folk tale. There was a time when she thought that the gang meant something. When all of their talk about loyalty, family, and purpose meant something. The first thing the gang demanded was an initiation to prove her loyalty. None of that bullshit about going to kill a random person at Meijer. Only a gang with no structure messed around with the kind of mess that would bring po-po down on their heads. She was blessed in. The gang had rules its members had to abide by. Only wannabes had no rules. No beliefs. No faith. And their judgments were as swift as they were harsh. She once had to administer a violation to one of her girls for talking to a member of a rival gang.

"What the fuck were you doing?" La Payasa asked.

"I knew him from back in the day."

La Payasa knew him too, from elementary school – all of sixth grade. Across the gulf of junior high. A lifetime ago. "You one of us now."

"I know..." she let the words hang. She knew she had to be punished.

"Head to toe or violated out?"

"Head to toe." She flashed her gang signs to reaffirm her commitment.

La Payasa understood they both were being judged. Her girl as a member and her as a leader. She had to put on a show. Drive home the lesson that the gang came first. That the streets were dangerous and real. And that other groups, all chavalas, were hated. No one outside the gang was to be trusted.

And La Payasa hated her role.

She summoned two other girls to join her. As soon as they flanked her, La Payasa punched the girl dead in her left eye. The ferocity of the blow caught her off balance and sent her sprawling backwards. More tripping over her suddenly clumsy feet than anything else, she landed on her back. A hail of kicks soon followed. La Payasa dropped low to continue to punch the girl in her side until she exhausted herself. The girl didn't cry out once.

"Help her up. She's one of us," La Payasa said. "A sister."

But there was a simple truth about the gang: it needed a rival to have meaning. It needed the police or another set to define its territory, to test it, to make it stronger and smarter. Without an outside enemy, there'd just be fighting among themselves. It boiled down to feuds. Blood feuds. It became personal and though wars should never be personal, wars were always personal.

War was inevitable.

Much more comfortable living in his head, Cantrell hated talking through his case out loud. The onsite director of *The Squad* flitted about, capturing footage of his phone conversations, loving how telegenic Cantrell's frustration was. "Think of it as running down the case for your captain," he was encouraged. Though Captain Burke didn't apply make-up to him before he provided details of a case. Cantrell reached out to Garlan's people. No place of employment, not in school, and a whole lot of "he don't stay here no more". Not that anyone could tell him where "he stay at now". Cantrell left messages for Garlan to contact him in regards to his car.

"I'm trying to track down a Mr Garlan Pellam. It was his vehicle that was used in the commission of the Perez kidnap

and shooting. Since his name has popped up a few times on the Gang Task Force radar, we want to question him about it. Maybe get some intel about the state of the streets and who's beefing with who."

Within a few hours, Garlan strolled in requesting to speak to "the detective that was bothering his peoples."

"Mr Pellam."

"I heard you was looking for me."

"You're a hard man to find."

"I'm here now."

"This dude was all wrong. From the way he slumped in the chair, evaded his eyes, and shifted about, I knew he'd been hauled in before. But Garlan didn't have the flex of someone who had been in the system. More like someone who'd been around the game and now suddenly was in a lot deeper, like a climber finding their footing. It wouldn't take long for him to find his equilibrium and become a hardened soldier."

"We on TV or something?" Garlan asked.

"They got us out here filming a documentary or something," Cantrell said.

"I gotta sign something?"

"Yeah, before we're done, I'm sure." Cantrell set his coffee cup on the table next to a stack of file folders. "Else they just blur your face and not even your woman would recognize you."

"I'm good with that."

"You know a Lyonessa Perez?"

"Nah, should I?"

"Now see, Garlan, we starting off on a bad foot. Cute little Mexican girl. Been all over the news."

"Yeah, I heard about her. That was some shit."

"Your name came up in the investigation."

"How so?"

"You're what we like to call a person of interest."

"What's that mean?"

"That you might know something that might help us out. And we the appreciative type."

"What you think I know?"

"What kind of car you drive?" Cantrell flipped open his notepad.

"Black PT Cruiser."

"How 'bout that?"

"What?"

"A car just like yours was spotted at the scene. You mind if we check yours out?"

"Can't."

"Why not?"

"Got stole. You find it?"

"Bad news there, partner. We found it, but it had been torched."

"Damn." Garlan lowered his head.

"He couldn't act for shit. His problem was that he didn't know how to react in this sort of situation. Was he supposed to be happy? Was he supposed to be pissed? Was he supposed to be relieved? So I'm guessing he knew it had been torched to cover any trace evidence they might find. I just don't know his level of involvement yet."

"Your name came up because your car was used in the commission of a homicide.

You ever let anyone borrow your car, Mr Pellam?"

"Sometimes."

"Ever rent it out?"

"Sometimes."

"That happen here?"

"It was stole. So I don't know who had it."

"So you don't know who had it."

"Nope."

"Why didn't you report it immediately?"

"Didn't notice it was gone."

"Notice?" Cantrell noticed the careful parsing of Garlan's words. Too careful, too well thought out.

"I was at my girl's place. She picked me up, we made a long weekend of it. When I came back, my shits was gone."

"I'll need her contact information. She going to back up your story?"

"She'll back it up to China, you know what I'm saying?"

"What you do for a living?"

"Odd jobs."

"Anyway, that little girl, Lyonessa Perez." Cantrell produced her school picture from his folder, blown up to an 8x11 and laid out three autopsy pictures all in a row like he was dealing a game of black jack. Garlan took one picture into his hands. As if catching himself, he tossed it back at Cantrell.

"He was lying. You can tell from the way he kept staring at her picture. Then watch him when I pull out the autopsy pics. The pain on his face."

"Someone did this to her," said Cantrell.

"It's a cold world."

"What kind of man do you think it takes to do something like that?"

"Don't know."

"A monster?"

"Yeah."

"You know any monsters, Mr Pellam?"

"No."

"You know Lonzo Perez? Lyonessa's older brother. Some people know him as Black."

"Don't know a Black."

"What about Dred?"

"Who?"

"Dred. Runs product through your hood. Your boss."

"Don't know the name."

"So you don't know about any beefs between them?"

"I don't know nothing about nothing."

"I'm just saying, I need people to come forward and identify some folks. If you had anything to do with it, any knowledge at all, it's best to get in front of it right now. It'll play better for you later."

"I swear, officer. Right hand to the Jesus I pray to, I didn't have nothing to do with no murder. I just needed to tell you that to your face so that you'd leave my people alone."

This fool couldn't pick Jesus, whatever Jesus he prays to, out of a line-up.

"I appreciate you coming in, Mr Pellam."

"I'm free to go?"

"Yeah. You don't know nothing about nothing. So I'll have to go back to the peoples of that little girl and let them know that no one is willing to step up and help put down the monsters that did this." Cantrell put the autopsy picture back in front of Garlan of their baby.

He then handed him a card with his cell phone number on the back.

"I'm out."

"He came in because I was pressing hard for him, sure. Maybe also to see what evidence we had. But, I don't know. He don't read like a bad kid. He still has a heart. You can see how bothered he was by what happened to Lyonessa. He's haunted for sure. He definitely knows something about nothing. Since I don't have much else to go on, I may just dig into the known associates of Mr Garlan Pellam."

The Phoenix Apartments used to be known as The Meadows. An east side neighborhood once booming. A forty-acre development with fifty-six buildings, shops, and offices, and the Meadows Shopping Center. But by the 1980s, no one wanted any part of the Meadows, not when there were newer suburbs being developed north and west of the city for folks to run to. Leaving the corners free for Melle and The Boars.

Sitting on the front stoop, Melle – sometimes called Melle Mel, sometimes called "that crazy motherfucker that runs with Noles" – took a razor to his head. Most days he might run down to Hot Stylez barber shop, but today he was on the clock putting in work and had one of the young'uns to look out for. Melle used to sport a wild Afro, sometimes pulled back, most times not. Eight inches of mess, a neon sign easily spotted and picked out by the police, no matter how thick a crowd he ran with. He finally said "fuck it" and cut the shit off. The razor scraped his head. He didn't trust too many niggas with a razor to his skin, so he did it himself.

The Boars – sometimes called Bo Little, though only by his momma these days, sometimes called "that nigga who likes to hit people", though mostly by his football team mates at Northwest High School – perched like a gargoyle on the stoop steps. He, too, kept a bald head, though with a full beard shaved low. He spat idly while petting his dog. Its tail wagged wildly and its muscular hindquarters flexed as she licked his hand.

"What you feeding that bitch?" Melle asked.

"Steak, Gravy Train, and Hennessy. My dog's straight-up gangsta."

At the sound of Melle's voice, the dog hopped up on him, half-humping on his leg.

"Get that bitch off of me. Your dog's gay."

"It's not about sex. It's about dominance."

"Whatever. All I know is that if I want you as my bitch, you'd best roll the fuck over."

Leaning against the dented, paint-chipped entrance doors, the brick alcove sheltered them from the wind and rain. Empty grocery bags blew by in the wind like fall leaves.

"How's the count?" Melle asked with an expression of grudging interest.

"Down for the third straight week."

"Don't try to play me."

"I'm serious. With the stuff between Dred and Black jumping off, them casual customers been staying away. Afraid to catch a bullet. Or worse. Listen to some of them old heads, they talk about no one's got any respect for the game. About how children used to be off limits, but now you got fools out here wildin' like…"

"The shelf life of the stuff we got? Like we done stepped on it a dozen times. Weak as shit. When's the re-up coming through?"

"Due in next week ain't it?" The Boar's tone registered genuine confusion.

"Yeah."

"Seen Omarosa?"

"Nah. You jump like a motherfucker. What you been into got you so nervous?"

"Mind your own. We got enough on our plates."

"Way I hears," Black began, gun trained on the two of them, "some folks pile up their plate like a fat man at a buffet. Eyes bigger than their stomachs."

To listen to the counselors at school, Black was pretty easy to nail down. Directionless, fatherless, loveless. In search of a place to belong. Filling the holes that home couldn't fill, yet which still left a gnawing emptiness inside. Nothing he couldn't learn on the street, except how to have a dad. But he didn't want to give up the control. Before them, he was a misfit, out of place, one of society's embarrassments. No identity, no culture, no history, no sense of who he was. Except profoundly lost. He hated himself and took it out on other people. That was how the counselors saw him, but they were wrong. He was Black. He was fury. He simply... was. Revenge was mandatory. All slights met with angry, swift, retaliation, but an attack to his family? That was a matter of death.

"You," Black aimed at The Boars. "Vamonos."

"I ain't afraid to get shot. That's the game. I just don't want you to go after all of my people is all."

"This here ain't about business, hese, otherwise I'd have Swiss-cheesed all of you motherfuckers. This shit here, this is personal. Between me and him. Tell them. More will burn before I'm done. You let Dred know. More will burn. Vamonos."

The Boars trotted off backwards, not wanting to turn his back to them before putting more distance between he and them. Then he turned and booked out at full speed.

"You need to think on this hard, Black. We this close to war already," Melle said, his hopes fading with each quick step of The Boars.

"You already at war." Black tucked his gun into his waistband. The Boars would bring back others soon, but he had a message to send. "I know who you are, *Melle*." Black spat after he said the name. "I knew who you and Noles are." He spat again. "You think word don't travel back to me? Descriptions." Black tugged his gloves off. "Took two of you to rip apart a little girl. Y ahora?"

Emboldened by the gun being tucked away, Melle adopted what he thought was a fighting stance. The two circled each other warily in the alcove. Though lanky, Melle towered over Black. Melle swung wide, hoping to use his height advantage or wrap him up until The Boars came back. Black ducked under the blow, waded in, and rabbit-punched him twice in the face: the first exploded his nose in a spray of blood, the second cuffed him in the ear as his head lolled back. Blood splatter landed on Black's tattoo, then seeped into his skin. The blows themselves didn't rock Melle – he'd been hit harder by his baby momma, but a sickness rose in him.

His insides didn't feel right. Nauseous and dizzy, he cried like a scared little boy before the wrath of a thunderstorm, only wanting to be tucked in and comforted.

"Mira este, pendejo. Y ahora, hah, y ahora?"

The sick feeling crept into Melle's belly, as if he were witness to something sacred. Or blasphemously profane. His heart thumped in desperate staccato. Teeth clenched in anger, Black pressed his tattooed hand to the man's face. Melle screamed, but all Black heard was the last cries of Lyonessa, equally helpless on same concrete mattress. Melle's bruised face swelled. Fissures erupted along his skin, as if his blood boiled and his veins burst open. Dark pustules sprang up, eroding his face. His eyes clouded, lifeless long before his body stopped writhing in agony.

"More will burn."

The war was on.

CHAPTER SEVEN

Goodness was a fragile thing; rule, its own burden. Drenched in sweat, King threw off the covers as he woke. "Ripped from his sleep" better described his racing heart and the uneasy feeling that he escaped another nightmare. He napped more than slept most nights. Checking his clock, he'd managed to sleep for nearly three consecutive hours. Sick from anger and love, the waking world took a few moments to get used to. Sometimes he wished he could just turn his mind off, stop the jumbled images and memories of the good times shared, the promises made, and the dream of them. And the nagging voice that twisted all of those things into something unrecognizable. There were a few days when King didn't hear that voice at all, but on those days he was completely alone.

Allowing the blanket to drop into his lap, he sat up. Darkness filled the room despite the mid-day hour. Thick blankets covered the venetian blinds so that no light crept in, either from the front windows nor the rear window in the kitchen. He didn't know what to feel. He wished he could hate them, then he could get on with things. A thin reed of hate and resentment would protect him from the casual vulnerabilities of his heart.

Picking up and sniffing a pair of jeans, he decided they were good for another wear. A black T-shirt with the portrait of Sojourner Truth on the front and his pair of black Chuck Taylors completed his outfit. He then stuffed the rest of his clothes into his duffel bag. A backpack, a duffel bag, and three boxes. All of his worldly belongings fit into them. The three boxes were in his car already. He hadn't made up his mind what he wanted to do, but he wanted to be ready for when he did. It became increasingly difficult for him to remain at Breton Court. He couldn't take the weight of the stares, the pity in them, the sense of shame they drew like needles raked across the skin. Tongues wagged, but he told himself that as long as he knew the truth, he didn't care. Where was his strong right hand? Where was his heart? Where was anyone who gave him the chance to believe in himself? A knock came from his front door and he knew he had to postpone his anger.

The wisps of an attempted goatee sprouted along the sides of Prez's mouth. A slight hunch to his gait, though his swagger slowly returned, a slight bump of their shoulders served as their greeting. They quickly backed away from the gesture. King couldn't bring himself to hug Prez. The boy reminded him of yet more failures in his life. Failure to protect him, failure to keep him out of a gang, failure to keep him off drugs.

Big Momma was a neighborhood fixture, a force in her own right. In a matching sky-blue sweat suit and with a fan in her left hand, she trundled past him with a slight grunt. King let the door close on Prez, who waited patiently. Big Momma fell into the couch without saying a word. She fanned herself and let the minutes tick away.

King fell against the opposing wall, waiting for the inquisition to begin. His hands interlocked across his knees. Both of them shadowy figures in the gloom, which was the way King preferred it. Better than having to meet people's eyes or, worse, have them see him at his weakest. He broke first. "You awful quiet."

"Just thinking. Isn't it better to know her for who and what she truly was and be cured of loving her?"

"It's like that, is it?"

"Come on now. When you were that age, you're telling me if you got in trouble and had the chance to blame someone else and get off scot-free, you didn't do it?"

"I was never that age. Or that dumb."

"That's your problem. You expect everyone to be like you. You hold them up to your standard and castigate them when they don't live up to it."

"I do the same to myself."

"Like that's any better? You one of them stiff-necked types. Sometimes God has to break you to use you. Sometimes He sends the storm. But you know what? Storms pass."

King had long lost track of how long he'd been gone. Not so much gone as withdrawn. Part of him wanted to stay in his cave and stew in his pain. He was broken and there was no rush to him becoming fixed, no matter how many folks wanted him to pick up and keep going. On the one hand, he wanted everyone to just leave him alone. On the other, he didn't want to be alone. If they could spare him the platitudes and speeches and let him be, he could probably see himself clear.

"He took the people I loved most away from me. He took my mission, my purpose from him. What was the point of bringing me up only to turn me out like this? That doesn't sound like a God I want to follow."

"Come on now. Don't be like that. My parents had their problems. Abandoned me. But the adults in the neighborhood decided to raise me and hid me from CPS whenever a social worker came around, because they would just have sent me to foster care. I know about rough times."

"You don't understand. I had people. I used to be able to look in their eyes. They looked up to me. With respect, though they'd never admit to it. I was their big brother. They took it all away from me. They did."

"It still sounds to me like you were looking for the wrong things. Like all of this was about you. Maybe you need to be stripped of all that to see who it is you are really working for and how you go about doing the work."

"I liked you better when you didn't say anything."

"Life is long. We don't have to be defined by our pasts. Or our mistakes. Who you were then doesn't have to be who you are now. You had your mission. It made you feel right. Have you stopped to consider that she's hurting, too?"

The thought of that softened him a little. He turned the idea around in his mind for a moment, inspecting it before digesting it. Being around one so young was self-ish on his part. He didn't allow her to be her age. Being young and dumb was the point of youth. He above all others knew the toll on her, acting up to his expectations. How he saw her. But he did the same: he wanted to be the man, the hero she saw in him. Listen to him. Old-man thoughts. He always had an urge to protect others, to ride in on a white horse.

"She wanted you to think... she could hang," Big Momma pressed. "You be impressed with her. Not be dis-appointed in her."

"I don't think I'll be able to trust her again, and I hate that. She was my best friend."

"Come on now. Can't nothing heal without pain. Let it go. Let her go. Let them go. So that you can move on and do what you need to do. Cause there's still a lot of work that needs to be done. Ain't no point in letting all of your gifts get all moldy here in the dark."

"All right, Big Momma. What's the first step?"

"Do what you do best. Someone's got to lead. Some-one's got to be brave enough to put themselves out there to make the first move. Bring people together."

"It's time for a family meeting."

Not very many things scared Lott. In his few years on earth, he'd seen men die, by the hands of both men and monsters, though the men were usually monsters in masquerade. His FedEx uniform, in only a short time, had become a second skin. How he saw himself and how others saw him. He was lucky to get a spot at the printing company. The hours weren't as good and the drab brown uniform made him self-conscious of walking around like shit on a stick. His beard grew longish, not quite unkempt, but definitely scraggily as it came in. The swelling in his face had retreated, leaving only the occasional bruise along his ribs from the beating. Word traveled quickly along the neighborhood wire, but he didn't know what to think about the meet-up.

With family, truth was a while in coming. There were watershed moments in a man's life, a crossroads of regrets and humiliations. Lott wondered how he could make it up with folks. For so long he had stuck close to King, forgetting why he needed to get clean. These days, with his spirit dry and cracked, with him on the verge of relapse, he was barely conscious of asking himself "what the fuck are you doing?" Living on automatic pilot with the disease of amnesia, the bad times didn't seem that bad and the worst times reminded him of where he came from. That to forget how bad he got, just for a second, and he'd be right back there. So he concentrated on just trying to breathe and to sort things out.

Everyone had an assumed role to play. When he was little, his mother often came home, having gotten her drink on, usually in the company of some man she called her boyfriend who basically threw a couple of bills her way to keep the lights on. When ends came up short, the shouting could be heard up and down the block. Lott always feared for his mother. From a young age, if things got too loud, he stepped between the man and his mother. "Leave her alone," he'd shout. Or he'd simply ram his head into the man's testicles. On more than one occasion, he took the beating intended for his mother.

With him and his mom, he was quick with a joke whenever her own pain threatened to lash out at the nearest
available target, usually him. Anything to laugh away
the pain. Then came the mission, salvation in something
larger than himself to believe in. To be straight. Then
came King. The man wasn't his salvation, but he gave
him purpose.

*"Every man wants to be part of something larger than him-
self."*

He recalled the words as clearly today as he did then,
as if he were... called. He and King were boys almost
from the jump, but King had a way about him, kept himself guarded around him, not letting Lott all the way in.
The great King was afraid of being hurt. Again.

And Lady G. From the first moment he saw her, he
thought that if he could have her, then it would mean
he was worth something. That if she chose him then he
could feel good about himself. It was all so selfish and
messed up.

And he knew he had to carry it.

Yeah, he'd be at the meeting and take what was coming to him.

A few times Lady G thought of crying. She didn't know
how she'd react the first time she saw Lott. Part of her
thought she might just slap him. It was as if he represented her poor choices, all the hurt she that twisted her
up inside, all of the damage they – she – had done to
their little circle of friends. It was easier to put it on him,
his manipulation of her feelings – she was in a vulnerable
place, confused, scared, out of her depth, and he took

advantage of that – than think about her role in things. They would never be the same after all of this. Nothing would be the same. Not their friendship, not their circle of friends, what remained of it. Not the common vision they once shared. They were lost.

Two blocks north, on High School Road, a couple of large backhoes razed two houses. They'd fallen into disrepair and no one wanted to buy them. The fact that one had been set on fire with the word "snitch" spraypainted on the side surely didn't factor into it. They could have met in the Youth Solidarity building, which technically fell under the ownership of Pastor Winburn's church. But King wanted to meet where they had started.

The burnt cream color burnished to near gold under the stern glare of the sun. A year or so back, the Church of the Brethren was one of the churches caught up in a string of arsons. Fire investigators suspected drug addicts illegally squatting. The fire unleashed a nightmare torrent of paperwork, with confusion over insurance and permits. The faux-stucco façade, which was once a simple near yellow, was now seared to a muddy ash. Scorch marks, like black tongues, lapped at the edges of the building. Plywood protected what remained of its doors and windows, supposedly sealing the building into a free-standing sarcophagus. The rear of the building, more heavily damaged by fire and water and vandals – the elements of the neighborhood – reduced the back to piles of scree and poles. More plywood served as the rear wall. An unoccupied eyesore, it stood as if in hopes of its presence shaming the community into some sort of action.

Lady G ducked under a fallen beam in the alcove and wound her way around to the sanctuary. From the way he stood, hands joined behind his back, a commanding presence, she recognized the silhouette on the far end in an instant.

King.

Her throat tightened even as her heart raced. A wave of heat flushed her face and her mind... blanked. Hoping that he'd take notice of her before she was close enough to say anything and initiate conversation, her feet carried her forward in a zombie shuffle.

King rolled the spindle they used as a table to the center of the room. Painted white and green, it served as their round table. Meeting around it meant fair fellowship, one body coming together as equals. Cooperating in equal service. There were no chairs to sit in, which left them all in the same position, but he didn't think the proceedings would last too long. This meeting was just to clear the air, and he doubted anyone would be seated anyway. Plus he still needed to go across town. As head of Youth Solidarity, he'd set up a meeting with Black. He had to start over building bridges and coalitions among the gangs. And this new player not only had muscle, but the will to use it. All the work King had done getting the leaders to the table was undone.

And he wondered how much weight he still carried in the street. A cuckolded man, punked by his own. It didn't play well.

He recognized the slinking shadow immediately. He knew every curve, every nuance of her movement. She could never hide from him because she had filled up so much of his world. His heart hurt at the sight of her. He longed to hold her in his arms again, to feel her pressed into him, to know the presence and comfort of her love again. But he couldn't escape the specter of pain that accompanied her. The anger he expected wasn't there. He didn't know what to say to her.

Lady G wandered all the way to within feet of him before finally stopping. Once it became obvious that he knew she was there and hadn't said anything. Part of her wanted to turn around. The soft scritch of her shoes against the cement floor was the only sound.

The pair locked eyes only for an instant. Lady G studied the ground, King the scenery to his right.

"I'm sorry." Lady G's voice cracked and trailed off.

"What? I couldn't hear you."

"I said I'm sorry."

"Damn right you are." The words sprang from his mouth before he could stop them. "I'm sorry." The words just seemed so small. Three syllables to cover all of his pain, loss, and shame. It didn't seem like nearly a large enough bandage to staunch the wound.

Lady G had braced herself for the rage. Actually she feared it would be worse. Possibly violent. "I know."

"You don't know how much I loved you."

"I guess. I took it for granted. I couldn't handle it."

"You threw it all away."

"I was scared."

"After all that we've been through, I thought I could rely on you. You're dead to me." King still loved her. Part of him would always love her, but he kicked himself for missing the signs of her duplicity. At no point did he sense her betrayal, so how could he trust himself against Black? Or Dred?

"Do better."

"How could you leave me when you knew me? You were the only one I let know me and you turned your back on me." The words tumbled out of his mouth. He'd rehearsed what he was going to say for weeks. The prospect set his brain on fire most days, parsing the imagined conversation for maximum impact. But to hear the words, they fell short. They failed to capture his pain. Worse, he sounded weak. A school boy worried about his hurt. His pride. The cold thing in his chest, desperate to beat again, to find life, feared the hurt. Easier, by far, to be the hardened unfeeling lump, than play the fool.

"I feel like I've been stolen from myself." The pain ran deep, deeper than the two of them. He knew it. She cried for all of them. King. Lott. The "knights". Big Momma. Even herself. "I don't know if there was ever a real me. A real us."

"I…" Her tears moved him, though not the way he expected. King wondered if he'd ever be able to forgive her. He wasn't strong enough on his own. But he remembered the words of Pastor Ecktor. It was a start. Lady G wrapped her pinky around his. No expectations. Just a gesture. He squeezed her. His hand jerked back as Lott stepped into the entryway.

Playing wheelman to Dred was in Garlan's job description. It meant he was trusted. Counted on. Still, there was a part of him that hated being so close to the heart of the crew. It was like orbiting the sun: too far away meant he was frozen out and had only scrub duties, too close and he was likely to be consumed by the heat of the madness.

Garlan studied him with his dull eyes, scarred by seeing too much too early. He sensed Dred's mood, recognizing the ritual of getting amped up. The fondling of the weapon as if he stroked himself to make sure he could still get it up. The wild eyes jacked up by getting his head up before he rolled out. Yet, Dred never went near drugs. Whatever hyped him up was neither grown nor cooked up in a lab. Subtlety was a lost art. Left to his own devices, he'd have his tension tools and feeler picks, ready to sneak up on a person under cloak of night. Or invisibility. In and out like a ghost. All of this driving up on someone and start blasting or bursting in doors, guns a-blazing, were all hallmarks of the impatient and unskilled.

Dred inspected his Caliburn. The 9mm Springfield Armory custom-ported stack autos gleamed with the frames, slides, and some other parts plated in 24K gold; with gold dragons rearing up along the contrasting black grips. King, too, brandished such a weapon. He wondered if there was any connection between them.

"Something on your mind?" Dred asked, conscious of Garlan's studious gaze.

"Never seen a gat like that." Garlan stared forward, hands on the steering wheel, as he tried to play things casual.

"No reason you should. Ain't but two of them around."

"King got the other one."

"Yeah."

"They valuable?"

"Priceless. Why, you planning on taking mine?"

"Just wondering. No disrespect, but what is it with you two?"

In a feral warning, Dred arched an eyebrow. "Why you asking?"

"I mean, dude had a point, but was out of line in how he asked. One minute you want him checked. Next, you all up on him. Then you all about hurting him. Word came down that no one could touch him. Now you about to take him out. I ain't seen that kind of love/hate since Thanksgiving dinner."

"That's the way of family."

"Exactly."

"Especially brothers." Dred pressed the Caliburn to his own cheek and closed his eyes, letting the metal cool his cheek. "Want to get in the middle of this with more questions?"

"I'm good."

"Good."

Not knowing his father was the missing piece. It left a scar, not being whole. Unable to believe that he was loved or capable of being loved. Garlan never understood why his mother made him go to church. It was a program he could never get with. Talking to someone he could never see, hear, or touch but who knew him so intimately as to know the number of hairs on his head and had the power to control every aspect of his life. Power was to be used. Power was at the hands of guns, drugs, and money. Anything else couldn't be trusted.

• • • •

Lott and King squared off. The air between them charged. The silence between them spoke volumes. Lady G stepped from between them. An eruption of chatter came from the rear, as Wayne cracked a joke which had Prez and Percy laughing. The conversation came to an abrupt end when they took in the scene. The entire court had assembled.

"What do you have to say for yourself?" King asked.

"Lady G was innocent. It's on me." For Lott, things boiled down to honor. He'd already dishonored King and Lady G, but he wouldn't have her reputation besmirched. As far as he was concerned, it was all on him.

"She a grown-ass woman, not some little girl. She made her own decisions."

"King, I don't know what else to say. We've been through some wars, man."

"Yeah, we have."

"Seen some times." Lott spread his arms, a tentative gesture – unarmed, posing no threat – and stepped closer.

"I know."

"We fought for you. We bled for you. We've died for you."

"You took from me! You took what I was. You took Lady G."

"King, I..." There it was. Lott shoved his hands into his pockets and shut down. Silence took hold of the room.

"I can't do this right now. You need to get out of my face for a minute."

"Can you ever forgive me? I can't lose you. I don't want things to end like this."

"I can forgive you. I can forgive both of you. But the trust, the bond? That's ghost." King rubbed his temples, both exhausted and as if they threatened to burst. "Both of you, go. We need some time to think."

"King..." Lady G began.

"Just go."

King turned his back and waited for the sounds of their departure to subside. The dream was nothing but a nightmare dressed up in whore's make-up. Wayne was the first to approach him.

"That went better than I expected. You all right?" Wayne sidled up next to him and put a gentle hand on his shoulder.

"I'm good. Tired. What about the Black thing?"

"Black? Screw Black. What about us?"

"Life don't stop. There are things bigger than us going on."

"That's been the whole problem: it's only been us. You keep missing that." Wayne turned to face him. A slight quaver filled his voice as if hiding his own hurt. "We all want you to be okay. Lott, Lady G, Wayne. Even Merle."

King remained impassive.

"Man, you one of the most tortured souls I've ever come across. You ain't never met an opportunity to brood you couldn't pass up. All right, man, I'll let it go."

King dreamed of birthing something that would protect his people, of building a kingdom, a way of living for generations to model after. And he had the hubris to believe he was the man to bring this dream to his community. Perhaps he couldn't admit that his reach exceeded his grasp. In his few short years on earth, he'd

long ago realized that he didn't know everything; that
he wasn't as good as he thought. That he was afraid. For
all of his hard work, he was just another knucklehead
out to prove himself because he believed that no one
loved him. Everyone had lies built into them that whispered to them during dark times.

Percy and Prez followed silently behind them. Not knowing what to say, not wanting to ruin the silence.

King paced back and forth. Everywhere he looked
there was something to piss him off. On the wall were
pictures which now mocked him. Each snapshot a memory that bit into his heart. One of him and the mayor.
Him and Pastor Winburn. Him and some of the kids he'd
worked with. Rok. The Boars. Tristan. Iz. Prez. So many
faces. A few dozen kids so far. Ghosts of his past. How
many of them did he let crash at the center? How many
of them did he let raid his refrigerator? How many of
them laughed at him now? A collage of failure. Maybe
he started too old. Maybe he should have gone after the
pee wees. Get them before they became loyal to the
game. The sadness was tangible, a blanket fallen over
their neighborhood thickest in this very room. Wayne
hated the air of resignation. Of surrender. It was like
death.

"You hear about that little girl?" Wayne asked in order
to switch topics. If death was already in the room, they
might as well deal with it.

"Lyonessa." King rubbed his face and waited for the
next pounding.

"She wasn't even in the game."

"She was in it whether she choose to be or not. Her brother, Lonzo..."

"Black."

"Black. He puts her in the game. Same with me and Nakia. So I take her off the board."

"How she doing?"

"Nakia? She good."

"You being done on visitation?"

"It ain't like that. I can see my baby girl when I want."

"But?"

"But... you see the life I lead." On the defensive, King lumbered back and forth, his anger fueled by the fact that he was angry at the wrong people. Or there were so many people to be angry at. In a moment he could make a few phone calls, rally some knuckleheaded boys and rain down pain on Black or whoever else needed hurting. Whoever. Else. Many nights the thought tempted him.

"You married to your mission."

"I'm on call 24/7. And..."

"... you've made your share of enemies."

"Folks that would take things out on my family. And my friends."

"Your friends seem to be doing a good enough job of that on they own."

"Yeah." King stopped. "Man, it feels like they got me on some sort of timetable to get better." He turned to Wayne, who did his best to hide his smirk. He had a way of putting things in perspective. The man was frustrating. Could make his point and make you smile. It was his heart. Wayne had one of those hearts that made you feel better just by being around him.

"They mean well. We want you well. But you not."

"I'm trying."

"I know."

"Dred's on the move."

"I'm just saying... We gonna need all the friends we can get. You need to give them a chance to show how sorry they are."

"You worse than Ecktor, man. What, you, he, and Big Momma all have a meeting to get your stories straight?"

"You're a good man, King. With greatness in you. Sometimes you have to be encouraged to do the right thing. To live into that greatness."

"I still love them. Both of them."

"We all do. They still family."

"Make sure they're okay."

"You planning on going somewhere?"

"I just know I won't always be around."

"I got it handled."

Life never stopped. King reached past Wayne to grab hold of Prez. The boy smiled, locked in a playful head-lock. His emotions spent, it was the most he had in him. But Prez took it. Wayne hustled Percy to hurry on. Sadness leadened the boy's steps. He hurt for everyone and didn't know how to be there. For King. For Lady G. For Lott. For Rhianna. For Wayne. They were his family, the way family should be. And they hurt. He needed to do something or else they might all fall apart and go their own way. Wayne locked up the building.

King was the first to notice the car slow. It wasn't the car which drew his attention, but like a piece of his soul returning home which alerted him. For King, life slowed to a crawl. His nose flared. Spit flew from his mouth. A sudden heat swept over him. He seemed to sweat from everywhere at once. For a brief few seconds, there was a sudden calm. His eyes grew wide as his mind took in what he was seeing. He hoped his voice wouldn't crack as he called out. "Get down!"

Dred raised his gun. King recognized the Caliburn immediately and the sense of another betrayal overwhelmed him. The report thundered. King's ears rang. His balance thrown off, time slowed. A bullet slammed into his shoulder and spun him around, like a warm knife slid into him with ease. Another pop followed as a second bullet tore through the side of his neck. The smell of blood was the odor of death. Perhaps his body went into shock, but King did not feel any pain, only the peace of acceptance washing over him. Perhaps it was relief. The earth fell from underneath him and shadows engulfed him.

Across town, from within Nine's embrace, Merle cried out, "No!"

"What is it?" She wrapped her arms around him even tighter.

"The dolorous stroke."

"Then the end draws near."

CHAPTER EIGHT

The Security and Housing Unit – often called the Shoe – housed everyone who was under the age of eighteen detained in the Marion County Lock Up. In the protected block of juveniles, its guests spent twenty-three hours a day in cells. Artificially set by their lights, their days were out of the prisoners' control. They were told when they could eat and when they could shower. Privacy was a dream of another life.

The previous night Rondell "Mulysa" Cheldric dreamed he was a child, lost in a forest, trying to make his way home. The brush grew thicker as he ran. All he knew was that something chased him. Though unseen, the prey's sense of an impending threat, that a creature stalked him and had been after him for a while, remained with him. His lungs burned with each breath. The muscles in his legs ached. Pain shot up his shins. The joints of his shoulders grew sore. Exhaustion overtook him. A weariness that seeped down to his bones. Slumped over in a collapsed heap, he waited. The predator still in the shadows. Nearby. Salivating at its soon-to-be-had kill. Mulysa woke as he always did: bone-tired and resigned.

In juvenile, he used to imagine himself as a top-secret spy caught by enemy agents and imprisoned. His days idled along with daydreaming plots to make daring escape. His imagination was his true escape. His fantasy was, if nothing else, consistent. When he was younger, he imagined it was his father that was the spy, always called away on important missions. As he got older, within a few years actually, after a lifestyle filled with danger and intrigue, though heroic, he decided that his dad had been killed in action. Only in the last year did he conclude that fantasy was for children.

Life in the Shoe was about boundaries and limits. The cell closed in on his mind. Lonely, confined, a lack of privacy; the tedium alone could drive someone to madness. The darkness made noises. Tears sobbed into pillows. The rutting sounds of rage and power being rammed into any who gave the appearance of weakness. His life was a prison.

He was two men: Mulysa and Rondell, battling it out, and Rondell was about dead. Reduced to an animal going about with survival instincts on high alert, constantly on the lookout for any of the innumerable enemies he'd made. He was a fallen man. Weren't but two ways to go from here: up, or embrace the darkness and finality of his life. And the game itself was slow suicide. All of the devilish things he'd done, each act a step in his journey toward here. Being locked down, swept under society's rug, allowed him to see the bigger picture, and his life for what it was worth.

A big steaming pile of shit.

Today, he was due in court. His public defender assured him that this was just a matter of going through the motions. The police could have him under suspicion for any of a number of things, but with only a circumstantial case, he was going to walk. He wore his orange jumpsuit with a measure of pride.

A young boy with an old face – and eyes which had lost their innocence too soon – was next up before the judge.

"What's up, homie? Are you a thug?" the boy asked.

"Who asking?" Mulysa eyed him with bored wariness.

"I'm just sayin'. I got my own hoes," he said with too much enthusiasm and empty braggadocio. "I do some crazy shit. I ain't got time for that mess. My ass hurts from doing all this sitting. Waiting on my Johnny to get me off."

"Nukka, you still got your baby teeth." Mulysa couldn't be bothered to muster a bemused smile – more of a sneer masking a mild state of melancholy.

"I know how to jail," the boy said as his case was called. "Straight-up thug."

Never show weakness, never back down, never step aside. The boy had already internalized some of the basic rules. The boy reminded Mulysa of how he was at that age: already a lost cause, beyond redemption. He knew what fate awaited the young'un, what few true options he had, and how he had embraced them.

They had pulled Judge Rolfingsmeyer, a fair-minded jurist, with just an independent enough streak to piss off liberals and conservatives alike. This made him popular among the people. A jovial face, the judge's robes draped like a muumuu over him. At the moment, he appeared to be suffering a migraine as he rubbed his temples.

"I never wanted to hurt nobody. I just want to be a terrorist and blow stuff up," the boy shouted out.

"You're too young to be doing these kinds of things. I mean, look at you: you haven't even grown out of your cute stage," Judge Rolfingsmeyer said. "I just want to eat you up."

"Fuck you, judge." The boy flipped him off. A bailiff immediately escorted him out. The judge ordered him held over for family court to decide the best course of action.

"Well, my, my, my. They grow up fast," the judge remarked to his bailiff.

The hood was the main world Mulysa knew. Life in the Shoe was like a vacation in his summer spot. But in the court, mostly white faces greeted him from the judge to the bailiffs to the lawyers. He was in their world now. When they called his name or his case number, all he heard the word "nigger". Everything dripped with contempt. From the bench, the judge's words ran down his nose to him.

On the streets, he could defend himself. He'd go toe-to-toe with any fool who dared step to him. But in this world the assumptions weren't always physical. The pain crushed him in inner spaces, places he couldn't trace and rarely let himself acknowledge. He didn't know how to defend himself against this kind of attack. He only had his anger, and he stacked onto the kindling pile of his previous resentments and hates. His fist clenched out of reflex and his public aid lawyer nudged his arm and he relaxed.

Mulysa strode toward the judge, eyes meeting his, unafraid. Pride marched him forward now, as he was under the careful scrutiny of those in the gallery as well as those whose cases were up next. It was time for the show. Never show weakness, never back down, never step aside.

His court-appointed lawyer took apart the state's case, such as it was. He was little more than a person of interest, suspected of having knowledge in a few crimes. The death of Lamont "Rok" Walters, even the fire at the Camlann apartments. Because the search was ruled illegal, the police didn't even have the drug charges to hold over his head. Not to mention how he was treated while a guest of the state.

"Son, sounds like you been into all sorts of mess," Judge Rolfingsmeyer said. "But it's not like the state has much of a case left. Got no reason to hold you on remand. A bit of an overreach, wouldn't you say, counselor?"

The state prosecutor mumbled to himself. Mulysa didn't like to be talked to that way. He tolerated it from Colvin. Mulysa grimaced under the pain of his own headache. They were getting worse now. Like a metal spike driven into his eye to stab him in his brain.

"You're going to be on a nine o'clock probation. You understand?"

"Yes, your honor."

"So if your friends show up at ten-thirty at night and say 'Hey, we got a big ol' bag of weed'," the judge put on a street affect to perfection, "'let's go smoke,' what should you do?"

"I'd have to tell them 'Man, y'all shoulda been here earlier cuz I'm on curfew."

Mulysa's public defender lowered his head.

"Right…" Judge Rolfingsmeyer glanced up from the stack of papers before him. "The correct answer is 'weed is illegal and I still have to drop a piss test.' But I suppose that's as good as I'm getting."

With that, Judge Rolfingsmeyer signed the papers and Mulysa was once again back on the streets.

Prez hated to visit his father. He knew in his heart of hearts that no one begrudged him his visits with his old man, especially now. Imminent death had a way of forcing that: cancer ate at his father's insides. Death rarely weighed on Prez, though its specter hung like a shadow over his soul.

Especially now, considering King. It wasn't as if Prez could talk to King. Though King had said it best before he was shot: "Forgiveness is the only way to let go of the past. Relationships are fragile. Repair the rift between you and your father before much more damage is done. You don't know when the people you love will be called home. Time is always short." Some things were morbidly expected, no, not expected, but rather unsurprising; only the method of his father's eventual demise had been up for grabs. Diet was never a particularly high concern as he ate pig's feet and barbecue ribs, and fried everything, washed down with vodka and Coke. Or brandy and Coke. Or rum and Coke. The man loved Coke. Say what you will, the man was brand-loyal, thus his two-pack-a-day Kool habit. And exercise? Only if you counted his four-hundred-videotape porn collection, some of which he inherited from *his* father; and his predilection for chasing women other than his mother. So Prez had long resigned himself to the fact that his father was not long for this world. The only surprise was that he lasted so long.

The family had a cancer scare a few years back. Months of agonizing waits, treatments, and surgeries culminated in the removal of a lung. The crisis seemed over, the doctors confident that they got it all. His father lost a lot of weight ("the chemo diet", he called it) and gave up smoking. The family took its cue from him, hanging their hopes on his own lust for life. That was then.

Somewhere in the back of his mind, Prez suspected that his father started smoking and drinking in earnest again in the hopes of dying. Like maybe he took a look at the measure of his life, realized what a waste his was, and decided that it wasn't worth it. Prez wasn't even sure things worked that way, but the thought stayed with him. The cost of treatment had strained the family's resources to the breaking point, but all they thought about was getting him better. However, Prez recognized the anger in his father's eyes, behind the laughter and bravado. Anger that he was ineffectual as a provider; anger that his body betrayed him; anger that he was no longer his own man.

So when the cancer returned, he chose to die the way he lived: at home.

Prez hadn't been home since he left a couple years

back to stay with Big Momma. She had brought him up here, cause kin was kin, and she wasn't trying to get between folks, and she wanted to help mend things when she could. The way she saw it, that's how good church folks did: stay up in your business and help, whether you wanted it or not. Folks didn't always know what was good for them. She was God's little busybody.

The family set up home hospice care. Big Momma didn't say anything as they entered the house, politely not commenting on the odor of mothballs, old people funk, and medicine. The day nurse – a squat, buxom woman with the face of a teamster – wasn't dressed in all-whites like Big Momma assumed she would be. The nurse escorted Earl Parker Wilcox from the bathroom to the couch. She untangled the array of tubes from his medicinal pump and oxygen canister, then excused herself to see about lunch. Prez and Big Momma waited until the door closed behind her and Earl to settle into the couch before they exhaled their pleasantries.

"Dad? It's me and Big Momma."

"Boy, you know I'm a grown-ass man. A dying grown-ass man, but still a grown-ass man. And I'm too grown to be calling a grown-ass woman 'Big Momma.' How you doing, miss lady?"

"Just fine, baby. You lookin' good."

"Shit. 'Preciate the lie though. You all clear a space and sit down. All that standing around on occasion is making me nervous."

Prez had forgotten how much he missed the raspy baritone of his father's voice. A filigree of wrinkles radiated from his mouth. His face was much thinner than he remembered, but he was still his father. Prez never understood all the angst most folks had about their fathers. He decided early on that his father was not someone he wanted to pattern his life after. They could be... he didn't know the best word to describe the kind of (adult) relationship he wanted to have with his father. "Friendly". Something that took the onus of responsibility off his father having to try to be a father. And Prez having to live up (or down) to it. Maybe that's why he took off. To be his own man; find his own way. And he fucked it up. Charting his own course ended him where he began: fragile and tired and no better than his old man.

"Another player done got caught up," Prez said, hoping his father had grown some. "All that 'he said/she said' stuff."

"The DA dropped the charges. Bet he won't see the inside of another court room for a while," Earl said.

"She'll probably see some cash though. Nuisance change to make that civil suit go away." Prez baited him. "That's all she was ever after."

"The cost of doing business. They all the same, only the rates ever change."

"They all alike, huh?" Prez's face grew hot, but he didn't know why. Maybe King's judgmental tone haunted him. Something close to rage mixed with resentment threatened to bubble up. Big Momma put her hand on his knee.

"Most of them." Earl turned to him as if annoyed by the interruption.

"Even Mom?"

"I said 'most'."

"I need a glass of water." Big Momma stood up as if hearing her mother call her from the kitchen. "Either of you need anything?"

"Help yourself. I'm good," Earl said. "You look like you got something on your mind."

"It's just that... you don't have that much time left."

"Uh huh."

"And I feel... I don't know... damn it, Dad, it's like you're a stranger to me."

"I'm your father, boy."

"I don't know what that means."

"It means watch your tone."

Prez knew that his father never respected him, or, at best, considered him as a soft punk. The only time that his father seemed to like him, to really talk to him, was when Prez was keeping one of his secrets. Prez studied the man. This old man. He'd never seen his father look weak... so old. The epiphany struck him: he was a boy. Not a boy in a man's body, a boy masquerading as a man. They both were. Boys who had gotten older, only the toys changed. The thought of playing at the role of being a father never sat well with him.

Prez never knew his father. Because he was little more than a man who left sperm in his mother. Prez knew the man who offered to smoke pot with him on occasion in lieu of actually bonding with or parenting him. But he didn't know anything about him. His childhood, how he was raised, events that shaped him, how he saw the world.

Sperm donor. Bill payer. Big brother. Protector.

My daddy's dying.

"I am who I am. Who do you want me to be?" Earl asked.

Real. "I don't know."

Fathers and sons. Everything kept coming back to that. He knew, whether being taught directly or simply absorbing it from the culture around him, that he was supposed to complete the work his father began. Follow in his father's footsteps, even if it wasn't a path he'd have chosen for himself. He was a son wanting to please his parent, to hear his father say that he was proud of him. Some part of him, some tiny voice, wanted his father's approval. Just like part of him wanted to prove his own worth, if only in his mind, by doing a superior job of being a parent. A husband. A man. It occurred to him that in order to grow, a son had to reject his father sooner or later. What he feared was, if faced with the possibility of rejection or disappointment in his offspring, his father would reject him first.

Shit. This was like breaking up with a woman. It didn't matter if both knew the relationship wasn't going to work, what mattered was who did the actual breaking-up.

Fathers and sons. That was some shit.

Garlan's mother was a nurse. That woman knew how to work a system. An opportunity which presented itself, she played it for maximum advantage. The way she put together her work schedule, she could hit overtime by a Wednesday, which meant by Saturday, working doubles, she was deep into the man's pocket. She wasn't married to the dude they lived with, so with everything in his non-working-ass's name, they qualified for welfare and other benefits. The name of the game was getting over. His whole life was training for a doctorate in the art of getting over.

"Who's that young nigga that likes to run with you?" Dred asked. Everything was a system, from school to a job, or the street. Teachers, bosses, ballers, cops. His job was to run game on them. That was the life.

"Who? The Boars?" Garlan asked, knowing who Dred meant.

"Yeah, that's him. He got promise?"

"Yeah, he tight. Got some game to him." Keep your eyes open. Don't trust anyone. Keep the count straight. Make sure folks respect your name. The Boars had the makings for a good soldier. He internalized that shit. Garlan had his eye on him for a minute.

"Whatever, man. Put him on."

"What's with the change-up?"

"I gotta explain myself to you now?"

"Nah, man." Garlan took his cue to be quiet. He loathed meetings with Dred. It was worse than being called down to the principal's office. He'd call for a meet someplace random, like today they were just two niggas kicking it at Mr Dan's burger joint. But Dred had a way about him. The way he looked at you, through you most of the time, like you weren't there. Garlan tugged at his ring. It was, who was that crazy white dude always up in Batman's grill? The Joker? Yeah, how if you were part of the Joker's crew, you never knew when he'd turn on you and cap your ass.

"Naptown Red stepped to me wanting points on a package."

"That nigga is scandalous. Would run a game on his momma to turn a few ends."

"That's why I decided against it. But keep your eye on him. Too much side action will bring Five-O down on us. Keep him close."

"What about Mulysa?"

"What about him?"

"You always quick to bring up his name. You kin or something?"

"Naw, man, it ain't like that. Just making sure the crew's taken care of."

"I got him out. But he's too hot right now. He needs to cool out for a minute."

"So he on his own."

"He a survivor. He be all right."

Naptown Red considered himself a ghetto griot: sooth-sayer, truth-teller, keeper of the neighborhood history. He grew up hearing tales of the great shot-callers. Green. Speedbump. Bird. Bama. Luther. Night. Dred. Dred had consolidated various crews under him. Bardigora Street. Estonce Posse. A hundred Knights. And that was how he imagined himself. As a player, a man with secret agendas, moving people about like pieces. A man of style and influence. Today, he held court.

Having assumed that he had some Indian in his blood, his straight hair had been pulled back, which accentuated the blotchiness of his skin. It pissed him off that no one saw him as a threat, that no one took him seriously. In his capacity as evolving historian, he knew about most of the various tendrils of the crew: extortion, fencing, prostitution, drug-dealing. His father carried a bullet in his back, which kept him from doing most kinds of physical labor. As a result, he rarely kept a job. Red asked him whether he'd received the wound in a war like Vietnam. Close, he said, a street war. Vice lords. Gangster Disciples. Whatever. All Red knew was that he was meant to follow in his footsteps: drinking, smoking weed, breaking into houses. Even absent parents taught and passed along lessons. From early on, Red's folks would go into one of the back bedrooms with their friends, drinking, and carrying on. He could smell the pot from the other end of their house.

"You gotta girl?" Naptown Red asked, trying to school some of these young brothers coming up.

"Rhianna," Fathead said.

"How y'all doing?"

"We a'ight."

"A'ight? What's 'a'ight'?"

"We cool. She be sweating me for money. Wants some new gear."

"Her babies need stuff, too."

"Let her go to they babies' daddies then. Shit. I'll pay for my own, but I for damn sure ain't paying for anyone else's. This whole relationship bullshit's more trouble than it's worth. I'm a hit-it-and-quit-it sort of man."

A more introspective turn might have seen this as a case of the sins of the father and all that bullshit passed on to his son. And his son's son. From firing up some herb for social occasions, Red's folks graduated to the sometime line of coke, by which point they'd moved into an apartment. They owed everyone in the neighborhood.

Shit, they owed everyone in the family. Some months they sold off their food stamps in order to make ends meet, as they smoked up the rent money again. He wasn't mad at being poor, but things didn't have to be as bad as they were. His clothes never fit. The house was never cleaned. There was never anyone doing any cooking. One day, he found a broken piece of antenna behind the curtain on the window sill of the Section 8 half of a duplex. Its intentional placement had the air of importance, laying on the altar of the sill. It took him a while to divine its use as a crack pipe.

The education system also taught him and passed on lessons. Early in his elementary school years, Naptown Red had been labeled learning disabled (LD). The educators shuffled him off to be in separate classes. When that freckle-faced Andy Baumer spread lies about his mother, Red bit the shit out of him and was labeled emotionally disabled (ED). His mother jumped all over that once she figured out she could get more welfare benefits. When the boys in his neighborhood began affecting the same look, he wore his hat to the right and was labeled a Gangsta Disciples (GD). Little more than a weekend gangsta, he ran with them for a hot second, flew his black and blue colors, broke into cars, boosted stuff from stores, smoked a little weed.

Then he decided to dream bigger.

"What's this business you trying to speak on?" Naptown Red asked.

"I heard you were the man to get with." This here fool Fathead done brought around Prez. He never knew who he wanted to run with. Every time Red turned around, this boy was with someone else. He'd give this much to Prez: he was reserved, didn't raise his voice. A little soft for the streets, he still had a nice way about him, though it looked like the dragon had chewed him up and walked him around the block a few times. Still, he didn't act superior, but kept things low-key and played it smart. He knew who was taking over.

"I run this over here," Naptown Red said.

"I'm looking to do some work," Prez said.

"You think you can handle this here-ron." Naptown Red exaggerated the pronounciation of heroin for old school effect. These youngbloods didn't know.

"I ain't tripping." He could tell the way he spoke to Red irritated him.

"You vouch for him?"

"Yeah, he cool," Fathead said. "Not like his strung-out ass was Five-O or nothing."

Fear made men bluster. Naptown Red trusted him because Fathead needed him to make things happen, just as Naptown Red needed someone with good street eyes. Information was gold. The man with the keys to the dope line was gold. Theirs was a relationship of mutual mining. Red studied his body language. When he was asked a sticky question, Fathead folded like yesterday's newspaper. He was all about protecting himself.

"All right, come on. I got a party to go to. You roll with me and I'll show you how it's done."

Mulysa had to die. For Tristan the hunt was long overdue. The portrait Iz sketched of her, especially the smile on her face, mocked her. The front part of her hair was tucked down while the rear half flared into an Afro. Her features generous and sculpted. Gold eyes, dark skin, smile lines around her mouth. Iz always believed she was terrible at drawing hands. Yet there they were, strong but delicate. And powerless to stop the men in her life from hurting her or her own.

The thing Tristan resented most about her relationship with her father was how grateful she was to him. And for all that he'd done, she still wanted to turn to him. Thirteen years old, scared, alone…

It had been a terrible Thanksgiving. It was just her and her father. She'd spent the day cooking while he laid back on the couch, slowly draining the bottle of Crown Royal, absently watching football. The game didn't matter. Nor did he stir for commercials. His was a slow-cooking stew of loneliness and self-loathing.

"Daddy, I have something to tell you." Tristan unfolded a TV table and placed it in front of her father. With meticulous care, she arranged a plate and napkin. Fork, knife, then spoon. She slipped a coaster under the nearly empty glass. One by one, she brought out saucepans of food, as if for his inspection. Macaroni and cheese. Mashed potatoes. Fried okra. Greens. Turkey. Fried corn. Ham. Cranberry sauce. Each entrée greeted with a barely perceptible nod or flicker of the eyes. Grief had swallowed him whole since her mother died. It took him in little bits, slowly robbing him of the will to work, go through the motions of life, or move. He neither made nor took calls. His friends, what few he had, rarely stopped by anymore. And he looked at her, with his bloodshot, rheumy eyes which looked too large for his face. The stink of alcohol on his breath. He slipped into her room at

night and held her. She laid awake in panic not knowing whether to move or remain frozen, and the paralysis of indecision left her in his embrace. Each night, the entanglement became more familiar. More intimate. His hands resting on her waist. He breathed her in, or the memory of her mother. And she feared what new intimacy each night might bring.

"Daddy, I… I'm not like other girls," she blurted out. Her heart slammed into her chest with a machine gunning thud. She could barely catch her breath. Her hands trembled with the weight of anticipation, so she gripped each pot handle firmer. She hadn't rehearsed what she was going to say. She wanted it to seem natural. Now she cursed herself for not better thinking it through.

"It's not a phase or nothing. I been this way as long as I can remember. I just… don't like boys."

There, she had said it. The words hung in the air and it was too late to take them back. Nothing could be unsaid. Or unremembered. His slightly yellow eyes turned toward her, barely noting the food placed before him like a placating sacrifice before a bloodthirsty god. The eyes studied her with a gleam of unfamiliarity, clouded by a slight lascivious glint.

The plate of food slapped Tristan in the face. The gravy from the mashed potatoes scalded her eyes. She ripped the plate from her face, food dripping from her cheek in time to make out the blur approaching her. The fresh sting of her father's palm against her jaw sent her tumbling to the floor.

Tristan knelt there, kernels of corn falling from her hair and cranberry sauce trailing down her cheek like streaking blush. Her face warmed from where her father struck her. As if he could slap the gay out of her, her father – a tall man, looming like a wild grizzly above her – prepared to pounce on her. He never said a word. The Detroit Lions rumbling backward on the television screen was the only sound besides her father's labored breathing. She didn't know where the attack, the anger, came from. His daughter had declared herself a dyke. Her tacit admission that she was no longer his. His own grief finally devoured him. His self-loathing from not working, not being where he wanted to be in life, missing his wife, and being lost, all of it bubbling up and lashing out in a feral outburst. He would control one thing in his life and house.

Tristan.

He lumbered toward her.

Tristan had had enough. She was done with this world of pain and abuse at the hands of someone who was supposed to protect her. Her fingers balled into a fist. Her hair, slick with gravy, fell to one side of her face. Tristan's body heaved as if wracked with sobs. He pressed his attack, leaning low to scoop her up, to lay his hands on her, to act as if he owned her or her body.

She punched him in his throat.

Her father reeled backward, unable to catch his breath. She pounced into him, letting her weight and momentum do most of the work in toppling him backward. Next to the fork she had once so carefully placed on her napkin. She pressed the tines to his eye and waited until she had his full attention.

"You come near me again…" She shifted her position, drawing her knee into his crotch. "You touch me again, and I'll kill you."

"You are dead to me."

Tristan put her full weight on her knee to push herself up, then ran out of the house. Into the waiting arms of the night. To the streets…

...where Mulysa found her.

"What's a fine girl like you doing out here?" Mulysa asked, his voice all silvery and polished in that way roughnecks could be.

"Chilling." Though terrified and alone, Tristan wasn't going to admit any vulnerability, silvery and polished or not. Mulysa sized her up with a glance.

"Where you stay at?"

"Around."

"Girl, why you playing? I know these here streets like the back of my hand."

There it was. She was penniless. Hungry. Hurting. And Mulysa was there with his big wad of cash. Taking her to expensive restaurants, well, shit, Olive Garden anyway. Treating her like she was worth something.

"You got potential."

"Potential to do what?"

"Be in this here game. Come work for me."

"Doing what?" Tristan knew the moment would arrive. Nothing was free, especially from a man. He'd fed her, clothed her, and put her up. Rent was due.

"I got something for you." He slid a wooden box over to her. "Didn't I say I'd take care of you?"

She opened the box up. Inside were two thin blades. She'd never seen anything like them. She could grip them like brass knuckles, but the edges jutted out at angles. She loved the way they caught the light and their perfect balance in her hands.

"You right, you right." Though his tone said, "you most certainly do."

"What do you want me to do with these?"

"You got all that hate and anger in you. I just want to put it to good use. Get you paid."

Tristan went out early in the morning and would stray into rivals' territories at seven in the morning. Catch them when they'd been out all night, catch them drowsy or otherwise slipping. And get them. She staked out places from behind bushes for hours. Rain, sleep, snow, heat, she would do whatever it took, suffer whatever conditions to get to her enemy.

The things she did in Mulysa's name were bad enough. When she found Iz only a year later, she was a different woman. Hard. Skilled. Feared. No one knew her name, she had no name as far as she was concerned. She was simply an extension of Mulysa's will. His name rang out because he could always call her down. His shadow. His weapon of choice. Iz changed all of that.

Iz she found in an alley. She reminded her of a kitten which had been abandoned to fend for itself. Dirty. Bleeding from a hundred little scratches. Infested with who knows what. Living under abandoned cars. Lost. Frightened. Could practically fit into the palm of her hand. The kind of kitten that immediately got into her heart and made her want to protect it. Not only safeguard it, but be the kind of person worthy, privileged enough, to be with it. With her. Iz always thought that Tristan saved her life, but Tristan knew it was the other way around.

Mulysa took Iz away from her. She would have done anything for Iz and proved so on many an occasion.

He got her back on drugs after Iz fought so hard to get clean. And he touched her. Touched her the way Tristan's father wanted to touch her.

And he had to pay.

The blades curved naturally around her palms like an extension of her arm. He would pay. And pay again.

Dreadlocks started in the middle of his head, the front half faded, Prez shifted in his seat, adjusting it further into a lean position as if the person who sat in the seat before him wasn't gangster enough. None of which fooled Naptown Red. He sensed Prez's lingering discomfort, his church-boy heart beating through his thug-lite exterior. Didn't matter, though, since it wasn't as if the church bus was going to pick him up out here.

Both sides of the street were lined with parked cars for blocks in either direction. Naptown Red parked around back then led them around to the front of the house. The wall thrummed with the pulse of the music inside. A couple of the neighbors hung out on their porches, drink and cigarettes in hand, shooting the shit. It wasn't as if they were going to call the police at the first sound of drunk and/or loud niggas on the lawn. Enjoying his role as concierge and consummate host, Naptown Red smiled, hearing the music bump as soon as they opened the doors.

This wasn't some basement party, all dim lights, slow jams, and grinding on the dancefloor. No, the party was all the way live: bright, loud, and a little crazy. Li'l Jon skeet-skeet-skeeted from the DJ's turntable, the bass turned so loud that it threatened an assault charge. Naptown Red took in a deep whiff. Sure, there were the usual chips and shit in bowls scattered strategically through the house so that no guest had to stray too far to snack, but that wasn't the kicker. Marble's Soul Kitchen catered the party: collard greens, macaroni and cheese, sweet potatoes, and fried chicken. Red needed them to know that he would take better care of them than their mommas. And the best part, ladies walked around with silver trays, serving beer, wine, or (inexpensive) champagne.

Topless.

"They cool?" the brother at the door asked, stopping Fathead and Prez. Samoan had to run in his family, because he topped four bills easy. Dressed in all black, he gave a wary stare at Fathead. His T-shirt was a dirty shade of beige over a pair of blue sweatpants. He wore dress shoes though he had no socks. No watch either; his minutes stretched into hours and melted into days. Lost.

"Yeah, they with me."

"What was that about?" Prez asked.

"Cover. Shit, I ain't trying to feed a house full of hungry-ass niggas out of pocket. Brothers don't go anywhere else for a dinner and a show for free. Twenty dollars a head, plus they got to tip the ladies. And they were happy to pay the twenty dollars." Now that they knew what they were getting, Naptown Red already had it figured out that next time he would charge $50. Word was out as soon as he had a full house. Sell it as an exclusive ticket and let word of mouth take care of the rest.

"Didn't you used to go out with her?" Fathead pointed to a high yellow-complexioned honey, a little on the thin side, but tall and proud. Her small breasts popped pertly with each step. A tight Jheri curl, that looked like a baby Afro from a distance, crowned her. She grinned defiantly, taking a higher step for an additional bounce.

"Yeah, I hit that." She wore the navy-blue shorts of a flight attendant's uniform and blue hose and matching pumps. He loved the way she rolled and pitched, too bad he couldn't remember her name. Sometimes he just opened his mouth and whatever line of shit trickled out he worked with, counting on his charm and wit to see him through. Mostly, he stalled for time to think of a way to turn the situation to his advantage. "I get down like Sprite, except that I don't obey my thirst, I obey my look. That's my motto."

Naptown Red left Prez to find his own footing at the party. Church boy or not, he still had eyes that worked and there was no harm in perusing the smorgasbord of flesh that he – as consummate host considerate enough to turn up the air conditioning to make sure the nipples stayed popped – had laid out. Red toured the party, giving his guests the opportunity to thank him and tell him how much the bomb his party was. Playing it cool, he gave a slight head nod, letting his eyes tell the rest. The party had splintered into discrete clusters of conversations and activities. Leering thugs pretended to watch the large-screen TV set to pre-season football, ogling any nipple in sight. He thought about getting another TV and setting up a PlayStation console on it, but he didn't know how that would go over. Maybe next time. Thick rolls of smoke billowed from the dining room.

But the women were the center attraction, exactly how he wanted it (thus he nixed his plans to add video games: if it came down between titties and John Madden, it was a toss-up. And they could get John Madden at home, but only Red could provide the titties). The white women looked straight out of a "Blondes On Blacks" porn site, just this side of white trash – that upscale Jerry Springer demographic that brothas couldn't resist. The sistas stepped right out of a rap video. The more modest ones wore lingerie which revealed more than if they had simply come topless, so Red didn't complain. The party threatened to overwhelm him. Red made his way to him, pointedly rubbing against one of the ladies "mmm-hmm"-ing his approval in her ear. She craned her neck to flash him a smile.

"I'm all about the squilla. He'll be here," Naptown Red said, but Prez had lost interest in anything that he had to say. Following the strength of Prez's gaze only to land on the figure of a young lady dancing on a nearby table. She wore a white cowboy hat and matching leather skirt and boots. Her ensemble practically glowed against her mocha skin. Auburn hair flowed out the back of her hat. Long slender legs uncrossed and crossed quickly when she sat in mid-routine. A tattoo, like the top half of two red balls, peeked from above her skirt.

Her eyes searched Naptown Red for the tell. He nodded, letting her know that a large tip was heading her way. She turned, without saying a word, and pushed Prez onto the couch. Whatever mild protests he offered ceased when the DJ picked up on the cue and interrupted an Usher cut with another Li'l Jon cut. She turned her backside to Prez, her body catching the rhythm of the song. She slinked backward, her body contorting into a languid curving "S" that made its way toward him. Swishing side to side, she made a tentative dip into his lap. Turning to face him, she ran her hands down his chest, crouching between his legs as she continued to let her hands trail lower.

Prez jumped.

The gathering crowd laughed. Red feared that his plan might backfire, causing Prez to be the center of humiliation, but the guys soon started cheering Prez and the girl on. She stood up, shaking about a few more times before settling into Prez's lap for real. She let out an approving "ooo" much to the delight of Prez, whose back was clapped for the honor.

"Come on, I got more to show you," Red said.

"Aren't your guests going to miss you?" Prez asked.

"With all them titties to stare at? They probably don't even know that I'm out." Naptown Red beamed with a cobra's smile. "We got business in back."

"That where the hidden sex rooms are?" Fathead asked, not able to keep the eagerness out of his voice. Naptown Red explained that the rumors circulating about his parties – rumors he, himself, started – was all about marketing. He made it sound as if there was an extra level of party available to the truly connected. Much like the exclusive – rumored to be high-stakes-only – poker game. It all added to the mystique, coming to life behind the closed doors, away from the noise and temptation.

"What we playing?" Fathead asked. "Texas Hold 'Em?"

"You been watching them white boys on TV too long." Naptown Red pictured himself as a prince who ruled with style. He didn't need all the chest-thumping and territory-marking pissing contests that came with having to prove their bona fides. No, he'd simply get a feel for them over cards. Some James Bond villain shit, except none of that punk-ass baccarat mess. They'd play Spades.

"Hup. He got the king of spades," Fathead said. He had a habit of thinning his eyebrows whenever he was on meth. These days, two scabby rectangles above his eyes scarred his face and made him appear constantly startled. He knew one girl who removed her eyelashes, convinced they were antennae broadcasting her business to the FBI. With lips like cracked rubber, the flesh of his cheeks eaten away, and a ring of fat swelling his neck, Fathead soldiered on.

"It ain't what you got, it's how you play 'em," Naptown Red said.

"There are still three cards that can take that king." Prez ordered his cards. He'd come a long way from when King found him scrounging around for bits of rock behind where Dred's soldiers had been slinging, hoping for anything that might have spilled out. A life that revolved around doing enough work to scrape together enough for another blast. Those days weren't too far in his rearview mirror, but King's words echoed in his head. He was full of potential and could do anything he wanted. It was time to start living into that potential. But he didn't know where to begin. Or how. Only that he had to do something, somehow begin his journey. King believed in him and he wanted to justify that belief.

Trapped in a cycle of need and placating need, he constantly sought attention to soothe some deep ache inside. Wayne helped him focus on his future and had him reading all sorts of books to stimulate his mind and his curiosity. *A New Kind of Christian. The Autobiography of Malcolm X. Black Boy. Blue Like Jazz.* And the Bible, of course.

"Don't confuse being a character with having it," Wayne told him.

He knew he was being shaped into something new. Something wondrous. And he prayed for Wayne. And King.

"I hope someone does for you what you've done for me."

The residents of Breton Court, the Phoenix Apartments, and so many places in between, had long given up on themselves. But King – a street legend – thought he was ready. And Prez wanted to prove to him that he was. No matter what it cost him.

"West side niggas had to go east side cause King had that place locked down. That's a whole lot of unexploited real estate."

"So what you looking for?" Prez asked.

"Drilling rights, motherfucker. What you think?" Naptown Red asked. "You think you ready to put in some work?"

"If there's work to be done," Prez said. "I'm here to do it."

So he decided to get on with Naptown Red. Maybe learn some of the inside news and feed it to King. He doubted King and them would approve, but he figured he could handle the risk considering the potential payoff.

"Time to raise up, gentlemen."

"Your time is done."

Naptown Red thought about setting up a dog-fighting ring in a daycare. Something to carve out his own niche in the game. Low risk, low overhead. Low pay-off. If he wanted a steady stream of ends, he'd have to get his own connect and set up his own operation.

"Uh oh, she coming," Prez said. "When he sat back, I knew he had that one."

"Come on wit it," Fathead said.

"All right, Cleetus," Red said, throwing the queen of spades on the table. Prez had good eyes and good instincts. Way better than Fathead. He could handle himself under pressure. Cards revealed a lot about a man. While Prez kept quiet and watched people, Fathead was all bluster and bluff.

Naptown Red stacked the deck.

"Uh oh, the sleepy giant wants some," Fathead said.

Fathead's life was divided between BC and AC: Before Crack and After Crack. BC he remembered that Christmas time was the best time of the year, poor or not. His folks got together, got a little tree, strung up some lights. They had a few presents. Nothing big or fancy, that wasn't the point. They spent time together, had their little traditions and showed each other they were family. Folks came over and cooked; family came together and they laughed.

AC, no one came over.

His first year of high school, BC, he had nice clothes and used to always wear designer merchandise. When he dressed, he came correct, knew who to hang with and how to hang with them. He was down with his music, down with his sports, shit, by his world's standards, he was a man of high culture. But he still felt like a piece of shit. A wound, a black hole of pain sucked all of the contentment and hope for happiness out of his life.

The first time he got high, AC, he got paranoid, convinced people were out to get him. He ended up hiding under the bed, bawling his eyes out like a little bitch. The drug was that overwhelming. He snorted deeply, letting it drip down the back of his throat, leaving a dull medicinal taste. His eyes pitched and rolled behind their lids, tracing intricate patterns of light and color. The high never fixed him, never felt comfortable.

"That your book?" Fathead asked.

"Nuh uh. You got to follow suit," Prez said.

"I better not see you play a diamond."

Look at 'em thinking hard. It was so easy for Red to identify bullshit. Fathead's pupils dilated to the outer rims of the corneas. His eyes appeared to flatten. His black fingernails scratched at his Styrofoam cup then itched along his arm. He had carved the word "guilty" onto his left shoulder. He'd spent too much time in his uncle's meth lab. Some trailer over by Mars Hill. Places easily destroyed and abandoned. As disposable as the people. With the windows shut and the blinds drawn, the smell of ammonia seeped into everything. All the places had the same tangles of tubing between glass jars and bowls, stacks of jam jars and measuring cups unless they went upscale, using Vision Ware bowls or something.

"Cut by my own partner," Naptown Red said.

"Yeah, he straight-up novice," Prez echoed.

"This lady came into the shop today," Fathead began, trying to shift topics from his inept play. "Showing pictures of herself buck naked or with just a thong on. She big, but she don't care if she looks big or not. Cause she's a freak."

"You can keep those chicks that look like boys. I need me something firm," Red said.

"Tell 'em what you call them."

"Slabs. I need something to hold on to. The only problem with freaks is that they don't know when to turn it off."

"Preach to this, boy," Fathead said.

"Freaks are always freaks, have always been freaks, and that's the only way they know to be. They need to know that they got to be a lady sometimes, too. I don't want a freak raising my children."

Prez grinned at him. "You right, some women ain't got a freak bone in their bodies."

"Unless you put one in them," Fathead said. Red reached over to give him a pound.

"But see, you didn't answer the question," Red continued. "Why don't women want to be freaks? I'll tell you."

"Who you supposed to be?" Prez asked with a smile on his face because he guessed what was coming.

"The doctor. And the doctor is in."

"Doctor of what?" Prez enjoyed his role as straight man.

"Booty-ology," Red said.

They all threw their cards into the center of the table. The alcohol hit them, their peals of laughter bounced about the room.

"You see, if more women were freaks, dudes wouldn't cheat. They wouldn't have a chance to. Cause a freak would be all into him. They'd be all into him, calling him up, talking that talk." Naptown Red affected a female voice, leaning in like a drunk prostitute. "'What you doing?' 'How you doing?' 'How you hanging?' 'Are you strong, baby?' Then she'd lay it out for him. 'Come see me, I got a gift for you. I really mean a gift, too.' Then she'd give him the gift, show him a good time, rub on his leg, get him all hard, then tell him to get back to making his money and that he can take care of her later on. You know what I mean?

"*Or* she calls up and is like 'meet me at Nordstrom's on the fourth floor. We can go shopping.' She meets him, and before they go shopping, she gives him some head. Then she turns and says 'before we go shopping, let me brush my teeth.' You know what that tells me?"

"That she's a freak?" Fathead asked in a tone that sounded like he was taking notes.

"That she's a proper lady *and* a freak. What nigga's gonna cheat?"

"Having a freak sounds exhausting," Prez said. "Too much work."

"You got to be up for it. Not every man can handle a freak," Red said. "That's when you come see me. I'll put you on that regimen. Myoplex and one teaspoon of noni juice."

"What's Myoplex?" Fathead asked, again with that tone.

"It's a natural herb. Keeps you raw for as long as you want. A whole weekend. You might have wood, but

Myoplex will give you a brick. Noni juice is the mojo. That's the finishing move. All-purpose health."

"I'm ready to snatch the pebble from your hand." Fathead raised his fist for another bump, but Red left him hanging.

"Anyway," Red continued. "You don't think if women were more like that, men wouldn't cheat?"

"Nope, we'd cheat," Prez said.

"How can you say that?" Naptown Red asked.

"Cause we men. You show me the most beautiful, loving, freak-when-the-time-is-right woman in Hollywood, and I'll show you a man who's tired of sleeping with her. We chase women the same way fiends chase that high. Cause we have to. Got something in us we got to fill. And either way, chasing that feeling, costs us one way or another." Prez laughed at his own joke, like a great fool not comfortable in his own skin.

"I got a connect. Some Jamaicans come through North Carolina." Naptown Red put his cards down. "Fathead and you oversee distribution."

"Dred know?" Prez asked.

"This here's on the side. I got the package, y'all dish it out. We split what comes in. *We* do."

"So how we gonna do this?" Fathead asked.

"A man must have a code. We live by rules: Never come up short. Never be burnt. Never be late. Never be slow."

"That's a lot of nevers," Fathead said.

"Don't get high. Don't carry. Don't use names on the phone."

"We all nevers and don'ts."

"This here's serious business. Life and death. So that's how we do this. That's how we stay out of jail. That's how we stay alive."

CHAPTER NINE

Wishard Hospital was the hospital of last resort, reserved especially for the indigent, the uninsured, those too poor or too out of the system to go to one of the better hospitals. An X-ray technician clutched a half-dozen transparencies as she dashed down the hallway toward the emergency room. A drunk chatted up the nurses at the check-in desk. They dutifully ignored him. The security guard coughed into his fist. King's room was a piss-yellow color with two beds in it. The monitor bleeped mercilessly. Pastor Winburn stood over him, his heart heavy as he touched the tubes which ran into King's mouth and arm. It was all so senseless. More wanton violence, more needless bloodshed, another man cut down and all of his potential cut down with him. Without King, the land seemed darker and the mood more hopeless. Bowing his head, he continued praying for him.

"Why, son?" he thought.

Outside the room and down the hall, Lady G fussed over a piece of fabric as she struggled with a needle or thread. Big Momma had been teaching her how to sew and Lady G patched one of her shirts, the idea of mending things she'd broken before appealed to her. Grief came and went in sudden waves. Setting the shirt and threaded needle down, she hugged herself nonchalantly and rubbed her upper arms. Dark circles swelled under her eyes, and she scratched her nose. Blotches pockmarked her skin like half-healed scars. She knew her place was at King's side, tending to him as best she could. Concern gave her the strength to face up to what she'd done. Part of her owed him some sort of explanation, though whatever words gave voice to her reasons fell pathetically short. She remembered not the hurt, but the years of good times. Then the dulling shock of sorrow swept over her all over again. Part of her hated King. And Lott. Funny what the mind did to protect itself. Or the heart. How the person they once cared so much about became the enemy; how every once supportive or encouraging comment or act became twisted into something nefarious.

"What are you doing here?" Rhianna asked, the words laced with more harshness than she intended.

"King's still my friend. I wanted to be here in case he woke up."

"What the doctors say?" Rhianna lowered herself into a chair next to her. Still sore from giving birth, or at least milking her recovery for all the attention it was worth. Rhianna's mother's theory on motherhood: have plenty of babies – it increased chances that one would survive and thrive. Rhianna had internalized her mother's lessons well. She'd done her time with the wrong man, wannabe players who smoked a little weed, packaged drugs, but mostly sold burn bags to unsuspecting fiends. And she'd spent more than her share of time on her back trying to find love or connection or some sense of worth from another. To most, she was still some fast-tail little girl playing grown-folk business, but she felt like she'd been given a second chance through Outreach Inc, one she'd come close to blowing on more than one occasion, which was why she was on probation. But with the birth of her second child things finally seemed to be falling into place for her. She had even enrolled in GED classes.

"They don't know. They sound confused."

"What you mean?"

"They got the bullets out. The wounds were mostly superficial. Missed all of his arteries and organs. They say he stable. But they don't know why he won't wake up."

"They let you back there?"

"Sometimes, for a bit. Told them I was his sister."

"You love him. So. Hard." Rhianna sucked her teeth.

"I love them both."

"You can't love two men, boo. Then you'll have neither."

"Then I'll have neither."

"You are so full of not trying today."

"That was dirty."

"I'm just saying.

"What we were doing wasn't love. It was pain and anger. Trying to get a feeling back. I don't know. Like we both, we all were chasing something that may not have been real."

"I thought something was going on, just hoped I was

wrong. I wanted to go on record as being concerned with the potential smell of that situation."

Everyone was full of that kind of brilliant hindsight, as if saying they thought something was up was the same as doing something. Most times she wanted to say "why didn't you say anything?" or "didn't you care enough about any of us to speak up?" Instead, she just nodded and let it go. "Uh oh, girl, what's up? You still with Fathead?"

"Lady G. Look here, I'm going to need you to come get your people today. It's your turn to deal with this foolishness, okay? Okay." She made a phone out of her fingers.

"I'm on a break from him and his foolishness. I'm too through."

"Do better."

"I'm done. Nigga came home smelling like pussy. Don't need no taco stink on his breath."

"Nuh uh. For real?"

"Next day, some Mexican hootchie had the nerve to try and call *me* out. I'm asking what's up with that. Then she accuses me of being on crack." Rhianna pushed back in her chair like she was pushing away from a table.

"Bet she got on the phone right away bragging to her girls. So I cut that fool loose. Better off on my own anyway."

"You a down-ass girl. You know that, right?"

Rhianna found it difficult to accept praise for her own abilities or herself as a person. Especially as a friend. She never was around enough or got involved enough. Spent so much time close to things but not really engaging in it.

The automatic doors which sealed off the Intensive Care Unit swung open as Percy and Mad Had came in, escorted by Wayne and Esther. Big Momma trundled in behind them. Lady G kept her eye on Wayne and Esther. She knew both from Outreach Inc. But something about their behavior struck her as familiar. Esther leaned a little too into him; he occupied her personal space. Without touching hands or even so much as a lingering glance, they seemed so... intimate. Lady G dismissed her thought as maybe her projecting her own ways onto others.

"How are things?" Wayne asked.

"Same old." Lady G couldn't meet his eyes. She picked up her shirt and fumbled with the needle and thread again.

"Nothing changed?"

"No."

"How he look?"

"He doesn't even look like him. Not even like him sleeping. Like part of him is missing."

"It just don't make sense. Things keep falling apart," Wayne said.

"It's like there's a cancer in the group." Lady G guessed what others thought of her because she certainly knew what she thought of herself.

"G... come on. I didn't mean..."

"Yeah, you did. I sure did."

His round, expressionless face and his indifferent eyes fixed on nothing in particular. His red jacket, with yellow sleeves and dirty cuffs, stopped two inches shy of his wrist. Mad Had screamed then writhed about on the floor, pounding it with his fists and feet as he bawled. A couple of nurses raised their heads above the cubicle wall, like prairie dogs catching a scent. Big Momma waved off their concern to let them know she had the situation under control.

Tears welled up in Percy's eyes then trickled down his face. Everyone was hurting. There wasn't anything he could do for them besides cry. He ached from powerlessness as much as anything else. As he rocked back and forth, he hummed to himself, but found little comfort in it.

The tinny strains of "It's All Right (To Have a Good Time)" erupted as Wayne's cell phone went off. It wasn't one of his pre-programmed ringtones, but apparently a message had gone straight to voicemail. He put the phone to his ear and the first words he heard was "Don't be daft. Put me on speaker."

"Dag, Merle don't ever stop," Wayne said. At the mention of his name, everyone stopped and turned to Wayne. Half-throwing his hands in the air, he put his phone on speaker.

"Sir Wayne, it is the prerogative of the truly wise to play the buffoon. I must go away for a time, but no matter because the story keeps telling itself. There are keepers of grails, guardians of blessings, and miracles through whom wonders come. Sacrifices of blood through which healings come. And when those treasures go missing, they need to be sought without further delay."

Merle's words brought back a memory to Percy. When he was on the streets, raising ruckus with his mom, Miss Jane, he once broke into Rhianna's place.

• • • •

Miss Jane convinced him to break in. Rumors of the household hoarding money and jewelry, eccentric ghetto millionaires. Such tales bubbled up from time to time, excusing would-be treasure hunters their Robin Hood ethos, though the poor who were targeted by their charitable impulse were usually themselves.

Two windows in the apartment, one with an air-conditioning unit in it, though it too was stolen from a first-floor apartment down the street. The bedroom window slid open easily enough. A young girl stirred, disturbed by the rush of traffic sounds from the outside, Percy closed the window behind him. Pausing, he bent over the frame in case the girl fully woke and he needed to make a hasty retreat. He sensed her in the dark, could hear her breathing. Fumbling along her dresser, his large, nimble hands found no jewelry. He ran them along a chalice; inside was a lone ring. He picked up the ring, holding the metal goblet in case it clattered against it. He peered over his shoulder. The sleeping figure didn't move.

Percy leaned over her. Rhianna. The warmth of her brushed against his cheek. He took in a deep breath. Flowers and powder, a gentle scent. Peaceful. The ring grew hot in his hand. He lost the heart to continue going through her things. It was a violation. He ran his finger along her face. Gripped by the panic that always seized him when around her, that sense that he might break her, he scuttled out the window.

"Anything?" Miss Jane demanded.

"No, Momma." The ring burned in his pocket. A memento.

He returned the ring, but it and the cup came up missing not too long ago. He'd always meant to find it again.

"Though the journey be fraught with peril," Merle

continued, "when isn't life a risk? Only the innocent can
enter their castles. Do not eat anything within the castle,
no matter how tempting or hungry. The chalice must be
brought home. Its true guardian will know what to do
with it."

Mad Had calmed and then moved to lie down with his
left hand supporting his head. He dragged his empty pillow case. Mad Had had taken to carrying a pillow with
him everywhere. An old, ratty thing, yellowed by sweat,
but he insisted on toting it about, sniffing it on occasion.
"Momma, my pillow's broke."

"I know, baby. I told you I didn't want you dragging
that thing everywhere." It comforted him, but Big
Momma wasn't going to drag a mangy pillow around
with them everywhere they went. So she let him take
his pillow case, which she was careful not to wash – a
hard-learned lesson. Babies with his condition tended to
wither without the attention of their mother, but Mad
Had had thrived as well as a crack baby could. Big
Momma had the distinct feeling he could speak more
regularly if he wanted to. She saw the glint of the tem-
pest in his eye no one else noticed.

"Be strong and be true, my precious knights. It is in
your nature to win the battle."

On the way to Haughville from downtown, off Oliver, a
gravel road branched from a railroad crossing, appearing
to be little more than a service road. A graveyard for
garbage, it wound past rusted-out rail cars to a thick
copse of trees between warehouses. This whole side of
town stank, as the old garbage dumps had been built

over. Not too long ago, folks had brought every bit of metal they could get their hands on. Rumor had it that when China hosted the Olympics, they bought scrap metal in such quantities, it was going for three dollars a pound. Fiends became industrious. Outreach Inc.'s air conditioners got jacked twice during this time. Two days after the Olympics, the price had dropped to seventy cents a pound.

The industrial park closed at dusk as it was difficult to find one's way around at night. The woods took on a sinister aspect of their own. Paths turned and shifted in the darkness. Merle kicked at a dirty little blanket. It was in her. All he had to do was touch it and the darkness took on a life of its own inside. This particular shade of shame was different. There was no fear in her eyes, only questioning. Startle become calculation. Thieves needed the night.

"What are you doing?" Nine asked.

"I had to make a phone call," Merle said.

"You had to contact them."

"Send them on their way."

"Ever the nudge. Push them in the right direction, did you?"

"You're a skilled manipulator. You tell me."

"Promise me you won't do any of that on me," Nine said.

"I so swear. I'm cuckoo for Cocoa Puffs." Merle squatted on the ground and scooped up a handful of gravel. Sniffing it and apparently satisfied, he dropped it and clapped his hands together. "Hopefully they're off to fetch God's pimp cup."

"You sent them after the grail?"

"It was my penultimate act in service to King."

"Penultimate?"

"I have one more trick up my sleeve."

"That counting what I want you to do?"

"What is it that you want me to do?" Merle knew the answer but wanted her to play out her role.

"I want you to make a place for us. A magical place. I want to learn how to build it."

"A place of joy and solitude. Never undone. I will teach you."

"Why?"

"I am impelled by a fatal destiny."

Merle knew that his fate was in her arms. And it would not be pretty. Having fallen asleep beneath a bush of white thorn, laden with flowers, while resting in her lap. As the story went. Like how children fall for one another; find one another without introduction, he was hers the moment they met. Beauty reduced to a blues ballad. Not content with his devotion, hers was a mission to isolate him, to get him alone. Nine was dual-natured, both girl and ancient. She would kill him if she could, to satiate the hunger. And still, he cleaned up his alley, his secret place. He swept the broken glass, and picked up the cans and bottles before he brought her here.

"I am but one of the Guardians of the Totems."

"One of the Lords of the Wheel?"

"Coo coo cachoo."

Bored and restless, Merle panted after her worse than an adolescent in love. Truth be told, by now, he probably was an adolescent. He went where she went, jumped when she asked, begged for her company like an old, well-trained dog. And, as girls often were with old men, she was wary of him, impatient with him. And he frightened her. For all of his seeming feebleness, he was the devil's heart, she thought, and she feared when he might turn his powers on her.

For all of her craftiness, her agenda was obvious: she wanted his knowledge and traded it for time spent with her. When the "inborn craft of women" met the "inborn weakness of men". For many, it passed as love. Helpless before her, he was unable to break out of the girl's spell. He wanted to teach her, be her tutor. Show her wonders. To show her his house.

"Show me, mage. Teach me everything."

"The magic is deep and the magic is old. But there is little room for magic in this age. In this world. So little faith. Magic is pure faith. A well-cast magic circle isolates you. The spell is just you and creation. You are cut off. One with…" Whatever image he chased after, the words escaped him.

"Perfect communion."

Merle nodded. "Look around you. What do you see?"

"A thin copse of trees."

"This is my home. My true home."

"A glamour?"

"No," Merle sighed. "Look. Even when you were young, you thought you knew so much. In all your travels, in all your accumulated knowledge, in all your years, you still overlook the basics. The primal forces."

"The dragon's breath."

"Forget the dragon's breath. You forget how powerful

you are. You have it at your fingertips to shape that energy into reality. It requires a boldness to repurpose reality. You have to be careful. Concentrate. Block the energies. You tap into it. Can you feel it?"

Old, deep, eternal, a call. The ley line. Lush, thick, green. Candlelight flickering in the night. The delicate hum of whale song. The gentle fragrance of rose petals. The scent of a newborn. A lover's embrace, the feeling of home. The thrum of life. Intimate, deliberate. Intentional. Knowing, probing, wanting. A whisper. A caress.

"Here we are, male and female, in perfect balance. I know that is the final key. Co-equals. Co-heir. Communion." She circled behind him and stretched her arm along his. "Tell me the words."

"The spoken word is the final tool. You have to form your own path, not walk someone else's. What you fear shapes the experience."

"And what do you fear?"

"You. I'm a foolish, foolish old man. Besotted with age and drunk on the promise of the charms of the young's fickle embrace. I know this and I am powerless to stop myself."

"Tell me the words."

"Et Verbum caro factum est."

"Et Verbum caro factum est," she repeated. From her lips, the power carried different images. Tiny skulls crushed under boot heel. The slow spill of intestines from a gutted animal. Graveyard dirt spilling overhead. Old bones grinding together. The splintering of joints. A selfish voice. Proud. Shrill. Chaotic. A living fear. Doubt.

Insecurity. Violence. Death. "The home you created. The home you will stay."

The fabric of space bubbled out. Created a slit and then resealed as if swallowing the home in a single gulp. When the light faded, the trees remained as they were. The camp cleared out.

Only Nine stood in the clearing.

In her hands a green orb shimmered. Merle's face flickered across the surface, bewildered then resigned.

"Our time is done, my love. Let the children have their end game."

CHAPTER TEN

Bo "The Boars" Little was known for his propensity for violence. It came to him naturally, he believed, as if God Himself gifted him for violence. By his freshman year at Northwest High School, he had the sculpted physique of an African Adonis. Well over six feet tall and 250 pounds of solid bulk; skin a lighter shade of onyx, his head shaved bald, yet nursing a full beard, he had a grown man's body. Playing left tackle, when he hit someone, they stayed hit. The stands chanted his name when he was on the field, the students parted in the school hallways as he strode down them, girls were quick to offer themselves to him, talent scouts up and down the east coast knew his name, but none of that was enough. He wanted his name to ring out in the streets. Navigating the complexities of office politics proved more difficult than he would have imagined. He attached himself to Garlan, positioning himself as his second-in-command, not really out of any sort of corporate climbing move – for that he would have sidled up next to Nine or perhaps to Dred directly.

They didn't come up as boys but had been thrown together to put work in. They got high on occasion. A
couple of times while high, they spoke of things they
rarely mentioned. Not especially close, the only thing
they had in common was the ache, the one they only
spoke of when high. They spoke of missing their fathers,
of not belonging anywhere, they let breathe the dead
areas of their souls and gave voice to their pain.

"I'm tired of being poor," The Boars said.

"A nigga just needs a break." Garlan took another hit
in commiseration.

"I'm tired of being poor," The Boars repeated, confused, thinking he had only thought the sentiment rather
than said it aloud the first time. "I'm tired of having to
claw through every day just to keep my head above
water. It gets so I don't give a shit who I got to hold on
to as long as I stay afloat."

"I just need some money. Rich motherfuckers ain't got
shit to worry about."

"Taxes, where to go out to eat, and how much to pay
their nanny."

"What if we weren't here?" Garlan touched his ring.
Garlan was so low-key, he was practically invisible. No
one would ever guess that he had thousands stashed
away. He was cut more from a business cloth than anything else.

"What you mean?"

"What if we had been given a chance? Born somewhere other than here?"

"White?"

"Nah, shit, I didn't say all that. But, you know, into a

real family. With a mom and dad. No niggas trying to shoot each other as soon as breathe your way."

"I don't do no 'what if' shit. That's enough to drive a nigga madder than he already is. I think more about how it's all gonna end."

"How's it end?"

"For me?" The Boars turned toward the night sky, lost in dreams. "Maybe taking out a cop, going out in a blaze."

"Putting yourself out of your misery."

Misery took a toll. All the death and hopelessness drove him to a place of despair. Stuck between life and death with only jail or the grave as a way out.

Garlan treated the fiends fair, like customers, and if they shorted him, he had The Boars administer swift recompense. Between them, product moved like clockwork. They weren't pleased when they were charged to bring Naptown Red's spot on a running as smoothly. Though both Garlan and Naptown Red were in the inner circle, Garlan's presence tended to carry more weight. A fact not lost on Red.

The only reason Garlan was present was because he was due to collect a money drop. Garlan made sure no one handled both money and product. Their crew paid some apartments to stash guns and drugs. The corner smelled of re-breathed beer and piss. They could only venture to guess what liquid soaked the pavement. When windows were shattered they remained broken. The procedure was simple. The crew left a taped-down grocery bag full of money under the passenger's seat in a car. All they had to do was drive up, get out, make small talk, watch for police, and switch drivers. He wisely pulled out exactly ten dollars without exposing the rest of his wad.

Naptown Red, Prez, and Fathead had their own thing going on, right under the nose of The Boars and Garlan. Which was difficult, because Garlan was always watching. Even when he wasn't around, if you were working Garlan's spot, you did the work cause his eyes were always on you and he had a way of just showing up. They'd be careful, unlike those other crews. They'd sell to only those they knew. They'd use check points to guard the stash house. On the spot, no drugs and money would be handled by the same dude. All re-ups would be taken to the cutting house and then split up and delivered to safe houses.

Naptown Red enjoyed the role of schooling these young 'uns, molding them in his image. The stoop offered the best vantage point to take in the action of the neighborhood.

"Isn't that your lady's girl?" Fathead whispered.

"My girl can't stand her," Naptown Red said.

"Why not? She seems nice."

"You know how women get about each other," Naptown Red said.

"Nah, brotha. That's what I come to you for. So you can school me about these things."

"They too much alike and want the same things. Women know how cruel women are. If they know you got something, they don't care. They think they can take it."

"So she thinks she can steal you from any woman out there?"

"Man, she was ready to give up the goods from the jump."

"You retarded. You think every woman wants you."

"I'm part thug and part businessman. I can be calm, but I know when to go off. And I know how to treat a lady. Women love that crazy stuff, that versatility." Relationships, Naptown Red long ago realized, were little more than altars to yourself. Either you wanted someone to adore you, dote on you, take care of you, or you wanted someone to reflect you, be like you, so you can be with you more. "But most, I'm telling you, most are wolves in sheep's clothing. Can I break it down philosophically?"

"Go 'head, brotha." Fathead became his one-man amen corner.

"Women try to be of a character that they really ain't to try and get that good man. Fake him out, hook him, and they don't care about being a good friend to another woman. They mess up a good thing to try and get their thing."

"That happen to you a lot?"

"Fuck you." Naptown Red tipped his bottle of beer in Prez's direction as he came waddling up the street. As low man on the totem pole, Prez made the food runs. Brought back to-go boxes from Yats, a Cajun joint up in Broad Ripple. They ate like men ravenous and entertained.

"What, you no good?" Naptown Red ran his tongue along the roughness of his teeth, ground down from years of gnashing. His jaw clicked when he yawned.

"You won't find the answers to your questions in a bottle," Prez said.

"Then I need to ask different questions." The boy was good, but had a square streak to him which gave him pause. He wasn't built for the streets, not to survive them anyway.

"I'm just saying, we can't afford to get our heads up when on the clock."

"You looking down your nose at me, boy?" Naptown Red cautioned. "Trying to show me up in front of Garlan?"

"Naw, man. I just know how easy it is to get caught up and become an addict."

"There's addicted and there's addicted. I may smoke a few blunts, but I'm in control. Them dope fiends? Shit. There's no talking to them."

"Folks want what we be selling." Even when your market was dope fiends, one still had to battle for market share, and that came down to building a brand. Fathead called his brand of meth "The End". "Can't argue with the free market."

"Didn't you sell to your folks?" Prez asked.

"Hell yeah I did. A customer's a customer." Fathead didn't care if it were them trading in their ghetto credit cards he called food stamps. "That's their choice. Their problem. They gonna buy from someone, might as well be me. Least they won't get ripped off."

"Most times," Naptown Red sneered.

"A fool's a' fool. And I won't sell to my brother. He needs to find a better way. How player is that?"

Naptown Red was still a believer. In his heart he thought that the streets could be his savior. They gave him purpose, meaning, and a place of belonging. The accusatory glare of the car side light first caught his attention. Like any believer, there were times of testing of his faith, and Naptown Red's began as soon as the flashing lights erupted and car tires screeched to a halt as Five-O jumped out all over their spot.

The Boar's first months of school, sixth grade, were an endurance marathon of tests. Instructive on what life was really about. He wasn't The Boars then, just Bo Little. In his class, a majority of the students were black with the rest evenly split between whites and Mexican. In the seat next to him was some Mexican boy, Lonzo. Weighed less than he did, was shorter than he was, but his group of friends carried on like he walked on water. Deferred to him, laughed at his corny-ass jokes.

Bo's very existence seemed to bother Lonzo. He refused to bow before him. Hating the humiliation of the free lunch program, Bo sat away from other kids so they couldn't hear his stomach grumble. Lonzo made a special point to seek him out to sit across from him at lunch.

"You can't sit here, homes."

"Who says?" Bo searched for a nearby teacher, hoping to catch an eye and tacitly plead for help.

"You talk funny, hese. Like a nerd and shit." He laughed and his pack of hyenas brayed alongside him.

Bo needed a comeback, but fear and embarrassment paralyzed him. The best he could come up with was "What's your problem?"

"You my problem. You coming in here like you own the place, like you better than the rest of us simply cause you black. You ain't shit."

"Why you explaining yourself to this puta?" one of his boys chimed in, backed by their amen corner.

Bo made up his mind then. The instigator was larger than Lonzo and for that matter, larger than Bo, but he dove across the table at him. Slamming his lunch tray at him, sent that day's portion of peas, mashed potatoes with gravy, and meat perpetrating as meatloaf into the air. Scattering the rest of the boys. Bo landed atop the larger boy and rained down punches on him before anyone could intervene. A smile crossed his face. No one would mess with him now. He had taken on the largest one and handed him his ass. Maybe he could walk the halls in peace. He just wanted to be left alone.

Then the rest of the boys stepped in.

Let by Lonzo, they let loose a beating so rage-filled, Bo didn't know where the anger came from. For the slight trespass which occurred, they swarmed on him with other students circling around as living bricks forming a wall to hide the scene. Kicks slammed into his side, Bo covered his face as best he could and tensed his muscles against the blows.

"What the hell is going on over there?" a teacher yelled.

Lonzo and his boys dispersed like dead leaves on a strong breeze, skittering down the hallways with only a stream of obscenities to mark their passing. The teacher helped Bo to his feet and walked him to the nurse's office. Limping slowly, his fellow students lined up and parted to let him through. Bo couldn't meet their eyes, but still felt the weight of shame on him. Their eyes bored into him. The stifled snickers. The inner pain of damaged pride. The helplessness of being a victim.

All turmoil and confusion, aggression and anger, pain and contempt, the need to belong and the inability to value anyone. Darkness, robbed innocence, with only fear and violence to earn power and respect. The Boars was born.

The Boars was wild, always being suspended from school. Quickly gaining a reputation for having low eyes: he never told anyone when he had money. Never chipped in on anything, but ate like he paid twice his share. He never escaped that fight. Thing was, he was doing all right in that tussle until Lonzo and the rest stepped in. He needed his own crew to have his back when the time came.

And the time would always come.

It began with a bang on the door.

Barely even a courtesy shout of "Police" before they knocked the front door off the hinges. Naptown Red was used to police raids. Coming up, it was as natural a part of their family's rhythms of life as family reunions. The routine was as practiced as a fire drill: the police charged the house with guns drawn even as Fathead threw bags at the open window and Pres flushed others down the toilet. When over one hundred quarter bags of China White heroin were being packaged, even in the worst of economic times, their business was recession-proof.

The rest of the boys scattered. The threat of imminent jail or death had a way of focusing one's attention on their future. Sobering up from the heady mix of respect and power. Garlan simply disappeared. Prez, Fathead, and Naptown Red all ended up scooped up.

Naptown Red relaxed, quite pleased with his present circumstance. The way he imagined it, law enforcement from all over wanted to talk to him. Specific, highly detailed questions awaited him, which meant he enjoyed a new kind of rep, respect, and notoriety. No one noticed him or took him seriously in the past. Now everyone would know who he was.

"God, where are you?" Prez struggled with his own faith, wanting God back in his life, but He never answered. Knowing that no one would believe this misunderstanding. That he was working on the inside to supply King with information, not feed his own wallet or habit. The metal bench of the lock-up was harder than any at Stylez, his local barbershop. Head ducked, his palms on either side as he cradled it, he waited for his name to be called. They led him into the hallway after finger-printing, where he was forced to disrobe and toss his clothes into a pile in front of him. Like a slave facing inspection on the auction block, the guards performed their medical check, examining his hair, eyes, ears, and mouth for tracks. Thankful he wasn't a woman because he didn't think he could take the final act of being forced to crouch then cough to clear his vagina. Next, he picked up his belongings and walked single file to processing where he was given new underwear and clothes. Whatever shards of faith he had remaining he clutched to like a life preserver on an ocean of open water. As a storm approached.

Time had little meaning, but at ten o'clock at night, shadows steeped in the night. The vague stairs which dappled the house out into a smooth, neutral gray. The spotlights of patrol vehicles criss-crossed the house. Cops had set up in back and in front of the house, a pincer closing in on the stash house. They had the doors covered. The cops trapped a few pee wees trying to slip out a bedroom window. They checked the alleys, locked down the backyard and street, but no one looked up.

The Boars, rather than chance running out the back or the front, ran up the stairs. When he reached the top of the stairs, he weighed his options. He spied the trap door leading to the attic, but he knew it was only a matter of time until the cops searched there. They knew enough to hit this house, they knew enough to check the walls and the ceilings. There were three bedrooms, one overlooking the front yard, another the rear. The side bedroom had a window which opened onto a deck. He went up there sometimes to smoke at the window. He tested the rotted deck with his heavy foot. It held. Beneath him, cops scurried about tramping through the yard in a game of hide-and-seek with the pee wees. For a brief moment, The Boars thought about leaping onto the over-hanging tree branch and scampering down it over the fence into the neighbor's yard. But that played-out Tarzan shit would probably end with him busting his ass when he missed the branch – or it breaking beneath his two-hundred pound frame – else the cops simply waiting for him to climb his monkey ass out of the tree.

His cousin made the same mistake once. Robbed a liquor store then ran behind it back to his apartment where his girl chased him out of the place, not wanting him to bring any police bullshit back to their house. Around their child. His dumb ass climbed a tree, hoping to elude the police. They had his tree surrounded in a half-hour. Couldn't fool them canines. His cousin weighed his options. He couldn't do jail. Not a bit like that. So he shot himself in the chest. His body didn't topple out of the tree. They had to call in the fire trucks to get him down.

The Boars tugged at the shingles leading to the pitched room with three chimneys. Lights beamed along the stairway as police crept up into the waiting shadows. Bracing himself – he had to do this in one shot or the police would hear him for sure – he took a step back. He leapt. His fingers latched on to any purchase they could, ignoring the sandpaper scrape as he pulled himself up. The shouts of "clear" echoed about as the officers checked each room.

"Upstairs secure," an officer shouted.

"The Boars stretched out on the roof. Pulling his coat over him, he figured he could wait them out. Sneak off before dawn once the scene was secured by only a couple of cops.

Bo Little might have taken a beating, but The Boars handled his business.

At his desk, Cantrell turned the framed pictures of his wife and kids face-down before walking Prez past his desk to the interrogation room. Cantrell always knew he wanted to be a cop. Wanting to be where the action jumped off, he chose the most violent beat as a rookie. He wanted to make a difference. His was a simple plan. Let black kids in the neighborhoods see one of them. Have a cop treat them as a citizen, both valued and respected. Each person he met with a steady gaze, firm handshake, and served with honesty and diligence. He was the kind of detective who constantly asked questions and needed answers and didn't stop until he had them. For his effort, he was treated as the enemy: more blue than black. It broke his heart a little every time he had to haul in another brother in cuffs. Chains.

"You breaking my arm. You breaking my arm," Fathead said as he was ushered into a seat by Lee.

"You ain't got to do all that. We barely touching you." In contrast, Lee could give a shit about community. He couldn't tell you why he became a cop. Falling into it more than anything else, his sheer mediocrity allowing him to rise through the ranks. More diligent fuck-up than conscientious detective, most figured he'd have long been drummed out of the force. Except that he had an eye for the streets. He understood its rhythms and at the same time loathed that intimate knowledge. He was one with the musk and misery of the city's grimy underbelly. These days, the two graying strands in his mustache disconcerted him more than his clearance rate.

Lee was *that* kind of police. The kind who drank vodka because it had no smell even though it did. The kind who hid bottles around the house: in the basin of the toilet, in a kitchen cabinet, in the trunk of his car, in a desk drawer. The kind who wore his relationship with alcohol on his face. The kind who had no friends besides his brother officers and even those he had a propensity to piss on then piss off. The kind with no relationship to speak of; only sex with the occasional prostitute or other lost soul cast adrift in a bar. The kind with no family, no home, no roots, with his one-bedroom apartment having one room too many. Utilitarian at best, a television, couch, refrigerator, microwave, and a place to shit was all he needed.

All he had was the job. A job he hated most of the time but would be lost without.

"This case sucks. But they always suck till I get someone in jail." Cantrell snatched the folder from his desk. Opening the door, he found Fathead pouring a lot of sugar into his coffee.

"Can you get me some donuts?"

"Detective McCarrell read you your rights?" Ignoring him, Cantrell took off his jacket and wrapped it around the chair closest to the door. His chair. If Fathead was ever going through the door to see the light of day and freedom again, he had to go through Cantrell.

Fathead nodded while his fingers fussed with each other in nervous fumbling.

"We ran your prints. Your name is Bartholomew DiGora. Why they call you Fathead?"

"I don't know. Just a name, I guess," he mumbled, eyes cast shoeward.

"I love this room, Fathead. The truth comes out in this room." Cantrell perched on the edge of the table that separated them. "Mind if I call you Fathead? I don't mean to be presumptuous."

"It's all right." The boy wore a constant quizzical expression, more of a listener type.

"I just didn't want to disrespect you. Figure in the end, all a man's got is his good name. folks want to trample on that, they disrespect the man. I figure, you show a man respect, give him his due as a man. Less'n they do something to lose that respect. You feel me?"

"I guess."

"Now your boys, Preston Wilcox and Robert Ither – who you know as Prez and Naptown Red – them I got no use for. Prez's new to me. Looks like a bit of a burnout, but he ain't been in the system. Red, he a bit of a problem. He been in and out as long as he been breathing. He's what we call incorrigible."

"What you mean?"

"Mean he gonna see the inside of a cell for a long time. He one of them three-strike brothers. Unless…"

"Unless what?"

"Unless he makes a deal," Cantrell offered, helpfully resting his fists, knuckles down, into the table. "You see, we got a little girl dead. You knuckleheads want to sling to one another, do harm to one another, that's one thing. It ain't cool, but it's part of the game. You do what you got to do, we do what we got to do. But bodies start dropping, especially a little girl…"

Cantrell removed an eight-by-ten glossy from a manila folder and placed a photograph of Lyonessa Maurila Ramona Perez in front of him. "Well, folks come down hard on something like that. Put a brother *under* the jail for something like that. You hear what I'm saying?"

"Yeah."

"Now we got witnesses. Puts three people in an SUV." Not a lie, per se, about the witness. More like a poker bluff, and Cantrell knew from poker faces.

"I was at home."

"How you remember? I ain't told you what day."

"Everybody know. I was home sick."

"All day?"

"All day," Fathead echoed.

"Anyone vouch for you?"

"I ain't got no one. Sick alone. In bed."

"You ain't got no one? No one to take care of you when you sick? No one to be with you when you alone? No one to have your back when you in a jam?"

"No."

"Cause you know you in a jam, right?"

"What you mean?"

"The kind of weight we seized? Someone's going up for a long time. And that's *if* we can't put you in that SUV. But someone will. Cause you ain't got no one."

"No." Fathead's bloodshot eyes drifted into a sullen gaze.

"Not even Red. What you think he's going to tell us when I say there were three people in the SUV and that he can lessen his years by giving them up?" Cantrell came around the table again to meet his gaze. His voice lowered to a whisper. "A little girl is dead. Someone's going to pay."

Fathead was unmoved, in the way the truly innocent were unconcerned. A little cocky cause he knew he wasn't there. So Cantrell changed tack.

"On the other hand, I wonder what Red will tell me. Like whose dope that was. Think he'll put it on you if I ask him for a name? He doesn't exactly strike me as a stand-up guy." Cantrell's eyes bored into him like trained laser sights on a target.

Fathead squirmed, his lips taut and bloodless. Cantrell knew he had him. It was time for one of his artfully told lies.

"Then again," Cantrell's voice dropped to a confidential drawl, "if I were to ask you for a name, you probably will be looking at a walk. I'm no lawyer, but I can talk to the District Attorney. Let him know how cooperative you were."

"One of my lieutenants have a problem, he squash it. I got zero knowledge."

"Lieutenants? Come on, now, let's be straight: you low man on the totem pole. Ain't shit you got to say to me about that."

"I know I ain't no cheese-eating rodent."

"I wouldn't want to cast no aspersions, if you know what I'm saying."

"I'm not a snitch."

"I'm not asking you to snitch. Just… speculate." Boy, you better swallow your pride like it's your favorite dish, Cantrell thought to himself. "You got a name for me?"

Fathead calculated the numbers in his head. A lot of dope meant a lot of years. Federal time maybe. Conspiracy. Murder. Intent to distribute. They were looking to close a lot of cases on him. Who had his back? Some public defender, his Johnny Cochran? Nah, they would take one look at him and be skipping out of work. Wasn't like Dred was going to post bond or nothing. Barely put up for Mulysa, and he stood tall with him for years. Plus, it wasn't like they were on the clock for him. They were on their own. He was on his own.

"I said, you got a name for me?" Cantrell repeated.

"Dred."

CHAPTER ELEVEN

A wanderer by nature, Lott never dreamed of peace or justice or love or being loved. He barely planned into the following week. He hated being trapped in a story that had been written about him. That he was "the betrayer" or "the outcast" or "the unredeemable one" (despite the fact that some of those stories were only written in his own head). He feared that he'd never be able to outrun those stories; that he'd never have the chance to write a new story of himself; that the stories would always define him and he'd be powerless to do more than be moved around more like pieces than characters.

"If you must die, die for something greater than yourself. Better yet, live. Live to serve others."

He longed to believe King's words again. To be a part of King's crusade. To be led by King again. It had been a while since he visited the Eagle Terrace apartments, an obtuse layout of living spaces, a large swathe of pot-holed asphalt surrounded by labyrinthine walls of rooms winding along curving streets. The first time in a long time he walked its sidewalks alone.

"Jesus help me," he cried out to the sky. In his heart he prayed that there was a peace to be had on the other side of war. Lott startled the Hispanic woman carrying two bags of groceries. Keeping a wary eye on him, she paused then walked a wider path around him. On any other evening, he'd have offered to carry her groceries for her. Now her wary eyes could see to his heart and know his sins. Everyone could. It weighed him down, pressed on him with a constant smothering.

Writhing in Lady G's embrace was what he had so longed for. Anticipated. Now the image was burned into his mind and tasted like ashes in his mouth. The cost was too high. He tried to not think about all the relationships he'd damaged, all the people he had hurt, all the damage he had caused. He no longer belonged anywhere. Rootless and wandering not by choice but by circumstance.

Redemption was a dream he tried not to put too much hope in. All he wanted was to be restored in their eyes. For them to look at him and see the Lott of old. Their boy. Not this stain that sullied their memories. The idea came to him that maybe he could nudge the process along. Perhaps if he could come to their rescue, help them in some way, maybe they'd be able to forgive him. Sure, their lips said they forgave him, but he recognized that look in their eyes. The one that said they'd never look at him the same. That look of resentment mixed with distrust. The look of his mother after too many drinks. The look of the endless parade of "uncles" who streamed through his life. The look of something that needed to be flushed out of their lives.

Loneliness gnawed at Lott's reason. Solitude was painful. Isolation the worst form of torture. Scared, longed to reach out. He hopelessly wanted someone to find him. To reach out to him. To hold him. Any attention. The madness of alienation created a desperation which drove folks to strange places, to reach out in strange ways.

So he banged on the front door of Black's grandmother's front door.

Blunt smoke thickened in the air of the house party. Drinks bobbed by freely. Cholos lined the walls, corners, and couches bragging about work they had put in. Whoever told the best story received handstacks in response. Black was offered a hit, out of respect, knowing he'd refuse. Tonight he didn't drink either.

His grandmother had stayed with one of his aunts for a week, Black sprawled along the black leather couch. With his slight build, gaunt face, and his determined eyes, he exuded power and fierceness. In a Celtics jersey and shorts, his extensive tattoos were on full display. Two young women snuggled on either side of him. Stroking his arm, the side of his face and whispering breathy seductions into his ear, their attentions annoyed him more than anything. He needed to clear his head.

Standing abruptly, all eyes turned to him. The room held its breath. They took their cues from him, and of late his mood was foul and brooding. He thought what his people needed was an excuse to let off some steam, but it wasn't what he needed. He nodded and everyone relaxed and went back to chatting. Intimate conversations as his boys chatted up the ladies. The laughter. The bumping music. Marijuana, cigarettes, sweat, and re-breathed alcohol.

La Payasa shadowed him from across the room. When he stood, she stood. When he relaxed, she relaxed. She trailed him into the kitchen. He walked across the green and white tiled floor to the refrigerator and grabbed a Corona. Elbows on the counter, he leaned back and waited for La Payasa. Eyes closed, he imagined a great sea. Born to Tomas and Angelina, he'd always had an affinity for water. Tomas often took him fishing. It wasn't the act itself he enjoyed. Truth be told, the idea of sitting around holding a rod like a limp dick waiting to be pulled never appealed to him. But spending time with his father, those times he treasured. Tomas worked two jobs: one as a butcher, he had been a butcher in Mexico before he moved here; and as an off-the-books security guard at a nightclub. It was at the latter job where three black kids, looking for an easy mark, ran across him. They took his father from him. That was the story he was told. His mother went mad with grief. He had to step up and be the man of the family. He was eleven.

"Everything all right?" La Payasa asked. Black respected La Payasa. Few wanted to actually squeeze the trigger though all would brag on it later. She had heart. Her word was bond.

There wasn't anyone who couldn't be made happy by the thought of deep, placid water. The languid waves lapped the shore, yet stretched out into the horizon. "Yeah, it's all good."

"This business with Dred and his crew..."

"What about it?"

"It's bad for business."

"Then they shouldn't have started it. What were we supposed to do? Let them come around here? Dictate to us how we should handle our business?"

Brothers. Uncles. Cousins. All were members of the nation. This was his birthright. The gang took him in, raised him, and showed him how to become a man. He had been a member of the nation for seven years. At five foot four, Black didn't back down from anyone. The gang didn't take just anyone. They had to have heart. That was what the initiation was about. He was violated. Four or five dudes set to beat his ass. Black went through it two times in a row. He wanted his brothers to know he was down for them twice as much as anyone else. The nation these days had no structure. Not like the old days, when they had a constitution which forbade things like rape, hard drug use, and snitching. Well, some things hadn't changed. But the nation fractured, with every crew going for themselves. Black was a disciple of the old ways. He understood that if you had power, you had control, and control was the endgame.

Too late, Black's mother worried about his affiliation with the gang. She thought the devil took him over. One night, she tried to perform an exorcism. She drugged him and then threw him in the bathtub. Lit candles. Cursed at him. Spat at him. Broke raw eggs to smear on him. Lonzo had little idea what was going on. But then the eggs turned black. And she cried that he was lost to her.

"All the bodies dropping brings too much attention. The police. The reporters. It's a big spotlight on us. You let it get personal."

"They killed Lyonessa. They…"

"I know. But before then."

"All my business is personal. I'm not going to let anyone disrespect me or my shorties. If you're afraid of dying, this is the wrong game for you."

His father came to him in dreams. It was he who first told Black about how his mother hired the boys to kill him. His father watched as he crept into her bedroom one night and wrapped his hands around her throat. Eyes teared up with pleading, she reached up, clawing at his face and arms. A son killing his mother, he knew he was beyond forgiveness. That he was cursed with no soul. And would burn.

He closed his eyes, too afraid of the final death rattle of his mother, when he noticed the smell and her renewed struggle. It smelled of rancid meat set to flame. When he opened his yes, his mother's hands slackened, her arms fallen to her side. But her skin where his hands met her throat blistered. Large pustules swelled then burst like over-ripe fruit, pus spilled out like lactating wounds. Her skin charred.

Black turned his palm upward, only to see strangers at the end of his arms.

Someone banged on the front door.

Black adjusted his gloves.

Lady G's image haunted Lott, creeping into his mind whenever he lowered his guard or sat still long enough. The odd crook of her smile. The press of her skin. His fingers could still trace each supple curve of her body because she had so totally filled his mind and consumed his heart. She was a fever dream that had not yet broken despite the fallout from them getting together. Part of him clutched to every moment they shared, attempting to track back to when it all started. Everything began with a moment. A furtive glance, sultry and lingering, which signaled the okay to become intimate. Unspoken. Between them. Their little secret. Knowing looks and personal touches like their own inside joke. So it was natural, after Garlan kidnapped her and Lott rescued her, that their inhibitions lowered from the adrenaline rush of the adventure. From there it was like coming down from their high, in passion's ebb.

Then things fell apart.

No matter how much he wished, things could never go back to the way they were before. They were broken and someone had to pay.

"You Black?" Lott asked. The man was shorter than he expected. A young girl stepped past them then off to the side, positioning herself to his flank and in the shadows. Her hair, blonde with black roots, flew her colors.

"Who asking?"

"Lott."

"You one of King's crew." If Black had heard about the situation between Lott and King – and Lord knew that word traveled fast on the street vine – he gave no indication. Not that it mattered. Lott knew. Most days he wanted to give in to the desire to get blunted and stop feeling so much. But he deserved to feel it all. The guilt, the shame, pressed in on him with such weight he was convinced everyone could just see it.

"Yeah, that's me."

"What's your angle like, homes?" Black asked. Not quite what Lott was expecting with his bald head and full beard. Five foot four, about a buck seventy, posed in an aggressive stance in order not to convey weakness.

"I come in peace, if you are."

"Seems you ain't got a choice. You traveling awfully light."

"Figured this could be handled man to man. You the one I need to be speaking with?" It was a mild challenge. Give him the chance to puff up.

"Yeah, I'm the one calling shots," Black asked.

"I need to speak on this business with Dred."

"What of it?"

"A lot of bodies are dropping. And for what? So each of you can see who can poison their community the fastest?"

"You seem to know a lot about my business." Black stepped closer in an unveiled act of intimidation. The grip of the automatic showed the gun riding in the waist of his pants.

"It's a nasty business. How are you looking out for your people?"

"I protect my people. I provide for them, me and my crew. If it wasn't for us, fools would come trippin' through here, guns a-blazing. That's the life. I'm not afraid of dying as long as I die strong."

"Not everyone wants to die strong. Or young. Your playing hurts kids. Little girls especially." Lott sensed the situation was about to bubble over. He'd been here before. The precipice of machismo. The best way to handle the situation was to ease off the throttle; give the man room to be a man and space to think. Not to back him into a corner and shame him. Lott knew this. Yet some inner compulsion, the need to do things his way, the need to have others hurt the way he hurt, made him dig into Black. "Girls like your sister."

Black short-jabbed Lott in the kidneys, a punch so fast and with such little movement, Lott didn't have time to react. If anything, Lott was braced for a swing to his face. Lott grabbed him at the shoulders ready to wrestle him down, but Black took a half-step back to throw him off balance, swung his arm over Lott's to break the hold, then rammed his elbow into Lott's neck. Black jammed his knee three times into Lott's side before throwing him to the curb. The sounds of the tussle brought a couple members of his crew out, guns drawn. La Payasa threw a sign for them to stand down.

"How you want to play this?" she asked, a flicker of alarm in her eyes. She was her gang through and through, and yet, the pride she had in her colors had been reduced to yet another thing which had disappointed her.

"We ain't wasting a bullet on this fool and putting him out of his misery. He and his crew are broken. Let him crawl back like the betraying dog that he is."

Black saw her thinking. "Come on. You need a break. Let's go back to the house."

"Not back inside?"

"No. The house."

Finding himself without friends wasn't new to Lott. Running was the thing his mother did best, second only to getting high. Setting down roots terrified her, either that or she so quickly made a mess of her life – shorting dealers, not paying back friends, bailing on family when rent was due – that she had no choice but to move. At one point, Lott had changed schools six times in one year. Each time, Lott was the foreigner, the stranger, the outcast. Most times he was too tired to prove himself, content to live inside his head, writing lyrics and working out beats. Music was his only friend. His only refuge. His only constant. And he was too tired, too resigned to his life, to bother risking himself to invest in someone. Even just to get to know them. Not if he was only going to have to leave them. Each introduction held the promise that he had found a place to belong. Maybe he'd found family. It hurt too much when just the promise of family was torn away. Or worse, they abandoned him.

There were times of quiet lucidity when Lott would return here and cry. Thinking about how badly he had fucked up his life, the route which seemed to make the most sense was for him to kill himself and start over. That voice whispered to him in the void of no other voices in his life. It certainly beat the continual struggle against thugs charged by the thrill of petty power, constant chest-thumping, and the daily need to grind out an existence.

He still hurt, inside and out. Pain bled out of him. Not just from the recent pair of ass-whippings he'd subjected himself to. He could confess his sins to anyone, could recount the details – from loving King and Lady G, to working hard in service to them, to allowing himself to

fall for Lady G, to sleeping with her, to busting up the
only family he'd ever known and experienced – in a way
so unaffected it was as if he was telling the story of someone else. The reality of the immensity of the pain he
caused and suffered seared him to the point of him not
feeling. That was his one truth today. He allowed himself
one, it was all he could handle. He had lied so much to
himself in so many subtle ways, he was no better than
his crackhead of a mother.

Lott didn't remember how he stumbled to the house.
Only when the door opened and Lott nearly tumbled in
from his exhausted body leaning against the door did he
become aware of where he was. "Wayne."

"Lott, man, you look like you got your ass
wawawazupped. What happened?" Wayne ushered him
in and plopped him on the couch.

"Went to go see Black."

"By yourself?" He called out from the kitchen, where
he dashed off to in order to run some water into a bowl.
He returned with a wash rag to damp at some of Lott's
cuts.

"Thought it was the right play."

"You need to re-examine your definitions of right and
wrong." The words stung despite them not being intended the way Lott heard them. "You get any clarity?"

"I'm stocked on clarity. In fact, I'm in need of a clarity
clearance sale. Hope I ain't blowing up your spot. If you
got something going on…"

"Nah, man, it's cool. I was meaning to get up with you.
See how you were doing."

"Yeah," said Lott, straining to keep any trace of

resentment out of his voice. He winced as Wayne daubed at his cut lip. "Lots of folks been meaning to."

Got a touch of pride to him. Wayne wrestled with his internal voice. Course why he got to ask for someone to be with him? Why didn't someone offer?

"I feel so dirty inside." Lott couldn't escape his sense of shame. Everyone wanted to know how/why he let things happen the way they did. After all, he was old enough to know better. He understood the consequences. He certainly was an adult. But he also knew that no answer would help them understand. He wasn't sure he knew "why?" anyway.

"The way I see it, it wasn't really you who did it. Not the real you."

"What if it was?"

"You're a good person. You're still the man we know and loved. You just did something wrong. You have to have faith that people will have your back. In a few months, this will blow over, and be nothing but a memory. But that's only if you handle your business correct from here on out."

"What do you mean?"

"You're trapped, you're scared, you're living in fear," Wayne said. "You push this too far, we'll lose you, too."

Lott wanted to believe him, but Wayne was wrong. The lies, the memories, they were like scars. They might heal over, but it would take more than months. The dreams, the sweat-drenched things he woke from, only now were beginning to fade. Lott considered himself a cancer that needed to be removed for the sake of the health of the community. He'd already tried twice.

"Can I ask you something?" Lott asked.

"What's that?"

"Why don't you hate me?" The whole conversation, Lott had been waiting for Wayne to blame him. For him to yell at him, to tell him that "if you made different choices from the beginning, none of us would be broken or torn up right now."

"Who said I don't?" Wayne asked. Lott slumped in his seat, further resigned. "That what you want to hear, ain't it? I've already said this, I don't know how many different ways that I can say this, you just ain't hearing me. You my boy. You messed up something fierce and it'll be a while before things are okay, if they ever will be. That's on the real. But we say we believe in certain things. Honesty. Responsibility. Courage. That includes the strength it takes to make changes and move on. And forgive. Forgiveness has to begin somewhere. It's the only way we can find our way home. I haven't given up on you. God's not through with you yet. Speaking of..."

"What's up?" Lott asked.

"Now, I hate to get between a man and his need to punish himself, but I do have a problem you could help me with."

"What's that?" Lott perked up at the prospect of being useful to someone.

"Percy and Had."

"What about them?"

"They've run off. I think they've got it in their head to search for some missing cup."

"What?"

"Some Merle thing."

"Where are they?"

"Here, let me play you the message." Wayne played Merle's voicemail. Lott's eyes half-closed as he concentrated. He wound his hand in the air to get Wayne to replay the message.

"I think I know where they went."

"Can you go look after them?"

"Me? You sure?"

"Trust has to begin somewhere, too."

CHAPTER TWELVE

The mayor implored to the city that the erupting violence was not race-related. The last thing he or any official wanted was to let that genie out of the bottle. Even the Concerned Clergy, that coalition of black pastors, was notably quiet on that front, focusing on the need to quell the violence on the streets. The media kept flashing the school picture of Lyonessa Perez, all cherub cheeks and teeth within a beaming smile, long brown hair with a white bow in it. The image of a little girl snatched away by street violence transcended race.

From the police commissioner on down, no matter what side of the political aisle they were on, they vowed to continue to fight their own war on terror. However, down in the unlit places, out of the glare of the media spotlight, reigned little men – big men, too – who knew, without embarrassment, their manhood lay in their guns. Without their guns, birds would laugh at them. But with their guns they could stop you, instill within you the fear. Infatuation was a selfish wildfire, fed by sex, as a masquerade of connection, and blared as a one-night stand even when it attempted to last for a season.

Tired of heating the house by leaving the oven door open, The Boars was the high priest of the corner. He prepared a quiet place, tended to the holy of holies, as the local fiends prepared to make their pilgrimage to his spot. A procession lined up just out of sight of the plasma center. He accepted them no matter where they were in life: sick, tired of it all, in a place of limbo wondering "now what?" In the short space of a walk from the plasma center to the edge of the property line of Breton Court, they transitioned from the daylight world to a sacred space. They headed to worship in a back-alley church, to partake in the ritual of taking communion.

The tips of his fingers scorched, his legs weak, shaky, with the pants falling just short enough to reveal a cigarette package taped to his ankle, the first supplicant brought their offering: a hundred dollars for six marble-size rocks of crack. The Boars knew the lie. The man believed that those would last him for a few days. But the fiend would have them devoured a few hours later. The Boars knew the ritual of inhaling from the fire put to the pipe, the sizzle of crack. How for a few moments, nothing could touch him here. Memories of family gone, time stood still, a shower of color, heat, and light. What Moses must have felt like on Mount Sinai, having glimpsed a part of God.

And The Boars knew what their conversation would sound like if they truly gave voice to how they felt.

"I hate you."

"I hate me, too."

"I need you."

"I need you, too."

The Boars paid some dude a dollar to buy a bottle of Wild Irish Rose for them. He and the crew waited around in the dope house, passing the bottle back and forth, while they smoked weed to pass the time. They worked in pairs and waited for customers, though The Boars found himself missing Garlan's company. Everyone was on point when they suspected Garlan might come through. He hated working with any of the new recruits because he hated having to explain himself and hated schooling young'uns. The street was the street. Too much eye contact, you became a threat. Too little eye contact, you became a victim.

"We ain't supposed to use product on the clock," he said in a waste of breath as the young'un sparked up some herb.

"This ain't Mary Kay, motherfucker. We ain't got to have makeover parties an' shit."

"Boy, you better watch your tone. I will cut you like an umbilical cord."

It was as if Fathead, Naptown Red, and Prez didn't just get popped. But, no, these corner boys didn't worry about cops since they mostly sold to neighborhood folks. One man on peep-hole duty could watch fiends walk up, walk around, getting out of cars. The transactions were simple enough. They'd knock, tell them what they wanted, slide money through the mail slot, the drugs would be slid back out. And he'd keep three hundred of every thousand dollars earned.

If Garlan was here, he'd understand. When he was high, he was on point. He felt better. He learned better.

The Boars leaned back in his chair and thought about his high. "Yeah, that's money."

Someone knocked at the door. The young'un slid back the eye slot. "What you need?"

"I need a taste," a woman said.

"Ten dollars."

"I ain't got it. Can't we work out some... other arrangement?"

"Hold up." Young'un slipped the slot back. "The Boars, some fine-ass trick wants to trade some of that good stuff for a taste."

"How fine? We talking crackhead fine or *foine* fine?"

"Big booty foine."

"Think you can handle it?" The Boars asked.

"I'll lock it down."

The young'un unlocked the door then slid the brace that reinforced the door from push-in – or police battering ram – out of place. The Boars waited in the back corner, to guard the product and get a good look at this chickenhead. It wasn't as if he hadn't had a dope date or two in his time. And he might as well let the little dude have a piece.

The woman stepped in, a pair of handcuffs clicked in her hand as she spun one spindle through the rest of the cuff.

"Oh shit."

The young'un turned to The Boars, the wide grin on his face slowly dying as the panic on The Boars' face registered. By the time he turned back to Omarosa, she had her sawed-off brought to bear and wrapped one of her arms around his throat.

"You know the deal, son. Product and money."

The shotgun held The Boars' complete attention. He chanced a glance at the product on the table. Just like he knew there was a gun behind the table the baggies rested on.

"I..." He couldn't believe his run. First the police, now Omarosa. The only thing saving his hide was the fact that the police grabbed the package Naptown Red was working on his own. Not Dred's. Which meant this was the first he'd been hit for Dred's stuff. Still, there'd be some explaining to do and trouble did seem to be following him.

"Let me clear up the bit of confusion hitting you right now. You might be experiencing a bit of job loyalty. You don't want to report back to Garlan or Dred how you got took off by me. After all, shortie here," she flexed her arm a bit, easily lifting the boy from his feet and pulling him along further inside the doorway, "should've long been schooled on the subject of little ol' me. In fact, I'm offended that he wasn't. I'm beginning to think that Dred's feeling a little too secure in his spot right about now. Thinking he's the only shark in this pool. You've got to ask yourself at this point: is this shit worth dying for?"

Tires screeched outside the stash house. Omarosa peeked out the door to see La Payasa leading four of her crew – clones of roughneck Hispanic boys in oversized white T-shirts and baggy blue jean shorts like they were the required uniform – in a charge toward the house.

"Looks like we all got company." Omarosa yanked the young'un away from the front door as La Payasa stepped in.

"What's this shit?" La Payasa eased in through the open door with a dancer's gait. Thin but sturdy, her lithe physique belied the fact that she knew how to move and did so with determination and purpose. A crease, an old scar truth be told, etched the side of her face, but it was barely noticeable as her face was painted white with clown make-up. Black crosses covered each eye. Bedecked in her war paint, La Payasa was ready to dance.

"Looks like we got us a situation. And either way, it's Dred's very unlucky day." Omarosa kept her shotgun trained on The Boars, careful not to appear flustered by the new arrivals, who were uncertain who to train their guns on. La Payasa never brandished a weapon, instead stepped to Omarosa.

"You the one I need to talk to?"

"I'm the one with the sawed-off. Definitely puts me in the conversation." The young 'un whimpered a bit, trapped in her arm lock. His pants dampened at his crotch.

The Boars kept his hands in plain sight while calculating the math of his situation. Omarosa was all about survival and take-offs. She enjoyed the game as much as anything else, an agent of chaos who meant to keep everyone on their toes. She'd rob from the Mexicans as quick as she would Dred, though she'd been off her game since the death of her brother, Colvin.

La Payasa was a stone bitch. Other than Mulysa or Green back in the day, only Omarosa had as fierce a reputation. Her fearless stance, unfazed by the complication of Omarosa, calmed her boys, who were rattled enough to just blast everyone in the room and call it a day.

"You here for the stash, the cash, or both?" Omarosa asked. "This here is a... transactional date. Each party has something the other wants."

"We all draw our moral lines in the sand." An elite few pocketed the profits meant to benefit the entire nation. When she had first brought it up to Black's attention, to quiet her up, they offered her a cut. That was when the luster began to fade on the organization. "We're here to send Dred a message. That he has started a war he can't win. And you?"

"Same thing. Plus the stash and cash. So it seems to me the message might get a little muddled."

"I think I can provide some clarity." La Payasa was a blur of motion as she drew her gun, shot The Boars in the side, and returned it to the front of her pants. The Boars clutched his side and scrabbled off to the bathroom. Omarosa watched him slam the door behind him then returned her gaze to the warrior clown. "He'll live. And can deliver my message to Dred."

"And the product?"

"I've sent my message. You can send yours. We good?"

"We good." Omarosa pulled the young'un close and kissed his cheek. "We good, sweetheart? You gonna let Dred know exactly what happened here?"

The young'un nodded. Hot tears trailed down his face.

La Payasa withdrew her crew.

The Boars tried to not move or panic. He fumbled for his cell phone as he pressed his free hand against his wound. 911 might not come to his address, but he could hope. A banging came from the door.

"We got a little unfinished business," Omarosa said.

"What?" The Boars leaned against the door.

"You got the cash on you."

Shit. "No I…"

"Before you finish that lie, I still got young buck right here."

"I called 911."

"You think I can't blast my way in there and out before they get here? Or go through them if I had to?"

Omarosa was patient. That was the way of her kind. And she wasn't one to leave money on the table. Dred wasn't directly responsible for her brother's death but he employed that dog, Baylon. Even as she thought the name, her heart burned with the fury of vengeance. That was also the way of her kind. It was bad business to be on the wrong side of the fey. "Don't make me repeat myself."

The Boars slid the five hundred he had on him under the door.

There were many days when Percy thought about what it would be like to have a real mom and dad. She'd get him up out of bed and fix breakfast while he dressed. By the time he got to the table, his dad would already be reading the paper, but he'd set it down at Percy's approach. His mom would put a plate full of eggs, sausage, and hash browns in front of each of them. They'd discuss issues of the day over the meal, both of his parents enjoying talking with him while also simply spending time with him. And they knew what was right and wrong. They laid down rules like no television until homework was done and how he had to go to church with them.

But when they were done, his dad would take him outside and play football in the yard with him. His mom doted on her husband and kids, buying clothes, making food, cleaning the house, and yet finding time for them while helping in the community. His dad took him to school, where Percy proved to be extremely talented. He worked hard in school and was respected. The teachers liked him there, especially Mr Combs, who encouraged him to write more and pursue his dream.

It was the same dream.

Percy was embarrassed to bring anyone back to his house. Miss Jane lying in bed, covers pulled up about her like a burial shroud, a lighter in one hand and a bottle wrapped in aluminum foil in the other. Never sure if she was dead or alive, since she always smelled of decay and burnt skin. Her skin pallor leaned toward blue. Her shirt half-open, revealing the full swell of her left breast. Her hair a matted mess. A trickle of foam escaped from the crease of her lips. Her eyes vacant. Now she truly was gone, and ever since his mother had died it was on him to take care of his little brothers and sisters. Some days it was too much. Piles of clothes left about the house. Percy's hoodie shadowed his eyes, eyes which bounced all over the place as they walked down the street. The peach fuzz on his lips itched slightly, well, not really, but he couldn't help messing with it.

More comfortable around the animal than people, Mad Had ran his fingers through Kay's fur, removing any burrs or knots. Dogs didn't judge. They didn't care if you had a bad past. They didn't care if you walked funny or talked funny. They didn't make fun of you. They were loyal and loved you. Kay wouldn't answer to any other name. Not "boy" or "dog" or a whistle or any gibberish meant to call him. His name would be respected and anything else was an affront to his canine dignity.

Part of Percy wanted to encounter something strange. King, Lott, and Wayne often had to fight weird creatures. They'd whisper about it when they thought he couldn't hear because they didn't want to glorify any of the fights they had. Fighting seemed to make them rather sad, like it was something they had to do but took no pleasure in. They weren't like the other boys out here who loved to fight, bragged on it like they had something to prove. To King and them, fighting was a last resort. Percy wanted something, an adventure, to call his own. To show them that he could hang with them. His own creature, maybe with the body of a leopard, haunches like a lion, feet like a hart. And a snake's head. That would be cool.

"Yon caitiff," an aged woman said, strolling up to Percy.

"Me, ma'am?"

"Who else?" She placed her had on Mad Had's head. "Oh, you're a fine lad. You both are. So brave and so true. Do you know where you're going?"

"Not really. I thought–"

"You'd follow your heart. Careful, there are no damsels out here. Tarry your heart and find the castle." The woman steadied herself as if suddenly dizzy.

"Are you okay?"

"I'm almost out of tricks. Tell Sir Rupert that I can only be freed by she who imprisoned me and that he should quit searching."

Percy smiled as the old woman staggered off. He nodded to Mad Had, who ambled silently after him. A song caught on Percy's lips.

"Jesus loves the little children..."

CHAPTER THIRTEEN

Without a home, Mulysa was his own master with nothing to lose. While part of that meant he was free to go wherever he wanted, in his heart he knew that he was a man without a home. Dred hadn't reached out, too busy grooming his next pet, Garlan. Dred had a habit of discarding people who were no longer of any use to him. Or were used up. Broken. It wasn't as if Dred didn't discard Baylon as soon as he was done and Baylon was his boy, yet he followed that fool fake Jamaican like a hobbled puppy. Somehow Mulysa convinced himself that it would be different with him. And though Mulysa still possessed his skills and ferocity, he was tainted. Marked. That was what he assumed, as he slid in the booth at Marble's Café. The owner, a Seventh Day Adventist, fisheyed him, not wanting any foolishness, as he didn't put up with dealers or wannabe pimps. Mulling over a plate of Marble's thick, potato-wedge fries, alongside the remains of a sandwich of ham, turkey, and bacon fried up and topped with three cheeses, Mulysa could have been either. Carried on waves of nostalgia – like an old man reflecting on his life, despite barely being out of his teens – Mulysa knew he'd run out of life. The days wound down for him. He was as certain about that as he was about the fact that he had a tail. He had the sense that the sword of Damocles about to fall and split his skull. A fatal intuition he couldn't shake. The engine which drove his life had simply run out of gas and he was exhausted.

He had checked out one of his old spots, a place he stayed before the Camlann, but it was little more than a lot grown over with weeds. He pulled back the flimsy plywood sheet which covered the door, part of which broke off in his hands as he bent to it, to slip into the abandoned house. Beer cans littered the floor. The house had pockets of shadows as little light poured in around the boarded-up windows. The pungent tang of soured meat assaulted his nostrils. Dirty dishes piled in cold, gray water with a strange orange film on them. With a molding layer of macaroni and cheese burned to the bottom, the pot turned on its side provided shelter for a stream of cockroaches. He had stayed here for several months. That was how he had lived and he'd thought he had life by the balls. But seen in dim light against the backdrop of peeled paint and ripped-up carpet, his life amounted to a waste. No one would mourn him if he died.

Pain was something they all had in common, but it looked different on everyone. For Mulysa, no, for Cheldric, the old wound had the voice of his uncle.

"You're ugly. No one will want to get with you. Might as well get used to paying for it. We all do, one way or another, anyway." Then his uncle would get his head up in some

herb, some Crown Royal mixed with Pepsi in his glass, and stare at the television whether it was on or not.

"You're dumb. No sense in doing anything that will make you any dumber or careless. So don't do drugs." Then his uncle would clear the books from the table with an angry swipe and glare down on him like he was a ghost of his past, pull out his belt, and beat Mulysa until he was spent.

"You're fat. Watch what you eat. You're young now, but don't become slow or let your body betray you." Then his uncle would send him to his room, without dinner, confining him to the dark to amuse himself or at least be out from underfoot.

"No one wants you. I took you in after they abandoned you. You're lucky you have me." Then his uncle's eyes bulged in surprise and his neck opened up like a screaming mouth vomiting blood when Mulysa ran a box cutter across it. He was eleven.

Ducking out of the hovel, the sun mocked him. Someone jogged after him or something put him on edge. Hunted him. He forgot how paranoid the drugs made him.

Mulysa had never thought much of what it meant to be a man. Women were casualties of his conquests. Bitches. Hos. Chickenheads. Skanks. Less than human. Barely a collection of orifices on which to pleasure himself, reflections of his self-hate upon which he could vent more of the same.

Ever since he'd been out of the Shoe, he'd been directionless. Dred never summoned him, nor set him up with his own package to sell and get on his feet. Didn't use him for any work. Acted like Mulysa was dead to him. Without explanation or warning. Suddenly he was a pariah to all the folks he knew. So he'd come full circle.

There was a bridge under 19th and MLK, across from the Children's Bureau, where he now stayed. The four culverts on either side of the bridge were like little apartments. Crystals hung from the top between the cracks like salt stalactites. The dirt floor, white like chalk, had a moldy mattress, almost a part of the hill, resting on it. The fine sand got into everything: his backpack, his blanket, his clothes, but the concrete walls sealed him up nicely. Entombed him. Alone, in the dark, he reflected on his life. Sometimes he had to chew over the pain of his life in order to write his story. Sometimes that was easier to do with the distance of fiction.

He ate in peace. Despite being the only person in the spot – and the owner having a penchant of passing the time by waxing philosophical with his customers – Mulysa ate alone. In uninterrupted silence. The best sort to speed him on his way. He recognized the hardened eye, the one-hand-under-the-counter style readiness, prepared to grab a bat or gun or whatever in case Mulysa broke bad.

In his time, Mulysa might have robbed this place, mugged the man's kin, or killed someone he knew. Mulysa was bold with it. He came up admiring folks like Green, who knew how to get shit done. Folks knew his name, his face, and the details of his do, but no one spoke out. Mulysa modeled his own stalwart career with the same approach. It only took one to speak out, but if no one did it meant he didn't have a wake of ardent admirers.

No one was immune to life's little tragedies just like no one was immune to the potential of drugs to make a good person do bad things. The theory assuaged the emaciated thing he called his conscience. That was what he would say to them, any of them. That it wasn't their fault. His neither. It was the drugs. Faceless, nameless, blameless, because ultimately they were a force of nature and blaming them for the destruction wreaked in your life was like yelling at a hurricane. He tried it out loud to see how it might play.

"You can't blame me. Drugs, they like a tornado or some shit. Can't be mad at them neither. They just do what they do." It sounded like every bit of bullshit to him. Dabbing his mouth with a napkin, he dropped the wadded napkin into his half-eaten piece of peach cobbler and pushed away from the table. He left a five-dollar tip on the ten-dollar tab and didn't know why. He left the building unsettled, something nagged at him. Some detail he'd missed.

The last thing he saw was an empty forty bottle coming toward his head.

How did one refer to the recently dead? They were still alive, still real in the memory of those who knew them in the present. But they were still gone. Past tense. Alive in name only. Baylon had been without power or control for so long he wasn't about to go back to either state without a fight.

"What brings you to the front lines?" Baylon asked Dred.

"Just checking on things." Dred's voice a conveyer belt of shifting accents. A hint of Jamaican patois in one breath, formal English in another, and relaxed hood-cent in the last. Shifting with his identity of the moment.

"Surprised."

"By what?"

"That you still remembered the ones you came up with," Baylon said sardonically.

"I remember." Dred let the slight pass. He'd allowed Baylon the one as long as he didn't cross the line.

"Those you hurt."

"You hurt, nigga?" Dred desired to control everyone and everything around him by the tools at his disposal: fear, threat, intimidation, violence, and death. Remorseless eyes marred his pretty-boy looks.

"Look at me. I gave everything to you."

"Listen to you. You sound like my bitch."

"You right. Shit." Baylon hated this. What he wanted to do was break out a sawed-off. But he couldn't raise a weapon to the man. It was as if, despite all Dred had done, Baylon was still bound to him. To the end.

"Guess you had to get that out your system."

"Something like that."

"Now can I get to the business I came to speak on?"

"What's that?"

"Them Julios." Every Mexican was "Julio" to Dred.

"What you need?"

"We need to end this once and for all. You need to put the word out that you want a parlay."

"If we fly the truce flag, you can't do anything. So how's that gonna help."

"*We* ain't flying the truce flag. *You* are. They probably still think you speak for me. That's they fault. Call for it at the site of the new Camlann."

Not that Baylon had much of a name to trade on, but he hated that Dred could so casually play it for nothing. Not too long ago, Baylon stood tall. His word was bond. Now he'd been drained of most of his life. By Dred. "That how you going to do them?"

"I'm in a loose-end-tying mood. It's time to tighten up the ranks. I still got to rock the cradle on my latest crew."

The storm, relatively calm now, would soon pick up in intensity. Tristan carefully followed the road along its snaking path. The rain beat a harsh rhythm upon the roof of the car as it snailed its way down the long, winding road. Like cotton tufts churning in oil, the clouds choked the indigo-blanket sky, plunging the night into deeper shadow, a foreboding whisper in their overhead passing. Large, looming trees lined each side of the dismal, dark road like protective guards. Tristan wiped away the angry tears that pooled in her eyes, checking herself in the rearview mirror. She wouldn't give him the satisfaction of tears. The windshield wiper danced madly as she continued to fight them back. The rain fell unceasingly in annoying splatters. The low moan of the wind left her undaunted. Headlights sliced through the thin drizzle of rain as the car headed up the forgotten, dimly lit access road. Plenty of sound filled the silence. Birdsong. Gravel spit up by tires. Crickets in dusk light. The gurgle of torrents of water. No words needed to be said, even as the car slowed to a halt in front of a locked fence.

A narrow footpath, full of thorny branches, circled him, leading to a denser stretch of woods. Tristan shoved Mulysa in that direction. The constant rain splattered tree branches and leaves, slickening rocks as the pair nearly stumbled several times as they walked. Twigs snapped in their passing processional.

She kicked him in the back of the legs, forcing him to ground. If he tried to defend himself, it only brought on more punches. Her blood pumped with righteous fury. She hooked him in his head, groin, stomach, and throat. He curled into a ball, brain seized up. Mulysa's head fell forward, his chest tightened as if he had shards of glass in his lungs.

"Are you afraid to die?" Tristan asked.

"Yeah. I guess. We all are," Mulysa said like a general tired of war.

"That don't sound like the Mulysa I knew. The Mulysa I knew didn't let anyone's needs come before his own. Didn't back down from anyone. Didn't care whose territory he ran in. He wasn't afraid of anything.

"I'm afraid to meet God." The words came softly, without irritation or bravado. More resigned than anything else. "For Him to tell me that I wasted my life down here. That I pissed over all the opportunities He gave me."

She put a dirty look on him. Meek like a tree trunk, he disgusted her. He was too easy to insult. This wasn't the Mulysa she wanted. This animal was already broken and beaten down. This one sounded too much like the little girl trapped in her that she never gave voice to. The one who was also afraid, not of His judgment, because she was ready for that. She could carry that. No, she feared "... that He loves you anyway."

"Love. I don't even know what that means anymore."

She understood the resignation and the black hole from which he operated... but he was still a dog that needed to be put down. Tristan reached over his shoulder and stabbed him in the chest. He bolted, running on pain and adrenaline, already dead. It hurt to breath. He tripped, his head bouncing off a stone, leaving his ears ringing and his world blurred. Tristan landed on him and stabbed until he quit defending himself.

Classes in school would always have a timeout whenever a student entered holding a note. Prez's heart skipped a beat. If the student knew him, they'd try to catch his eye and give him a nod, but most times the kind of students trusted to run the administrative errands of the principal's office weren't the kind who ran in the same circles as Prez. In the usual routine, the teacher took the note then read it silently. Like they were on some reality show, all of the students studied each other for any tell as they waited to see who had been voted off the island, whose journey would end here. The teacher then called out a name and the student perked up with a "who me?"/"what did I do?" look of complete innocence. Too many times, Prez's name was called. All eyes turned to him, accompanied by a few stifled snickers and some exhales of relief that their name wasn't called. He'd march to the front of the class – under the weight of the glaring eyes – to receive the note like a communion wafer and then pass into the hallway.

His mind turned over the devious things he did, which ones might rise to the level of being called to the office. A dead man walking the green mile to his execution, the journey and the wait did their psychological jobs. He reflected on the cost of his antics. He pondered the various crossroads moments of his life and the decisions he'd made. He'd wonder "what if?"

Prez hated being called down to the principal's office. There was a bench right outside of her door where those awaiting her judgment waited. Not only could she watch each delicious squirm – and she'd let you wait there, stewing in your anxiety, dread, and guilt until you were fit to burst before she called you in – but her office was the first along the corridor. That meant that students and teachers had to pass in order to get to the other offices – the nurse's station, the guidance counselor, and so on – becoming tacit players in the shaming game.

And then he awaited his punishment.

Prez, Fathead, and Naptown Red relaxed at Red's crib. Dred had posted bail for them and assured them that he had lawyers at the ready to defend them. But they were instructed to wait at Red's until he could meet with them. He needed to switch up houses to deflect eyes and they needed to stay low until he had them set up. Prez's stomach bottomed out at the summons.

Naptown Red took his endo in deep, allowing it to work its magic inside him. It mellowed him out in a way that released him from having to play a role. Long as he was free, paid, and high, he was good. The game hadn't changed: get locked up, keep your mouth shut, stand tall, and you'd be taken care of. Naptown Red had all of the angles worked out. Just like how Dred sprang Mulysa, even if he didn't want anything to do with him once he got out, he didn't have much choice but to take care of Red and his crew if he wanted to keep his street cred. It wasn't as if they'd been busted doing their own thing; technically they were on the clock for Dred. Doing their do hadn't made them any more sloppy, just the opposite in fact, as they had to be more careful fearing Dred's retaliation far more than the police. Worst-case scenario, Red would break Dred off a piece of the action and they'd be square, because business was business.

"You think we in trouble?" Fathead asked.

"Where you think we is? Kindergarten?" Naptown Red had the belief that he was a shot-caller. It reeked in the tone of his voice. Play the part, be the part. First these two reacted to him like planets pulled into orbit by this sheer gravity then others, seeing them, would fall into line. That was how kingdoms were built.

"Just saying, won't he be mad? We lost his money and his package, then on top of that, he has to come out of pocket to bail us out." Fathead skittered nervously about. His exhaled smoke didn't seem to stave off his anxiousness. He didn't tell the police much. Certainly they had Dred's name already. No harm in giving them what they already had. And if they had Dred, they had to know who his main lieutenants were. And where some of the stash houses were.

"You give the ghetto a bad name." Red snatched the joint back from him as if he were a child wasting good food. "That's the cost of doing business."

"But Dred–"

"I ain't afraid of Dred. Green hisself couldn't work those corners any better than us. Shit, we out there on the front lines." Naptown Red had a way of sounding like he supported those in charge while undermining them at the same time to rally folks around him. "I got your back. So you better learn to squad up."

"Squad up?" Fathead grabbed a bag of half-eaten Doritos from the coffee table and absently began stuffing them into his mouth.

"Look here." Red reached into a nearby drawer and retrieved a gun. "This here might suit you."

"What is it?"

"A Beretta. Light on recoil. A bitch's gun." Red let the insult fly and sink in before cleaning it up a little. "A starter gun for you. Let you get used to the idea before moving you up to something serious."

"Yeah, I don't think so. It's not my thing." It wouldn't matter if he had fifty guns on him, Fathead didn't have it in him to kill a man. He survived by rolling over, allying himself with whoever could protect him.

"Suit yourself." Red tucked it into his dip. "Probably blow off your joint with it anyways."

Heavy thuds hammered on the front door. Fathead nearly fell out of his seat. Naptown Red eyed him with mild disgust, beginning to re-think their partnership. He didn't need any weak links at the table. Peeking through the eyehole, he sucked his teeth in Fathead's direction.

"Dred, my nigga." Red opened the door and gave him a pound. "You alone?"

"I need to be here with anyone?" Dred stepped inside.

His facial hair grew in odd patches, none of which took away any of the boyish nature of his face. But his eyes glared about, ancient and rheumy, caught up in his machinations. "Nah, shit. When you here, you with family." Naptown Red knew better. Dred's king was never alone. Not with as many enemies as he had not to mention Black on the hunt. Probably a soldier at the car as lookout. And Garlan's ass had to be around somewhere. Red glad-handed as best he could, but there was no play with Dred. Only a brooding intensity, like a volcano deciding when, not if, it were going to erupt.

"What is this here?" Dred gave a cursory once-over to the two in the living room.

"Nothing, just chillin' like you said. Staying low."

Dred projected a mien of barely suppressed anger approaching the group, with the tone of personal disgust and irritation. Their first reaction was to give him plenty of space to vent. They knew they were in for getting their asses chewed. Naptown Red lit some incense he had on an end table next to a burnt spoon. The scented smoke proved too cloying.

"You ain't saying one motherfucking think I want to hear." Dred marched to the couch where Fathead rested. He simply stared until Fathead got up to join Prez on the other one.

"We got rules for a reason. Protocols. We do things a certain way to *not* get caught. We do business with folks we know. Who this motherfucker?"

"This is Prez. He hung out with Green and his crew. I brought him on to do work."

"How you know him?"

"My man Fathead here made the intro." As Naptown Red beamed with confidence and reassurance, Prez sank into himself, dismissed and dejected. "See? We all about protocol."

"Then how did *we* end up in jail?

"Shit happens."

"Shit happens? Shit happens and I get calls at three in the morning. Shit happens and I got to pay lawyers and bail bondsmen. Shit happens and I gotta make fools ghost so the state ain't gotta case. Shit happens and someone starts talking to po-po like a kid trying to make nice with Santa. What they ask?"

"Didn't ask me shit. I lawyered up soon as they slapped cuffs on my black ass." For the first time Naptown Red sounded nervous, edging into unfamiliar territory.

"They got names." Prez hugged himself.

"Who?"

"Red. Mulysa. Garlan. Baylon." Prez straightened up but stared straight ahead. "That's who they came at me with. Wanted me to confirm who they were."

"They didn't mention Nine. Where she at?" Fathead chimed in.

"She on… special assignment."

"She ain't around, that's for damn sure." Fathead puffed up and shifted on the couch, confident that at least they were on the clock putting in work.

"What about me?" Dred turned to Prez.

"They talk about you like a ghost. A whisper."

"Yeah, I like that. Poof." Dred blew into his fist and exploded it into wiggling fingers. "Still, I don't like folks talking."

Prez wore a cologne of panic. His heart stammered, a foreboding filling his heart. Expectant eyes took in Dred's every move like he couldn't get enough of him. Fathead, in a jackknife crouch more nervous than before, shoveled more Doritos into his mouth to comfort himself.

"You need anything?" Prez asked.

"We straight," Naptown Red said.

"Good, cause I'd like to think that I treated you all fair." Dred walked the perimeter of the room. With a casualness, he peeked in corners and checked out the layout.

"Nah, we good."

"We alone?" Dred patted himself down as if he misplaced something.

"Just four fellas kicking it."

"That what you do when you working for me? Kick it?"

"Dred, man, I think you operating out of some kind of misperception," Red started.

"Spare me, Red. I know your kind. You align yourself to those with power and manipulate those without it. You think you the smartest man in the room. Like you the only one that knows something."

"I..." Dred's tone chastened him as well as rubbed Red hard the wrong way.

"You're going to want to be quiet now." Dred raised two fingers, his hand rearing up like a cobra about to strike. "Here's what I know. Niggas always wanna hustle. We'll put in more work, do more dirt, often for less than minimum wage, and act like it's somehow better than working a nine-to-five. No matter how much cash I lay out, product I provide, or corners to sell it from, it's never enough. Ain't that right?"

Prez nearly pissed himself when Dred turned his direction. He curled away from him a bit, crossed his arms over his chest as if to fend him off. Dred's eyes bored through him as if examining for any weakness or flaw. Prez couldn't move under their scrutiny.

"Names have power. You name someone, you have power, dominion, over them. When you call someone by name, you imply knowledge of them, a certain level of intimacy. Names have to be respected. God took three of the Ten Commandments to lay it out. This is who I am." Dred ticked off the first finger. "Don't put anything or anyone above me." Dred raised his second finger. "Do not misuse my name." Dred held up his third finger and stopped in front of Fathead. "What's my name?"

"D-d-dred," Fathead stuttered.

"Every time that name comes off your lips, I know."

"Dred, you ain't got to…" Red protested.

Prez moved into a colder, more frightened place.

"You, I'll deal with in a minute. I don't care if I'm dry-shooting as that joint, my name will not be disrespected. You feel me."

"Yeah."

"What's my name?"

"Dred," Fathead said.

"You want to say my name, fine. You do so to po-po and…"

Shadows erupted from the corners of the room. Strands, ebon ropes lashed at him. Two fear-forms held him fast, vaguely human-shaped, at each arm. Four strands latched on to the corners of his mouth, pulling just taut enough to reveal his bleeding gum line. Two more strands hooked into each eye, holding them open. Thousands of threads sprang from the carpet like a harvest of night. They dug into the flesh around his neck, a penumbra obedience collar.

"Here's the problem as I see it. This one here has been snitching. Gave me up. If I hadn't gotten you all out of there, who knew who else he would have given up."

"Let me at that snitch bitch," Naptown Red said.

"Don't worry, he didn't give you up. You ain't significant enough to warrant police attention. However, you did vouch for him."

Naptown Red pulled out his gun. He was at a crossroads moment and had only seconds to make his play. Were he a man of deep thought and methodical planning – or simply had the time to weigh his options – he might have shot Fathead on the spot and thrown himself on Dred's mercy, banking on the show of loyalty to buy him a few days or weeks. However, Red was a man of intuition and opportunity. Fathead had given up Dred's name but not his. What Dred hurled as an insult, Red interpreted as an advantage. He was an unknown, off the radar of Five-O. And Dred was here alone and preoccupied with binding or torturing Fathead. With a few shots, he could remove Dred as an obstacle and bind Fathead to him. Naptown Red fired off five rounds.

Dred turned and waved his hand. The bullets seemed to move in slow motion. The bullets whirred past, their trajectories marking the air like spinning tracers. He moved out the way of all of them except the last one. He allowed that bullet to tear through the muscle of his arm. With a scientific detachment, the pain stabbed straight into his brain and he watched his blood as if experiencing both for the first time in centuries. With a flick of his wrists, he shot a spear of shadow at Naptown Red. The plume pierced his heart, leaving a frozen expression of surprise on his face. Naptown Red dropped to his knees, the Beretta fell from his hands, and then he toppled forward. Dred strolled over to the gun, scooped it up, and then walked over to Prez.

"Don't let all that fool you. Magic takes a toll on a body. People weren't meant to wield it. We just weren't built for it. That kind of energy, even the dragon's breath, can burn up a person."

Prez remained paralyzed in his chair, still unable to move.

"We still have a problem, don't we? Red vouched for Fathead, but Fathead vouched for you. You see my dilemma, don't you?"

Prez's body tensed as Dred pressed the cold metal of the Beretta against the back of his neck. Prez could feel exactly how many hairs it disturbed, conscious of every quaver in the man's hand, down to his pulse. Though the chaos of his thoughts threatened to consume him, he fought to stay calm. A serene calm, one that came with the knowledge that his life was held in a trigger finger. One twitch and it was like blowing out a candle.

"Nakia."

"What's that?"

"Nakia. King's daughter."

"Oh, now that *is* a useful bit of information. Names have power."

With a gentle squeeze, the candle's flame was snuffed out.

CHAPTER FOURTEEN

Percy walked along the sidewalk closest to the traffic of Michigan Street, his protective nature wanting to stand between potential danger and Had. As much a herding instinct as Kay who trotted alongside them, working in tandem to keep Had on the sidewalk. With school out, the days were even less structured for Percy. He dropped his little brothers and sisters off at Big Momma's place. They'd be able to go to the park across from Breton Court, at School 109. There was a free lunch program there and they'd be able to play. On an overcast day like today, they probably wouldn't be able to break out the Slip 'n Slide and have a time. But they might. He pictured them in their little bathing suits, squealing with delight and shivering on Big Momma's porch when they ran into the shade. He missed being young.

Percy was seventeen.

A lifetime had passed during his high school years. But one more year and he'd be out. He never believed he would have made it, but between Wayne and Outreach Inc, and King, he could imagine himself graduating. He'd allowed himself the thoughts of going to college, Ivy Tech or some other trade school. He loved to cook. But these were dreams of tomorrow. As always, he had to make it through today first.

"I don't like storms," Percy said. Had turned to him as they walked, not breaking stride, but attentive. "See them clouds over there? Every time I see one, they get closer and closer, like they're chasing me."

Had ran his fingers into Kay's fur.

"It's okay though, cause they never catch me. They roll over me and make a lot of noise, but they never get me. I still don't like them, though."

They ambled along the street. Percy spent as much time on the west side as he did on the east these days, but the east side was still his comfort spot. He stayed at the Phoenix Apartments, but hung out all over. So when he thought of searching for the cup and Rhianna's ring, he immediately thought of the castle.

The castle was a house at Michigan Street and Dearborn Avenue. Word was that back in the day, it was originally built for the Grand Dragon of the Ku Klux Klan. Percy knew the neighborhood. A man pedaled down the street on a slightly rusted mountain bike. An olive-green knapsack slung across his back. Percy waved at him, receiving a head nod in return. The man sold bootleg DVDs in the neighborhood, his current stock including that week's film releases and a plethora of kung fu flicks. Wearing only a pair of tighty whiteys, an old white man rocked back and forth on a porch watching the traffic pass by, beer in one hand. Three days' worth of facial hair stubbled his face. Gray streaked his chest hair.

"Hey, Kool-Aid," the man shouted, a shot at Percy's red shirt stretched over his bulbous frame.

"Hey." It wasn't the first time he had heard the reference. It didn't bother him. Not really.

"Weather's gonna break soon."

"Sure hope so. It's hot. Heat does strange things to folks."

"Where you heading?"

"Off to a castle. Looking for a cup," Percy said in a matter-of-fact tone as if that perfectly explained everything.

"Oh yeah!" The man imitated the cry from the Kool-Aid commercial.

Had's face didn't register a flicker of emotion. Only a quizzical gaze as if not understanding any of it, then returning to their trek, moved by whatever unfelt wind filled his sails. If he had the words to describe his emotions or reason for accompanying Percy, they like most everything else went unvoiced. His small hands tugged at Percy's side then pointed to a boy on a cell phone.

"Why'd you have to tell her that?" A scrawny white kid in a wife-beater tank top shouted into a cell phone. Despite the heat, he wore over-sized blue jean shorts and a wool cap. Wisps of red hair sprouted along his jaw line and the sun deeply freckled his skin. The boy pled in a tone usually reserved for a girlfriend going emotional on a guy or a buddy about to bust his alibi. Then, in that way moods could swing without warning, the boy turned angry. He paced back and forth, a caged animal about to buck. "All right, motherfucker. I'm going to come over there and kick your ass."

The boy darted into his house and cut out the back-door into an alley. Hopping the fence, he dashed through another yard in time to meet another white dude as he exited his house. Black-haired, thin in the face, a tooth-pick to one side, his well-worn Reggie Miller jersey showed off his sleeve of tattoos down each arm. He spit out his toothpick. The two veritably snarled as they charged one another. The sleeve-tattooed boy ducked under the freckled kid's lunge, grabbed his legs, and took his feet out from under him in a backyard UFC move. Once the freckled kid hit the ground, the house whose yard he had cut through emptied, as did the house the sleeve tattooed boy came out of.

Chaos erupted all about Percy, Had, and Kay, who remained motionless, not drawing any attention to themselves. Kay bared his teeth and gums, barking rapidly then snatching at the air with his jaws. A feral glint in his eye warding off the encroaching madness.

"Come on, let's get you out of here before you get hurt." The voice came from behind them, but Kay knew him by smell and calmed as he neared. Lott had the sullen appearance of someone used to spending too much time alone.

"Lott. We're on a quest," Percy said, barely able to contain his excitement.

"Later, little brother. It's getting a little crazy out here."

A wood-chipper truck stopped in the middle of the street, held up by the melee. A mailman kicked his feet up in his truck, drinking a pop and watching the show. Someone shouted "they're coming to arrest your ass" as the police, an ambulance, and a fire truck pulled up.

Emotions over-crowded Lott's brain. Nostalgia. Guilt. Shame. Loss. Parts of him no longer wanted the obligations of friendship because it reminded him of old times, which was too much for him to handle. They knew who he was, what he was, and how he did things. They cheered him on as he rampaged through life. They exalted his exploits and not-so-secretly thrilled then encouraged him to greater heights of violence. Then they dropped him when he became inconvenient to them though called on him when they needed him. He wanted to bray about being used, perhaps muster up the energy to play the martyr, but he could only manage enough to feel sorry for himself.

Percy knew the neighborhood. Black folks, white folks, Hispanic folks – united by their ubiquitous poverty more than anything else – settling into isolated pockets within the community. Living mostly comfortably, sometimes not so, among each other. He also knew the houses on the block.

And he believed even houses became ghosts haunting neighborhoods.

Set away from the street and somewhat distanced from the surrounding houses, as if they shrank away from it preferring to crowd the rest of the block, the two-story house at Michigan Street and Dearborn Avenue loomed over the intersection. An old Tudor-styled home with a spire as a turret. Two stone, winged lions guarded its entrance. The entire property was fenced by razor wire, designed to echo the women's facility just west of it. That was how the house appeared to most, but when Percy walked by it, out the corner of his eye, or perhaps

though a disturbance in his spirit, the house was greater.
A many-roomed mansion, three stories. A red castle with
flourishes of turrets. An egg-shaped keystone with a
tower, the illumination of a winter's solstice within its
sacred geometry.

"You sure this is the place?" Lott asked.

"Aren't you? You knew it, too."

A fact Lott couldn't argue. "We got to clear this fence.
You up for it, Percy?"

"What about Kay?"

"Can't he wait here?"

"He needs to go with us."

"Okay." Lott eyed the dog, who lowered itself as if trying to shrink. "I'll carry Kay."

They scouted the perimeter of the house. The property took up much of the block with the alley behind
it littered with rocks and overgrown shrubbery. A
poplar tree grew barely within the property, thick, low-
lying branches stretched over. Percy lifted Had up to
the branch. Scrabbling up with a natural grace, the
small boy scampered along the branch and landed in
the yard before either Percy or Lott could tell him to
wait. Percy grunted as he hefted his bulk up, heaving
a massive leg over the branch, which bent in quiet sub-
mission to his mass. Taking advantage of the lowered
branch, Lott scooped up Kay and began to slide onto
the branch, as Percy slid along. The branch creaked and
strained under the weight of all three. Not wanting to
risk his friends, Percy tumbled awkwardly out of the
tree, landing hard.

"You okay?" Lott tried to keep his voice down.

"I'm all right." Percy was slow to get up, and limped toward Had.

Crossing over the razor wire, Lott allowed Kay to leap down before dropping down behind him. The tree branches shadowed a stone at its base. Surrounded by strange symbols, the number 1362 carved into it. Percy traced them with his finger. They seemed important, but he didn't know how to interpret them. He wished King or Merle were here as they were so much smarter than him and always seemed to know what to do. He missed his friends. They all seemed so sad these days. Big Momma always gave him a hug when he was depressed like this. Lott looked like he needed a hug. So Percy wrapped his huge arms around him.

Lott instinctively flinched, unsure how to react, struggling against the embrace at first. Then, he relaxed, succumbing to the act of being loved.

"What was that for?" Lott asked.

"You looked like you needed it."

"Now?"

"Why not now?"

"I… thanks, Percy." Lott clapped him on the arm and gave it a squeeze. The darkness in him shifted a bit.

Lott turned toward the house. Had tugged at his pant leg, gesturing for him to bend over. When he leaned down, Had wiped a tear from his face he didn't realize was there, then threw his slight arms around him, too. He didn't understand everything that was going on. But he knew when people were hurting and wanted to take away their pain.

"Okay, li'l man. I get it. Thanks." Lott was a strong

man. Not one prone to admitting when something inside him broke, like an ice sheath cracking. "Come on."

They moved in silence, though Percy strained to keep his lumbering gait quiet. Had's lightness made him mobile. Filled with the swell of mission and purpose, Lott took point. The rear patio doors were unlocked. Percy had the sensation of the house being larger on the inside than on the outside. They skulked along a thin hallway, Percy edging slowly at an angle to allow him to pass through. The servants' hallway opened into a linen room. Empty cupboards, cabinet doors removed from their hinges, covered in cobwebs against the creeping black of mold as the original wallpaper was exposed in patches, where not shorn from the wall.

They entered the dining room from the pantry. A boarded-up side door led out to a porch. One of the occupants had attempted at some point to lay down a stretch of carpet. Old glue streaked the wood floor along with blobs of paint, matted by half-rotted pieces of carpet in places.

Having squatted in his share of homes, Percy recognized one when he entered it. However, with this much room – larger inside than it should be, as if they'd entered a new space entirely – there should be many folks staying there. In some of his spots, if it was a good place, he couldn't stop others from coming in and claiming a room.

Kay growled. Had patted his side to reassure him.

Strange illumination filled the house as if emanating from the walls themselves. They approached the living room, with its curving wall, when the stench first hit them. Rotted meat mixed with the pungent smell of thick ammonia. And piles of shit. A cloying animal musk coated their tongues. The living room opened into a large foyer with a domed ceiling.

The creature parading about in it stopped them in their tracks.

A strange amalgamation of animals. White downy chest, with brown wings tucked in over its body, the feathers swept up its front to the face of a falcon. It had the forelegs of a large bird yet the hind legs of a lion producing its awkward gait. The rear half of the creature's long and sleek body, starting behind its elegant shoulders, was that of a jungle cat. Thick plates of muscles, mostly hidden by the draping wings, eventuating in a tail which was the body of a huge python, swishing about with an unsettling slither.

Lott pushed the boys back around the corner. When he peered around again, the beast's falcon head turned his direction, its eyes focused with the pupil dilation of spotting prey. But it remained frozen as if daring him to come out. It guarded a double staircase, steeped in shadows. Had snuggled into Kay, not so much scared as much as reassuring the dog that he was okay. Kay licked his cheek.

"Ever see anything like that?" Percy asked.

"I saw a heron once. It looked lost, like it meant to land somewhere else. But it walked around like it owned the place before it took off again," Lott said.

"I seen hawks and falcons fly downtown and nest in buildings. A snake once. I don't like snakes. Nothing like that."

"You all get out of here. I can't let you go on."

"What about the cup? What about King?" Percy asked.

"I'll get it. I owe King that much. But it's too danger-ous for–"

"Kids?" Percy fixed his heavy-lidded eyes on Lott, filled with determination, pride, and a distinct lack of fear.

"All right, but you stay behind me. Looks like its only interested in guarding the stairs. So whatever we want has got to be up there."

"You going to fight it?"

Lott studied the sheen of muscles rippling along the creature's flank, the sharpness of the claws, and the sharp downward arc of its huge beak – itself larger than his head. "Um, no."

He scanned the room quickly for a weapon. It had been stripped of everything of value. Not even a door re-mained. Nor any grates for any of the vents. He pulled at the trim at the doorway until a section gave way. Filled with a stiffness, Lott's muscles still ached from his recent attacks. He hefted it, getting a feel for its weight. Holding it out like a lance, he checked around the corner. The creature had ceased its pacing, waiting in a half-crouch like cats were wont to do, waiting for them to make a move. Impenetrable patience in its eyes.

"New plan," Lott said. "I'll distract it while you all run up the stairs. It's so large, it can't follow us up."

Lott charged the mosaic beast, jousting with the stretch of door trim. Percy took Had by the hand and immedi-ately pressed against the wall to follow its perimeter toward the stairwell. The creature sprang toward them, drawn by their movement, but Lott crashed into its side at full speed. The feathers around its head raised in shock and fury as it turned to him. He backed away from where the boys crept around. It snapped at him, its huge beak opening to reveal a dark pink maw. Fluttering in an un-felt breeze, its wings spread in a flare as the boys scampered behind it. It pounced at Lott, propelled by its powerful rear cat legs, its clawed talons skittering with a thunderous click-click-click against the hardwood floors.

Lott lunged out of its way, barely avoiding a swipe which would have sent his entrails spilling out against the wall like a dashed pumpkin. Scrabbling against a lit-ter of bones, he slipped on the thick paste that might have been its urine. The boys disappeared into the dark-ness of the stairwell. Lott dashed to the left then to the right, seeking to juke his way past it, but each move was met with the creature cutting off any path toward the stairs. It toyed with him now, its head cocked at a curious angle as if deciding whether to plunge its beak into his eye sockets or reduce him to a crimson smear with its claws.

Claws raked across his shoulders, producing scarlet stripes. Thrown off balance, he stumbled about and whirled at the sound of a terrible screech. It hurtled through the air. Lott pivoted away from the lethal talons, barely avoiding the scrape of chitin against the wood floor. Lott shouted, hoping to startle it, threw the piece of wood at it, then broke to his right in a full-out dash toward the stairwell. Hit in the face, the creature flapped its wings again, the powerful breeze knocking Lott off balance as it hooked its claws onto his face. It lifted him into the air, the susurrus of his screams seeming to please it. Opting not to crush his skull on the spot, it flung him across the room. Lott slammed against it, falling to the ground like limp meat, his fall broken only by landing in a pile of its excrement. Its horrible tail wrapped around his leg, drawing him toward it, squeezing him to the point where he could no longer feel. The rest of the creature's body turned to inspect him. It reared back, preparing to dive its beak directly into his chest.

With a snarl, Kay leapt from the shadows, landing on the creature's back. He tore into the scruff of the beast's neck, his jaws clamping down on its thick cords of muscle. The creature let loose a screech. Lott grabbed the nail-studded piece of wood and swung it into the side of the beast's head. The head jerked and it toppled though it raked a claw through the air, catching Kay in his side. He winced, his flesh opened in red gashes. Fearing the creature might renew its assault, Lott sprang between it and Kay, poised to club it again, but the creature didn't stir. Its chest rose and fell. Lott glanced at Kay then, filled with rage, turned back to the creature to smash its skull in. He stood there, rooted to the spot, its still form beneath him. Releasing the spear of wood, he scooped up Kay and climbed up into the waiting darkness of the stairs.

The shadows steepened with every step, closing in on him with a pressing closeness. It seemed to swirl and congeal, eddies of darkness, shadows within shadows.

"Percy?" Lott cried out. The darkness swallowed his words. "Had?"

Kay, bundled in his arms, lightened. Immaterial, as if dissolving in the umbra fog. Lott's heart quickened. Every muscle in his arms and legs throbbed with ache. He mentally traced each gash as each wound throbbed. The quiet times only made him reflect on his pain.

The dark grew deeper still. Lott inched along the stairwell. Traumatized and numb. Disembodied, he was a lost soul cast adrift in an obsidian sea. Bruises of metal and insulation underneath electrical boxes and tentacles of wires tripped him as he skulked. His hand pressed against the wall, like a blind man in a labyrinth, searching for anything which allowed him to believe he was still real. Paint flaked from the walls beneath his touch. The distinct smell of cat piss filled his nostrils. Somewhere in the distance, he swore he heard someone humming "Jesus Loves the Little Children".

"Percy?"

"Good-working, conscientious thieves." With the strange acoustics of the stairwell, the voice boomed from everywhere at once. "Young and inexperienced. Wandering an unknown land, ravaged by war."

"I don't understand."

"You only pass if you speak true. You have three chances. Who are you?"

"Lott."

"Liar. You have never been the man you believed yourself to be."

"But I…" Lott began.

"What do you seek?"

"I seek the grail."

"Liar. You seek what we all seek. Forgiveness. Redemption."

"I…"

"Where were you when she needed you? When she needed you to be the man you claimed you were. Hoped you were. Where were you?"

"I don't know. I was lost."

"Ask the question," the voice commanded.

"What question?" Lott asked.

"Ask the question. The one you truly want to know the answer to."

"Where is the grail?"

"Liar. Will you ever be forgiven? By God. By your friends. By yourself. For you… darkness."

The night swallowed Lott.

Percy emerged onto the second floor. He leaned against the wall next to the stairwell, then slid down it until his butt hit the floor and he slumped against his knees. The darkness frightened him, the voice moreso. It troubled him, in a too-knowing sort of way, so he pushed the entire encounter out of his mind. Two bedrooms faced the front of the property and two bedrooms faced the rear, the large master suite before him. A barrel-vaulted ceiling towered above him. Had trundled out of the darkness of the stairwell, innocent eyes non-plussed, and squatted down beside Percy.

"You hear the voice?"

Had nodded.

"It scare you?"

Had shook his head.

"Really? It scared me. A little. Kind of like a storm."

Had cocked his head as if admiring or studying the movement of Percy's mouth.

"It asked me secret things."

Had stared at him with no recognition in his eyes.

"Think we should wait for Kay? Or Lott."

Had peered into the darkness, then shook his head no, as if he, too, knew secret things.

"Okay." Percy scrambled to his feet and took Had by the hand. He checked each of the two rooms overlooking the backyard. Each room was empty. He walked past the door to the master suite to the other rooms. The two facing the front were identical. Both had huge walk-in closets and bathrooms with broken toilets. Both had a bedroll in the corner. And both had clear views of the winged lion statues.

"Edward and Hugh," Percy said. "They look like an Edward and Hugh."

Had smiled at him.

Percy led them back to the master suite and turned the doorknob. Across the room was another door. Between them and that door was a man seated in a wicker chair. With a thin but muscular build, his jersey showed off the measure of his tattoos. Half of his body, like a living X-ray detailing his skeleton. Though his face was too thin, his eyes, hazel and glassy, were determined. He exuded power and fierceness. The man wasn't one to cross.

"You a long way from home, hese." Black made no effort to move, just stood there as if entranced. His eyes fixed on the large boy, perhaps assessing him, perhaps dismissing him, perhaps not really seeing him.

"Not really. I live just up the street," Percy said. Still holding his hand, Had slipped behind him.

"You lost?" Black took their measure in a glance. If he perceived a threat, he didn't let on.

"No. Just looking for something."

"You 'just looking for something' in my house?" Black said. "You like Christopher Columbus and shit. 'Discovering' a land already occupied by people."

"This is your house?" Percy gaped about in awe. "It's nice."

"I stay here. You got to have a place to lay your head. No one knows that really. Only the people I trust most."

"I don't know you."

"I know. So when you say you up in my house 'just looking for something', guess that makes you a thief. We know how to handle thieves around here."

"I'm no thief."

"What are you looking for?"

"A cup. It used to belong to a friend of mine. It had a... ring inside."

"So now you calling me a thief?"

"No," Percy said unblinking and unafraid. "I thought... I was told it might be here."

"Who told you that?"

"Another friend."

"Your friend tells stories," Black said.

"Yeah. He does that sometimes."

"Why you want it back so bad? It valuable?"

"I don't know. I was told it could help a friend. He's sick."

"What's the matter with him?"

"He was shot and now won't wake up."

Calculations filled Black's eyes and he tugged at his glove. "You a friend of King's?"

"Yeah."

"That motherfucker needs to burn. Along with any motherfucker that stands with him." Black removed his glove and held it in front of his face, both admiring and loathing it. He glared at Percy, his anger prematurely exposed. Not solely anger, but despair. A huge void, the sheer immensity of the pain and loss, threatened to devour him where he stood if he didn't constantly tend to it. Which also fueled his anger.

"Why?" Percy didn't move. The way the man held his hand out, he was afraid threat underscored the gesture.

"Because of what happened to my sister."

"Lyonessa."

"Yeah. Someone's got to pay." Black reached out to him.

"She was pretty." The tiny voice stopped them in their tracks.

Percy turned. Had stepped out from behind him and met Black's gaze.

"She was pretty." Had stared straight ahead, not really focused on Black. His shoulders stiff, as if warding back a shiver. "And nice. She played with me."

Black peered down at the round-faced boy, oddly captivated by his sweet face. There was an innocence, a purity, about him which reminded him of his sister. He lowered his arm. Had approached him. Then, before Black could react, Had took his hand.

Black cried out, his voice choked and grievous, more

in fear for the boy than any pain himself. But he stared at him. No burning. No raised flesh.

"I don't understand." Black tried backing away from Had, but the boy kept pace with him, not releasing his hand. Black fell back into his seat. Had stood next to him, still holding his hand. A tear trailed down his face.

"She was pretty," he said as if letting the memory of her wash over him. Not just the memory of her, but the pain of her absence, the tragedy of her death. The guilt of Black's life. All of it, the pain and hurt of Black. All of it.

Had nodded at Percy as if shooing him along. Percy backed away from them, again with the overwhelming sensation that he was intruding on something personal. Something sacred. He fumbled for the knob of the other door, which gave way without complaint in his grasp.

Another set of stairs greeted him. A tight spiral of steps which seemed to go up quite a ways. Percy almost got dizzy simply from the view up. He took the first one, testing it to see if it or the delicate frame could take his weight. Then the next. The structure didn't buckle or sway. Rather than risk vertigo staring to see how far he had left or down to check how far he'd gone, Percy kept his eye simply on the next step.

Time became meaningless to him. He knew he ascended a tower. He kept climbing, pausing every so often to rest. Sweat soaked through his red shirt, giving it the appearance of a blood-drenched rag. Finally he came to a landing and collapsed in a heap.

"It's such a waste," a clown said. Her face, white with paint grease, had a scar dividing the side of her face.

When she closed her eyes, her lids completed the image of a cross over each eye. When she moved, she glided about the floor with the swivel-hipped body language of a dancer.

"It's all such a waste."

Percy scrambled to his feet, steadying himself on the banister. The room had a sacredness to it. A quiet retreat hidden from the rest of the world. And she was beautiful. A princess.

"What is?" Percy asked.

"The fighting. The killing."

"It makes me sad, too."

"You've come for the cup," La Payasa said.

"Yeah."

"Is it yours?"

"No."

"Then why should I give it to you?"

"It's important," Percy said.

"Why?"

"It can help my friend."

"King." Her eyes fixed on him as if gazing into the innermost parts of his soul. "Is that the only reason?"

"Yeah." Percy ran out of words. He didn't know what else to say, how else to plead his case. Words tumbled out of his mouth. "The cup had a ring in it…"

"Go on."

"A long time ago, my mom…" Percy hesitated. The memory and words came hard to Percy. But he spoke of his mother and her long losing battle with drugs. How she tried to be a mother in her own way. And he tried to be an obedient son, despite her trying to school him in things he knew were wrong. Which was how he ended up breaking into Rhianna's room one night and almost stealing that ring. Instead, moved by how pretty she was, he put the ring back. But it always hurt his heart how close he came to betraying her. Which was why he believed he owed it to her to find the ring.

"You are a great fool," La Payasa said in a soft, soothing voice. She pulled a ring from her left hand and placed it in his palm. Then curled his fingers around it. "I don't know if any of the people around you deserve you."

"Why are you here?" Percy asked.

"In this house?"

"With him."

"Oh, Black. Growing up. The police raided our house three, four times a year. They'd gather the children in a room, all of us terrified, not knowing what was going on. The police were supposed to be our friend. We were supposed to trust them. They were supposed to protect us. They were supposed to lock up bad people. Yet here they were, herding us about like cattle, all of them glaring down their noses at us, with that expression on their faces like we shouldn't be there. They reduced the house to a mess. I never learned to trust them. Handcuffing all of the adults, lining them up on the curb like they were on sale. And most times, the police would leave with nothing. Sometimes they'd take my father in, but he'd be back within a few hours. It was like some game he and the police played. With us caught up in it. Me? I hated the invasion. I hated the police. And I hated my father."

"I never knew my father. Met him once, I think."

"Mine never protected me. I never had my own bed. Always a bunch of us crammed into a room. Into a bed. Me and my cousins. We slept on opposite ends of the same bed. His crusty feet jammed into my face."

Percy smiled. It reminded him of home with his brothers and sisters. But the smile faded with the pursed lips of La Payasa and the sadness they held back.

"Every night for a year, he touched me," she said. "Touched me in private places."

Percy reflected on uncomfortable moments with his mother.

"There was never any…"

Percy shifted noisily.

"Only touching."

"So that's why you're here?" Percy asked, still confused.

"It takes a certain kind of self-loathing to be here. Maybe you know what it's like. You feel isolated. Apart. Trapped. The whole experience made me feel so different. As if everyone could see my shame. So I never wanted to feel weak or alone again."

"Black protects you."

"I love the nation." La Payasa hand-stacked the letters of her clique. "They my family. They took me in and taught me that they had a code. The leaders chosen had to be strong. Mentally, physically, and emotionally."

"They made you strong." Percy struggled to follow, but thought he understood.

"I held their guns and drugs from the beginning. I could use my looks to lead fools into an ambush. Women ain't trusted to go with men on hits. With me, I can go solo. No one challenges my word."

"So you ain't scared anymore."

"You… understand."

"It's like me with King. I'm not afraid. I want to live… like he does."

"I'm tired. You always got someone who wants to test you. And that gets old real quick." She wanted out of her life. She loved the power and the community her life afforded. And the respect. But her loyalty to her gang was also her biggest obstacle. Besides enlightened self-interest, she could give up the folks she didn't like, who were rivals in their way, or frankly, she didn't give a fuck about. But treason was the worst sin, punishable by death. A subtle shift of light in her eyes, the flicker of resignation. She took the lid of a can and began to scrape off her tattoo.

"Stop! You're gonna hurt yourself!" Percy yelled.

"The life, it don't give you time to think back on what you've seen or done. You live in the right now with the goal to survive to tomorrow." Rivulets of blood filegreed her shoulder. "I won't give the cup to you. I will put it in the hands of its true keeper. And maybe talk to this King of yours."

"What about…?"

"Come on, your friends are waiting on you."

Big Momma swept her porch. A little four-by-eight concrete slab set before her door and the adjoining condos door. Her hair done up in pink rollers, gray strands mixed with black in a gray jogging suit knowing full well she barely jogged to the refrigerator door. However, she hated house dresses, believing they were for old ladies ready for nursing homes. And she was neither. Two green plastic lawn chairs leaned against the brick artifice of her condo. A plastic bench upturned into the bushes while she swept. She arranged the furniture back to her porch, scooting the bench out into the lawn for a better view. From her porch, she could spy the entirety of her court, a cul-de-sac of condominiums forming the letter U facing Breton Drive. On the other side of the street was Jonathan Jennings PS 109 elementary school. The park next to the school was in her full view, the vista cut off by the row of bushes that grew along the creek that separated the school and Breton Court from the rest of the neighborhood. The comings and goings of Breton Court happened under her watchful eye. She knew who lived where, who belonged in the area, and who didn't. she watched over it. Protected it.

A dog barked then skittered around the corner of the bridge that crossed the creek and limped directly for her. It favored one side, had some wounds which had been tended to but were still sore. Lott, Had, and Percy trailed behind it, none of them moving quickly, especially Lott. Trouble followed that boy and he was all too happy to find his way into it. A girl, a pretty little thing, followed a few steps behind them. They all stopped at Big Momma's stoop.

"Big Momma," Percy said. "La Payasa."

"This belongs to you." La Payasa handed her a chalice. Unadorned and simple.

"It does?"

"It always has."

"Why me?"

"Because you're magic," Lott said. "It's what you do. You see us, who we really are, the way nobody else does. That's your magic."

"If you're not ready to be helped, you won't get better," Big Momma said.

Everyone wanted a happy ending to their story. To believe that no matter how far gone they are, their story wasn't over and there was still time to write a new story. "I think we have a stop to make."

Night shrouded a fog-filled world. King marched about a few tentative steps at a time. Uncertain. Almost lost. A hand reached out to grab him before he stumbled again. His brown leather jacket remained opened enough to reveal the gold chain along his black turtleneck. His brown eyes brimmed with compassion. Side burns, thick but tight, framed his wistful smile. He could almost see his reflection in his polished knobs. Yet King couldn't quite focus on him, as if he wasn't entirely there.

"Dad." King knew though he hadn't seen his father since he was two and had no real memory of him. But he looked exactly as he had in the pictures his mom kept.

"Yeah," Luther said. "Look at you. All grown up. You've become quite a man."

"I don't understand. You're dead."

"Yeah."

"But you're here."

"And you're lost."

"I'm always here. I came to you. A father loves his children."

King shifted in discomfort, a closeness to a father he didn't understand. There were times when it was easier to believe the seemingly irrational. King wasn't sure about a lot of things.

"You're confused. You have a lot of questions and soon we will have all of eternity for me to answer them. For now, take in my healing waters. What's broken can be made whole. What's dirty can become clean. Drink deep and know that you are loved. You are quite special to me. For who you are. You don't have to do anything to prove yourself to me. Just be the man I intended you to be. As for me, I'm already pleased with you, just as you are."

With that, King awoke.

CHAPTER FIFTEEN

The glow of the computer screen lit Garlan's face as he checked his Facebook page from the library computer. He debated whether or not to add his mother as a friend. Everything taught him that he was meant to live and die alone in the streets. The beatings he took from his mom's boyfriends. On the streets. A different kind of beating in school, by the teachers, as they either told him or assumed that he wouldn't amount to shit. And he seemed determined to prove them right. The lingering memory of his mom was how bottles lined the shelf of what she called "Club Nouveau". In an alcoholic's reflex, she counted her drinks and memorized the levels of the bottles. She knew each bottle as intimately as her own hand, knew if they had been watered down or out of place. She treated those bottles with more care and attention than she did her own kids.

Whenever someone got up or walked down the aisles of the library, any movement at all, it drew his attention. He set his jaw and eye-fucked them so that they gave him a wide, respectful berth. He wasn't one of those old heads, always nodding to each other like all black folks was related or some shit. So Five-O stepping to him was recognized long before they locked onto him.

"Garlan?" Cantrell sipped from a fresh cup of coffee from Lazy Daze, a local coffee shop, as he was "done supporting The Chain" as he called it, though he'd still sooner spring for Starbucks than choke down the watery sputum which passed as station house coffee.

"Who asking?"

"Come on, Garlan. Why you going to do us like that? I thought you were my dude. We've shared times. Surely you got some love for your peoples," Lee mocked, adopting the "brother–brother" affect he so despised.

"My partner, Detective Lee McCarrell." Cantrell cut him a caustic glance. Garlan certainly wasn't a tax-paying citizen, but he hadn't given them any cause to go hard at him yet. The thing was, sometimes Lee's pit bull approach, irritating as it was, cut through the mess. "Can we step outside?"

Garlan pushed away from the table and met the gaze of anyone who glanced his way until they averted their eyes. No one would see him if he didn't want them to. He touched the ring on his left hand, a nervous habit, as if to make sure it was still there. Garlan wondered why they stopped on the steps of the library rather than usher him to a squad car, then he spied the cameras approaching.

"You ever get a new ride?" Cantrell asked.

"No, waiting on insurance."

"How you get here then?"

"Walk."

"Must be quite the letdown, going from such a fine ride to hitting the bricks."

"It's all right." Garlan only addressed Cantrell.

"Easy come, easy go. Must be nice to have it like that," Lee said.

"Something like that," Garlan said.

"Word on the street has it that you been running with Dred's crew now."

"Yeah?"

"Yeah. 'Cept the ways we hear it, folks in Dred's crew have been having an unexpectedly short life span."

"What some folks would consider high insurance risks."

"So who put my name in they mouth?"

"Another witness," Lee said, getting half a hard-on at the thought of Omarosa. Or maybe it was the thrill of interrogating someone, not in the box, but in the street. "Same one that told us we could probably catch up with you here."

"Yeah?"

"Yeah. Old habits and all." Lee loved getting up in people's shit.

"What's that mean?" Garlan asked.

"Who is it they say he run with?" Lee asked.

"Noles and Melle. Long rap sheets on both of them. Not so much you," Cantrell said.

"Like you invisible or something." Lee smirked with an all-too-knowing grin. He received a momentary eye-flick of acknowledgment on that one.

"Either he's good or ain't been caught," Cantrell said. "Or innocent."

"Shit." Lee couldn't help himself. "Ain't an innocent thing in or on that body of yours."

"Anyway." Cantrell tossed him a hard eye then glanced at the cameras. "You hear what happened to Melle?"

"Yeah. I heard about that. That was some nasty shit," Garlan said.

"You ain't too broken up about it."

"We weren't exactly close."

"No crew love for your boy?" Lee asked.

"He was too wild, man. Always into some shit."

"I see," Cantrell noted. "What about Robert Ither, Bartholamew DiGora, and Preston Wilcox? You might know them as Naptown Red, Fathead, and Prez."

"I know Red. Not sure about them other two."

"So you ain't heard."

"Talk on it."

"Brothers went down wet."

Cantrell considered himself a detective, not a leader, despite the work he did in the community. Captain Burke constantly reprimanded him for clinging to that old saw, calling him afraid to lean into his gifts. Afraid might have been too strong. Most times he preferred the puzzles of detective work. Being behind the scenes and away from the politics and bureaucracy... despite being a natural politician who played bureaucracies like a fiddle. People were complex, but for all of their complexity they were simple at their core. Or there were certain things a person could count on. Like the look of genuine surprise that registered briefly on Garlan's face at the news of Naptown Red's death. He could almost spot the wheels turning as he puzzled out who could've done it and why.

"The scene was a real mess. Prez got off the easiest. Simple bullet to the brain. One tap, real close. Naptown Red, he put up a fight. Got some shots off, then it looks like someone stabbed him in the heart. But Fathead? Someone did a job on him. Took their time, too. His head took such a beating his own momma wouldn't recognize him. They pumpkin-headed him. And I get that you don't need shit to come back on you. I know they weren't your boys or nothing, but you got any thoughts on who might've done this?"

"Why you asking me?"

"I got this theory. It says that Dred has been stirring up things. Flexing a little, getting a feel for how much juice his name carried. That got him bumping up against Black and his set. Stuff goes back and forth like this stuff do. Then things get taken to the next level. Lyonessa gets caught up. Don't know who gave the order or who carried it out. We do have a vehicle description that vaguely matches your ride. But that's neither here nor there because it's been torched beyond recognition. As you know, it doesn't matter what we think, it's about what we can prove. But... someone out there must have a suspicious mind, cause they went after Melle. Probably got Noles on a shortlist, too. What I can't quite figure out is if the same person went after Red and 'em, changing up their methods, or if that was someone else tying up loose ends. You got any thoughts on that?"

"Nah, man..." Garlan trailed off.

"Cause if you do, we'd be all ears. That's why we having this civil conversation. Out here, in front of all kinds of passers by." Cantrell tipped his hat to a sister eyeing them from the sidewalk. "Not taking you in or busting up your routine. Just giving you something to think about."

"A friendly warning," he said.

"Cause someone's hunting your crew."

"I said I don't know nothing," Garlan yelled loud enough for any curious ears to hear.

"Well, if you do," Cantrell began to hand him a card, but Garlan turned down the block and stepped off in a huff.

"What you think?"

"Evil is rare, but stupid is everyday," Cantrell said.

"That so?"

"He's a ghetto nihilist. Life don't mean anything to him. Any of them. They got no reason to value it... Now they done gone and killed somebody. Part of them dead too."

"You ought to become a philosopher."

"I got nothing out here and I'm too old to start over."

"I ain't mad at you. It's a color thing, I got that," Lee said.

"You're my forty acres and a jackass," Cantrell said.

"I'm trying to relate to you... my brother. And all you got for me is names. It ain't your fault some politicians need to feel better about their beaner nannies and gardeners and decide to force a rainbow coalition on your behalf."

• • • •

Life pressed in on Garlan from all sides. Everywhere he turned, there were crossroads, each folding in on itself like a Gordian knot. In charge of a few knuckleheads, overseeing a corner or two, he enjoyed a comfortable spot with Dred. A little money coming through, set him up nice. Some wheels too, though he had to ditch them with Five-O on the hunt for them. But a car could be replaced; freedom couldn't. And he had no interest in being locked up.

All the death haunted him, however. Each body a new weight on his conscience and it wasn't as if he had nothing but time to pass in a prison yard. He knew Rok from back in the day, but he got caught up in that Colvin mess and being between a player like Colvin and Dred and King was a bad place to find oneself in.

Then Noles and Melle and that business with the little girl. That kind of drama would have po-po in his Kool-Aid forever or until they found someone to put it on. Catch a young black buck like The Boars, get him in the back seat of a sheriff's car, and he get mysteriously shot with them claiming suicide or some shit. Po-po notwithstanding, the hood was hot, jumping with pissed-off Mexicans and brothers alike. Shit, it was barely safe to walk down the street of his own hood.

Which was how he found himself in Broad Ripple. On a Thursday night, the strip hopped as college kids crawled from bar to bar in a press of bodies and a good-time vibe. The lights of the Vogue flashed with a spotlight's glare. Live bands came through on a regular basis: Madonna's Abortion, The Chosen Few, Saving Abel, The Why Store. Nothing Garlan would every listen to. Every so often some old school hip-hop he could get with would come through: Rakim, De La Soul, Method Man, Redman, Cypress Hill. Tonight was some wannabe heavy metal band, so he kept stepping, pushing past the crowd of folks milling about out front. The young college-age kids without sense enough to recognize a shark in their midst or not wanting to appear racist by profiling him. Not wanting any drama, he cruised through them without even bothering to flex his game face.

An old man danced on the corner across the street. Drunk. Homeless. People walked by as if they couldn't see him. Garlan crossed the street and put three dollars in his cup. It would go to whatever cheap booze wafted off him at that moment, but Garlan wasn't going to deny the man a taste. Whatever got him through the night.

Melle was dead. Naptown Red. Fathead. Prez. The bodies kept stacking up all under his watch. He was supposed to look out for them. Hunters were on the prowl. Too many hunters and a thinning school of prey.

And Garlan had the distinct impression that he was prey.

Nature's dark opera played unabated. The frightful melody of the rain combined with the mournful wail of the wind to tear through the trees. Lightning scampered all around, chasing some unseen prey, the radiance of the full moon shining vividly through the oppressively low clouds. The thunder roared with its terrible echo. Garlan swore that it was less than a mile that he'd walked, yet it seemed interminable. Or maybe it was the silence that lengthened the trip. Turning north up College Avenue, he walked away from the main strip of

Broad Ripple Avenue, away from the lights, until he got to the bridge that crossed the canal. Way he heard it, way back in the day, folks who lived in downtown Indianapolis used to build their summer homes in Broad Ripple. Large show-off houses with lots of rooms and windows. And there used to be an amusement park, like Coney Island, along the canal. Though the rides burnt down, the city kept the park. Lots of folks hung out at the bridge.

Garlan scrabbled over the edge of the lime-green girders of the bridge out of view of the patrolling officers, and landed in the dirt. Usually the bridge thrummed with activity. Bridge kids, the kind of folks Garlan would have no trouble blending in with. Most of them were rich white kids from the suburbs, Carmel, Noblesville, Fishers, singing that "My parents don't understand me" song while driving their daddy's BMW back and forth. Others were skateboarders. A few punks. Goths. B-boys. Some were hoppers, folks who followed the train lines cross-country. And on Thursday nights it should have been bumping. But it was deserted. The lights of Broad Ripple filled the sky above him, but didn't seem to cut through the shadows under the bridge. It was just Garlan and his ghosts.

"It all catches up to you after a while," a voice said from the shadows.

"Who that is?"

"It's just me." Baylon shuffled toward him.

"What you need?" Garlan balled his hand, but kept it at his side. He didn't find Baylon's presence especially reassuring.

"You."

"What you want with me? Dred need me to come in? He could've hit me up on my cell. He didn't need to send–"

"His errand boy?"

"I wasn't going to say that," much as he believed it. "Much respect."

"You underestimate your value. You Dred's number-one dude. His new number one."

"I don't know about all that." Though the thought did please him.

"A dog always returns to his master, especially when his master needs him most. Between Black, Dred, King, and the police, it's been hard out here for Dred's lieutenants. You his last one. The rest are gone or preoccupied. Soon it will just be a cozy little gathering. But… what to do about you?"

Baylon lunged toward him just as Garlan turned his ring and disappeared. Garlan threw himself against the concrete embankment, evading the initial grasp. He turned to kick him. Garlan tried to brace himself as much as possible. With all the strength he awkwardly managed, he stomped.

Baylon barely flinched, but the impact pushed him toward the river's edge. He couldn't hear above the roar or the current. Landing on his back, mired in the mud of a puddle, he locked eyes on Garlan. His heart pounded in his head. His mind, however, focused with clarity at the task at hand, detached, like he was playing a video game. Baylon's piercing howl cut through the noise of the storm.

Garlan bumped against a barbed-wire fence. He cursed

the Private Property – No Trespassing sign that swung wildly in the wind. He scanned for a weapon of some sort. A discarded piece of rebar was jammed between some concrete debris at the base of the bridge, but it meant rushing past Baylon to get it. The rain dumped down in sheets, creating a haze over the water against the lights overhead.

Baylon slowed as he realized he had cornered himself. Garlan edged along the fence, never turning from Baylon, his hands feeling for any break in the fence. His pupils dilated, thick blood vessels wrapping his eyes like jealous lovers. Leaves crunched and twigs snapped underfoot with each lumbering step, his feet sliding in the thickening mud.

Baylon's stride stiffened, each step requiring that much more effort. His laborious breathing sounded like wind tunnels. The mud by the fence bulged then oozed forward as if something plopped in it. Rain outlined the shadow of a figure. Baylon stiffened his hands. Without warning, he dashed forward and drove his fist through the center mass of the rain-occluded wisp. Blood sprayed the bridge embankment.

Garlan faded back into view as his pulse lessened, the last beats of his heart bringing him into full view. Baylon grabbed Garlan's hand and slipped the ring from it. Placing it in the center of his palm, he examined it. Then he flicked it into the air, caught, and pocketed it before police came to investigate the scuffle.

Now it was just him and Dred. Dred would have to turn to him again, and things would be like they were.

• • • •

The window latch clicked slightly as the glass slid up. An exhalation of a breeze jostled the curtains. The room was a murky swirl of shadows, unfamiliar and terrifying. The night hid the creature under the bed or bought camouflaging protection for the bogeyman in the closet. There were all sorts of predators in the night. Things that went bump in the night. Things that no amount of iron bars, safety glass, or fancy alarm systems could give the illusion of providing safety against.

He slipped in noiselessly. Despite his build he moved with the grace of a thief, light of foot and touch. Her mother certainly didn't lack for imagination. She wanted her daughter to have a magical, safe childhood, a little girl's room fraught with little-princess dreams and little-princess trappings. Mementos of a childhood denied him. It took him forever to find. There was power in a name: a tracer spell might have sufficed, but the apartment complex had some sort of ward placed on it. His own mother used a similar spell also to hide from him.

The little girl was just as beautiful as he imagined her. The sounds of light snoring filled the room as she snuggled into a thick pink blanket and pillow. For a moment he stood over her, just watching her sleep. He covered her mouth and sat down next to her. Her eyes sprang open, large with panic. Her balled little fists slammed into him, then slowly ceased as recognition filled her eyes. He removed his hand.

"Daddy!" she whispered with enthusiasm, sitting up to give him a hug.

"Nakia," Dred said.

CHAPTER SIXTEEN

Growing up, all of the adults in King's life filled his head with the idea that he had so much potential. That he was good and somehow destined to do great things. However, he had trouble enough leading his life much less the fact that he never truly envisioned himself as a particularly good man. He clung to the quiet belief that he never lived up to being the man he was meant to be. This knowledge both haunted and drove him. What he was slowly coming to accept was that he was a man out of place in this world. Try as he might to get caught up in the cynicism of this age, he couldn't shake his core faith that people were called to a purpose, were meant to stand for something. He'd been given a responsibility and had betrayed that. He didn't deserve anything approaching honor or respect, but he knew that no one was beyond redemption. Or forgiveness.

Even himself.

"Everything looks good, Mr White," said a small squat woman with large glasses who perked to attention around him like he was the last rib at a family barbecue.

The nurses fussed about him, drawing blood and checking his pulse and pressure, poking and prodding him.
The police had already left, marginally satisfied with the
answers he had for their questions. His friends – his only
true family – waited down the hallway.

"When can I get out of here?" King raised the bed so
he could sit up.

"The doctors want to keep you overnight for observa-
tion. No reason why we can't let you go in the morning."

"Can you send my people back here? I'd like to see
them."

"Only a couple at a time. We don't want a crowd in
here." The nurse pushed her glasses up on her nose. A
sweet smile curled on her lips, but she was not a woman
to trifle with.

King raised his hand to his forehead as if nursing a
headache. The images replayed in his mind. The searing
pain of being shot. After that, his memory became stills.
Flashing lights. A breathing mask. Bleets of a machine.
Doctors hovering over him. Then nothing. He dreamt of
his father, though it wasn't his father. More like the ideal
of his father. And there was water. Cool. Refreshing.
Pure. Like drinking life itself. Lost in his thoughts, he did-
n't notice Lady G enter.

"Hey," Lady G said.

"Hey," King straightened. He pulled the sheets down
on his leg, not wanting her to see him in so pathetic a
state. "Just you?"

"Nah, they all out there. Wayne. Pastor Winburn. Big
Momma. Percy. Had."

"No Merle?"

"He out of pocket. Some girl though. Calls herself La Payasa."

"Who?"

"Says she's with Black's crew. Helped bring Had and Percy back safe. So did Lott."

"Yeah, I need to handle some things. Old business." The question was still there, unspoken – Why did you do it? – but silence reigned with no obligation to fill it.

"King, I–"

"You know what I've realized?" King cut her off. Nostalgic for times that never really existed. Sometimes he feared that he couldn't relax and enjoy life because he lived it like it was glimpses of happiness spent holding his breath, waiting for the fall to happen. "I've worn out my capacity to love. At least in my own strength and on my own terms. I've just sort of reached my limit on what I can do on my own. It's a big world out there and I'm still amazed by all the good. And there's still so much to do. Like this Black situation."

"You and Merle go on about your duty. Your responsibility. It doesn't have to be you. The world will go on if you don't get on your white horse to try and save us all."

"When I first met you, you seemed like such a scared little girl. I mean, you came across all hard and stuff, but I could tell. I wanted to protect you. Heal you. I lost my way. Tried to deny my feelings for you, but they were too strong. Fell in love with you. I thought you felt that way too." It was always so easy to be with her. She understood him in ways few others did, without him having to explain much. King stirred as if bored. His brow lowered. Her voice didn't fill him with the crazy passion it used to. Loving her was like loving a black hole. Some days, he thought he loved her so much he hated her for making him so weak. Then there was something else. Something he didn't want to have to admit to himself or voice because to voice it made it real. That he loved the idea of her loving him. That if she accepted him, he'd finally feel good about himself, because of who she was... Good. Innocent. Pure. "Everything I did, I did out of love."

"I wanted to believe it. Trust in it. But part of me always thought that you loved your mission, not me." Lady G knew that was only part of it. Inside, she was still a little bit of that scared little girl. Trapped in a burning house with no one to protect her. To keep her from being burned. The idea of being loved so completely intoxicated her. It nourished her and she craved it. And she lost her way. She removed one of her gloves. The scars from her burns pulsed like throbbing veins. She held her hand out until King took it.

"I'm guilty of many things. I'm sorry I hurt you. I loved you, but not the way I should have. I should have guarded your heart better. I hope you can forgive me."

"I do." King squeezed her hand. "If I were to ask 'why?' would you have an answer?"

"Would anything I say help? Can't we just move on?"

"We can. Maybe we ought to. That would be easy. But not... real. We'd both always have questions that would haunt us."

"Do you ever wonder what happened to us?"

"Every day."

"You left."

"I..." by reflex, he almost said "I didn't stop loving you" but even that would have been a tacit admission of a truth. That he prided himself on how he guarded his heart and life were. How she slipped under his radar, right past his walls of protection. He didn't see her coming, then next thing he knew, she occupied a place in his heart. Nor was there any defense to be found by crying out to her, "You made me love you. You forced me to let you in, then you left me. You left me all alone. I had nobody. I needed you."

"There was an emptiness with you. Like you weren't all there, not... filling me."

"And Lott filled it? I couldn't?"

"You couldn't. Not really. You weren't there."

"I was good to you. Why didn't that matter?"

"It did, it just wasn't enough. Not from you. That was easy for you. What I needed from you, you couldn't give because it wasn't in you to give."

They met each other's eyes, affection tinged with regret and sorrow. The tension was gone. Nothing to rub up against. No one to blame. King cursed himself for falling into a laid trap of their weakness of character. They fought to gain some sort of control over their environment, their lives. He couldn't help but think it was somehow his fault. The price of a crown was often a heavy heart.

"One day, impossibly, it won't hurt this much," Lady G broke the silence. The last thing she wanted to do was hurt him anymore.

"What's broken can be made whole. What's dirty can become clean." The words came out of King, though he wasn't sure if they were directed at him or her. "That's the hope we live in."

"You're crying."

"So are you."

The conversation had already delved deeper than he was comfortable with. A wound dug into in order to remove the settled rot was a good place to allow the healing to happen. Saying any more might push them to a place they couldn't come back from. So they stopped. Movement caught Lady G's attention. She cut her eyes back at King, then lowered her head to excuse herself. Lott stepped to the bedside.

"You look good," Lott said, not knowing where to begin.

"Do you want to do that?" King asked. "Begin with a lie."

"No, not really."

"You don't have to be here."

"Where else would I be? You shouldn't be alone."

"I'm not alone. Not as long as I have people around me who love me."

"You ain't gonna make this easy."

"You are a lie. Let me know something about the you that hides."

Hurt spilled from Lott's eyes. A pain left buried in his chest. "I love Lady G. I always have. And I love you. You and me... we brothers. And I betrayed that. I betrayed both of you. I'm sorry, man. I... You don't know how sorry I am."

There it was.

The betrayal in a sentence. Somehow it seemed bigger before it was said. Now here, they were both broken, regretting the stupid decisions they had made and the pain caused in the wake of them spinning out of control while their worlds had been tossed upside down. A lot of hurt had passed between them. Sometimes too much time elapsed and there was nothing left of a relationship to mend together. Sometimes, you just had to pick up the relationship where it lay. And sometimes, you just had to see the weight of the hurt on the other person's face to know how genuine it was. "You need to quit punishing yourself."

"But King…" The words "I'm sorry" still felt too small to contain all that Lott carried and wanted to convey to King.

King waved him off. "Enough. We need you. I need you. We can't do this thing on our own."

"I just don't want to be alone anymore." Lott buried his face into the sheets. A hand rested gently on his head.

"You're not alone. Not as long as you have people around you who love you."

La Payasa never wanted to be her mother. Her mom was unable to survive without a man. It was that simple. Born in Mexico, her mom was married three times. Each time a husband left or died, she hooked up with another one within months. Her life was its own prison, trapped by being functionally illiterate with her third-grade education and thus captive to the whims of her men. Her third husband moved to Indianapolis to find factory work. Her whole life revolved around pleasing him. Her long hair was worn in a bun, the way he liked it. She spent her days cooking, cleaning, and taking care of the children, the way he envisioned a good wife should be. There was little of her mother in her own life.

La Payasa was not much different from her mom, moving from Black to King, her life defined by what others wanted of her and fitting in with their wants. Following their dreams and not her own. Yet she stood in the room at King's bedside as if having been granted an audience. Percy and Lott she knew. Not the girl. And not the one who, while lying down in a hospital bed, commanded the entire room.

"You're with Black and his crew," King said.

"I know the story that's been written about me." La Payasa ignored the weight of eyes in the room and focused on King. He had a way about him, like Black. He could draw you in. Unlike Black, there was a gentleness behind that hard exterior. A burning sense of caring. "But what if I'm actually one of the good guys?"

"You asking or telling?"

"Both, I think."

"What about Black? Aren't you helping him?"

"I'm hoping to help everyone."

King recognized that air about her: damaged but resilient. She reminded him of Lady G. "Nobody does it alone. Black and brown, we have a lot in common. And we need a place we all make together. Bring folks together in a positive way."

"I don't know, hese."

"You know what?" King turned to all of them. "I believe that Dred has united enough of the gangs and controls enough of the drug flow in this city to open the flood gates. To sink the streets, our streets, to lows and depravity and desperation we've never known. I believe the police are powerless because they can't build a case against someone they barely know. They're too busy cleaning up the messes left by the front lines of this war to get near him.

"Well, the police aren't in this alone. This is our community. These are our streets. Those are our brothers and sisters and children shedding their blood and losing their lives out there. Day after day in senseless waste. We're always fighting the same fight.

"This struggle has been going on forever. The players may change, the philosophies may differ, but there would always be war. On the one side you have the warlord, simple in his own way, who was always chasing that dollar no matter what the cost, and would use and climb over anyone he could to amass power. On the other side, you had the idealistic church wanting everyone to believe the same things and follow the same rules. You'd think they were on opposite sides but they were two sides of the same coin. Neither was as all good or all evil, as all right or all wrong, as the other side would make them out to be. In fact, both would do both good and terrible things to get what they wanted.

"And I'm *tired*.

"Tired of sitting on the sidelines. Tired of waiting for someone else to come along to solve our problem. Tired of not caring. Running around out here, asking folks to care, to look out for one another. That ain't snitching, that's caring.

"Most days we are gray people leading gray lives. We keep our heads down and mind our own, hoping things will work out. We keep on keeping on. Shadows in a world of black and white, of light and dark, waiting out a war and hoping that we don't get caught in the cross-fire.

"But we live in the crossfire.

"Every once in a while, we're faced with a decision. An opportunity. The chance to do something right, something we don't have to question or wonder about. Something we know is true." King turned to Lady G, then faced them again. "When we find what's true, we hold on to it. We're moved by it. And we act on it. This is one of those times. Some might say it'd be better to get out of their way and let Dred and the police scuffle it out. But this is our community, too. There comes a point, maybe when one side goes all in to wipe out the other, when you can't stand on the sidelines anymore. You have to pick a side. We will take this war to Dred and we will end it. Our brothers and sisters are out here, lost and misguided. But they're not beyond hope. They're not beyond redemption.

"Do you know how I've always thought of you? As knights. Knight means servant, and to be a leader you must serve. Sometimes we've forgotten that. Lost our way. I know I have. Faithful service is not always acknowledged. And you aren't a good knight until you've been tested. You've all been tested. Each of you in your own way. Now it's time to serve our people one more time."

They burst into applause, they couldn't help them-selves. King stirred something in them. They dared to hope. They remembered what they could be. The nurse burst in to shoo them back in the hallway. Pastor Winburn followed her, his "clergy" identification badge pinned to his suit jacket. He waited until the nurse finished her duties, nodding politely to her as she left.

"You have your serious face on. What happened?" King asked.

"King, there's something I got to tell you. It's about Prez."

CHAPTER SEVENTEEN

King slouched over his knees. The pain in his side and neck faded into afterthoughts as he reached over toward his clothes. The ones he was brought in with had to be cut from him. Pastor Winburn had brought a change of clothes upon hearing King had awoken.

"What are you doing?" Pastor Winburn handed him his clothes.

"I need to see the body."

"You know I can't let you do that, King. Family only."

"I'm the closest thing to kin that boy's got."

"Still…"

"Do me this solid."

A black T-shirt with the word "Resistance" across the top. Underneath were portraits of his heroes. Sojourner Truth. Marcus Garvey. Angela Davis. John Carlos and Tommie Smith. Rosa Parks. Frederick Douglass. Harriet Tubman. Malcolm X. Dr Martin Luther King Jr. The shirt stretched over his muscular frame, showing off his thick arms. Pastor Winburn took the liberty of purchasing a new pair of black Chuck Taylors to replace his blood-splattered set.

Taking tentative steps, King walked slowly down the hall, his legs still getting used to being upright. He slung his leather coat over his arms in front of him, following Pastor Winburn as if a bereaved relative.

The cold room had a blue tint to it. A single body on a metal table, a sheet drawn over it. The medical examiner, a ghost in blue scrubs, pulled back the sheet. The side of Prez's face reduced to a hole exploded out; even cleaned up, a cavern of flesh and skull ruined his former eye. Scores of bruises riddled his chest. Some strange wounds not made by blade, gun, or fist had the stink of magic about them.

Cantrell worked a double tour, exhausted but undaunted. Rubbing the fatigue from his eyes, he watched the pantomime play out from the next room. King broken up about the boy's death, his meaty hands slammed into his skull as he paced about. His mouth opened in a voiceless cry. The boy was like they all were: born into a family, into a situation, given a lifetime of choices and experiences to shape what he became, takes the path of his life, and then it was over. All that remained were the people left in his wake who mourned him. Lives he touched, for good or for ill. The same ride for everyone. Cantrell gave him a moment after the pastor left before he walked in.

"I don't know what you plan to do or how someone like you carries this. Don't know if you pray, go see your pastor, or go to where you lay your head and plot your comeback."

"Might do them all." King didn't turn at the sound of the detective's voice. Prez stared at him. The hole in his face held a steady gaze and gave voice to all of King's doubts and failings.

"Let us handle it."

"You got any leads?"

"Do you? I know, I know. No snitching." Cantrell threw his hands up as if backing off.

"It ain't that. There's what I know versus what you can prove."

"What do you mean?"

"I know who did it, but can't prove it."

"Give me a name."

"What good's a name going to do you? You can't act on it. Can't get a warrant. It won't provide you any witnesses. I might as well tell you my horoscope for all the good it will do you."

"Every little bit helps."

"You know and I know Dred's behind this. Behind all of this mess. But you're trapped by rules and laws."

"And you're not? King, don't let me find you on the wrong side of some vigilante shit. I *will* come down on you just as hard as I would Dred."

"I know."

King returned to his room. Wayne. Lott. Percy. La Payasa. Lady G. They assembled at his word and waited for him. He paused to take in the scene. Here they were gathered together for the first time in far too long. His knights. Battered. Bruised. Tested. But they'd come out the other side. They weren't many, but they might be enough.

"What's the word?" King asked.

La Payasa stepped forward. "Dred's muscling up.

Taking stock of who he got left." Unadorned, she didn't know how she fit in with this crew. They were family and she was the outsider.

"Making way the hounds of war." Knowing what it was like to be the new person in a tightknit group, King touched her lightly on her arm. His smile welcomed her as an equal.

"Something like that."

"Where?"

"Camlann." La Payasa's expression turned sour, as if she'd eaten some bad cabbage.

"What is it?" King asked.

"It's a place. Site of some new building project or something. But you don't understand. Word was loud on the street."

"Too loud?"

"Yeah, like they want people to know."

"A trap," Wayne said.

"That's what I think," La Payasa agreed.

"Then I'll give him a mouse to spring it," King said.

"King, I don't think that's wise," Wayne said.

"I can't ask you to join me." King turned to the rest of them. "Any of you. But I need to stop this madness."

"Then you'll need this." Lady G removed a bundle from her purse and handed it to King. The weight felt familiar and right as he unwrapped it. Even before he saw it, he knew part of him had returned. A 9mm, gold dragons rearing up along the contrasting black grips. His Caliburn. "I kept it for you."

"Let's do this."

• • • •

Lee's place consisted of a mattress and a box set as the lone furnishings in his bedroom. Plastic Totes held his clothes. Scattered newspaper and leftover Chinese take-out boxes buried the phone. Lee realized it took a particular brand of self-loathing to put himself through this relationship. On the good days, he rationalized that he was in this for the experience. Omarosa was a fine piece of ass and a great lay. And she provided solid intel as a not-quite-on-the-books confidential informant. He wasn't planning on bringing her home to meet his mother. That conversation wouldn't go well: "Hi, Mom. This is Omarosa. She makes her living taking off drug dealers. She may even be a prostitute on the side, but she's hell in the sack. How many grandkids do you want?" It was what it was: itch-scratching. A perfect, walk-away arrangement. By all rights, checking his man card, he shouldn't have any gripes.

But then there were the bad days. The days when he woke up, alone, and had time to think about his life. The days when he suspected he was ultimately without any-one who cared about him. A boss who despised him, a partner who tolerated him, and Omarosa, a woman who expressed nothing but open disdain for him, fucked him as if he were beneath her – all but held her nose while doing him – and if she had two kind words for him, they were never strung together in the same sentence.

Omarosa slowly twirled before him, her hips moving in full controlled circles, each muscle knowing exactly what it was doing. All Lee could do was stand there like a grinning idiot hick – what she often reduced him to – simply happy to be in the same room as her. She gyrated close to him, her ass rubbing against his crotch and then pulling away. He reached out to grasp her, but she eluded him, while staying on beat to the music. She danced close again. He raised his hands, but stopped short, fearing she might abandon him again. With a tantalizing slowness, she peeled his shirt off of him, lifting it over his now-raised arms. His thin chest and muscled arms had a wiry strength to them. He thought better of wrapping them around her.

"How come we never go to your place?" Lee asked.

"Because I don't want you to know where I live." Omarosa took a half-step back. "What's the matter, too on point? Did I hurt your feelings?"

"Would you care if you did?"

"Would you want me to? Besides, you wouldn't survive in my world."

"I'm up to my shitter in your world now."

"Lovely. Anyway, despite where you think you are, you're not. You couldn't... swim in the waters I do." It was said that when the angels fell, the ones who fell on land became fairies and the ones who fell into the sea became selkies.

"I'm a pretty good swimmer."

"Not that good."

"Why you gotta be that way?"

"You need to know, all things come to an end."

"Meaning?"

"Meaning this is our last time together."

"Just like that?"

"How did you think it was going to end?"

"I..."

Omarosa pressed a lone finger against his lips. "It ends the way all stories do. With bloodshed. And anger. And pain."

"What are you talking about?"

"There's a thing tonight."

"What sort of thing?"

"King. Dred. Maybe the Mexicans."

"Fucking beaners in the mix? Where?"

"Camlann. The new site."

"Over by the zoo."

"Yeah."

"How are you mixed up in this?"

"Do you really want to know? Have you ever? Or would you rather do what you came to do?"

He knew much more than he let on. He could be a clever "cracker-ass cop" that way. It wasn't as if she were his only ear to the streets. He heard the whispers of the street thief called Omarosa. Talked about like she was a legend. By the time he realized he was sleeping with her, there was no way to bring her in and explain away that he'd been banging her for months. "When?"

"Everything will be over in the morning. One way or another, the story ends tonight."

"Shit, Omarosa…"

"You've got a decision to make. I won't be back again. There's too much blood on my hands. It may take decades to wash clean."

"Blood?"

"Tick tock. Me or the crews. You can't have both."

"Damn it, Omarosa. I ought to take you in."

"You could try."

A steeliness hardened in her voice. He'd heard it before though she attempted to keep it hidden beneath the
velvety lilt of her voice and honeyed measure of words.
But it was always there, sharp as a sword's edge. Just
once he wanted to test her. To take her full measure. His
weapon lay on his jacket in the chair, never far from
him, especially when he was with her. Just once. Not
that he knew what he'd do with her. Shit. Maybe
Cantrell would know. He couldn't let her walk away.
Not like this. He wanted to taste her one more time. Just
once. He turned from her and scooped up his gun in the
same movement.

When he turned back around, she was gone.

"Camlann," Lee said, hoping she could still hear him.
"I'll see you there."

Rain drizzled, splattering on the oily surface of the street.
They were within eyeshot of the Indianapolis Zoo, its
trees lit with blue lights. Wayne turned the van off of
Washington Street onto a little used drive under the
bridge along the White River Parkway. The White River
itself created a zone of relative peace, separating one
world from the next. A nexus point, a natural ley line as
Merle had once explained to them. The overcast sky
drove a miserable chill into their bones. A mural decorated the wall, in a faux children's painted style. Blue,
pink, and violet stick figures held hands while walking
along grassy knolls toward a crude cityscape. On the
other side, similarly painted rainbow-colored figures
hung outside the windows of a school bus under a pic-
turesque blue sky lit by a bold yellow sun.

The abutment of the bridge formed a concrete shelf littered with bags of trash and Styrofoam cups and plastic bottles mixed among the scattered leaves. The number 1516 etched into the concrete had eroded to the point where it read more like ISIS. The words "eat you good" had been spray-painted higher up along the embankment. And Wayne thought about trolls as a train rumbled above them.

Overgrown bushes obscured the trail beside the bridge, a leaf-strewn path of brown and yellow. Little more than ragged scruff known mostly to those who lived in the other Indianapolis. Away from the gleaming buildings of downtown and the bright light of tourist attractions. The invisible Indianapolis. Beneath bridges. Under the city. In abandoned lots. A wire fence provided an illusion of security, but the links on one side had been severed and it was drawn back as easily as a curtain. They entered a mini wilderness of brown grass, scattered bushes, and vine-choked trees. They weaved their way between the trees until the path opened up into a field. Then they came to a second ley line as the railroad tracks created a buffer, cutting off the outside world from the secret things kids enjoyed exploring and fantasizing about. Magical things. A world which made perfect sense to those still able to wonder and dream. This site was well chosen. Secluded. Cut off. The city fathers planned on dumping low-cost housing according to the Not In My Back Yard crowd. For Dred, it was an abandoned warehouse of stored magic.

A dull thud reverberated as Percy beat the train track with a tree branch with each step. Part of him wanted

Had and Kay with them, but he knew they were better off with Big Momma. Safe. Despite how they had proved themselves, this was no place for so young a kid.

Plus, it was a school night.

In the distance, a train whistle blew as if conjured by force of will.

Standing at the convergence of the footpath and the train tracks, King stopped. A sea of rocks separated one stretch of woods from the more foreboding underbrush. He scoured the trees, the skyline, the railway. He brushed his forehead with the side of his hand, wiping away the sweat, and closed his eyes.

"Now's probably not the best time to catch a nap," Merle said.

"Merle." King's heart rejoiced at the familiar voice. "Are you a dream?"

"I've been called that."

"I've been tormented by dreams before." The dreams of he and his people were too coincidental. They harried their nerves and frayed their temperaments. His whole group was on edge for months. During that time, King had joined forces with Dred; Lott and Lady G... It was yet another thing King needed to pay Dred back for.

"Torment is being trapped in a barrel of eels without any soap."

"You're crazy."

"As are you. The story's about to come full circle."

"I can't tell anyone else, but I'm scared, Merle," King said. "They're all looking to me as if I know what I'm doing."

"You'd be a fool not to be scared. You don't really have much of a plan beyond marching in there and saying 'I'm King. Boo!'"

"I didn't have my wise counsel during the planning meeting," King said. "Besides, I got a few surprises left in me."

"Moving on in the face of fear, fighting for what's right, that is the definition of bravery." Merle took King's hand, first as insubstantial as a breeze, then solid as remembered flesh. "It's your cup. Drink its fill and don't be afraid."

King opened his eyes. Merle wasn't there. Lady G struggled on the slate-gray rocks. Her ankle gave out beneath her, but Lott caught her before she fell. Regaining her balance, she absent-mindedly reached for his hand. He took hers without reassurance. Whatever antsy dance stirred in Lott stilled at her touch. She quelled his disconnect.

There was no unhappiness in King. It was their life. She deserved the best. Someone stable, nice, who treats her well. Someone with a future.

"Hawk's out." Wayne broke the tension. "Looks like a storm's moving in."

"'Bout time. Been building for a long time," King said.

"What's the plan?"

"This is it." King gathered them around him. Lott, his right hand. Lady G, his heart. Wayne, his conscience. Percy, his faith. He could walk into Hell knowing they had his back.

"What? We show up," Wayne said. "Ain't but five of us. Ain't like we leading an army."

"Look, Dred's called for a summit meeting. He needed to pull together his whole crew to see what he was working with. It's all his top people plus his crew. They got numbers."

"What we got?" Lott asked.

"Five cold, wet fools," Wayne said.

"Six." A voice came from the underbrush. Lott and Wayne flanked King, ready for an attack. Her hand pulled back the branches, allowing Tristan to come into full view. "If you don't mind the company."

"Where you come from?" Wayne asked.

"Been here waiting. Saw you pull up."

"Waiting for what?" Wayne asked.

"Waiting to figure out my next play."

"What'd you decide?"

"Didn't. You all pulled up. You decided for me." Tristan came alongside them. "Time comes, a person's got to stand tall and do right."

"Way I figure it, we just need to take out Dred."

"Take out?" Tristan gestured a throat-slash.

"No, that crosses a line. But if he can be humbled before his people... challenge him for the right to lead..."

"You ain't exactly one hundred percent there, chief. Why not let Lott? Or Wayne?"

"Because it's my fight."

King no longer knew what was normal. In his gut, he knew exactly what he was doing, but had little idea why he was doing it. Things just needed to play out. All he needed to do was reach Dred, the rest would take care of itself.

At first glance, the greenery formed a smooth, thick

grove, fairly impenetrable to incursion. Wayne formed a visor with his hand for closer scrutiny. A section of the undergrowth seemed to dimple. As he neared it the strange play of shadows revealed an entrance. He had traveled this way before. Once, with Outreach Inc. He suspected that the camp wasn't a live camp but a party squat. Towels and random pairs of shorts buried in the mud marked the path. He wasn't but a few meters in before brambles and burrs covered him. An action figure, Pyro – a villain of the X-Men – dangled from a tree. Two chairs – a burgundy car bench from the rear seat of a car and a green vinyl La-Z-Boy – were arranged around a set of bookshelves. Like cupboards, the shelves kept clothes, candles, flashlight with a hand crank, and a set of toiletries from a more recent Outreach Inc. visit. A Bible rested on top of all of it. Off to the side, milk crates with toilet seat covers squatted over holes in the ground. Empty bottles of Cobra, Magnum 40, and Miller Lite littered the camp.

"It's like a tower of Babel of beer up in this piece," Wayne said. "Is it just me or is naming your beer 'Magnum' overcompensating?"

The rain increased. The dampness of his clothes irritated Wayne as much as the itch from the burrs, but he tried to keep a good humor about things. He stepped over half-filled bags of trash. The haunted echo of a train whistle blew in the distance. Everyone kept moving in a morose silence, except for the thick crunch of trodden gravel. Twigs snapped, leaves crunched underfoot, branches cracked with commotion as they skulked through the woods. These were city folk, not woodmen.

A thin sheen of sweat dappled his brow despite the cooler temperature. One person through the woods was bad enough, but a half-dozen of them wasn't sneaking up on anyone even half-paying attention. Weeds choked off grass, which only grew in spurts and rough patches to begin with. Thickets like knots of foliage. King adjusted his pace so they could more silently make their way through the woods. A grumble of thunder pealed though the skies, refusing to fully open up.

"Down there." King drew aside the intervening growth. Through the barrier of foliage, he pointed toward a swift-flowing stream following a steep hillside of gold, yellow, and brown leaves. A long, secluded drive made worse by the muddy trail as the rain picked up to obliterate their view.

"This is their organizational meeting?"

"A ghetto pep rally," Wayne said.

"Quit playing," King said. "We can make our way closer to hear what's going on and see where we can make our move."

Camlann had the feel of refugee camp, with three-quarters of its occupancy slated to go as low-income housing, people jockeying for position on the waiting list, each desperate to secure their own welfare, at the expense of neighbors. The Camlann experiment was what spurred talk of the threat to raze Breton Court. After the mysterious – though most suspected arson – fire burned the original Camlann to the ground, it dislocated many homeless squatters. City officials got it in their heads to construct low-income/transitional housing. Unfortunately, no communities wanted such a project in their neighborhood. Tenants worked together or crawled over each other, community leaders looked out for themselves. So the city designated an area near an industrial park as the new potential site. As the grandest of messes, it began with good intentions. The Camlann project was a bureaucratic mess. The city declared eminent domain. Thus the era of tenement housing and abandoned property left to rot ended with a whimper. A new era began, one of re-gentrification, locals pushed out by stingy agencies; inspectors in on the hustle; grant money thrown around; all while media and politicians promised a new day and new opportunities.

The abandoned construction site teemed with a few dozen hard-eyed thugs. Many played around, whooping and yelling. Dred was the last to arrive, cutting through the heart of the throng. Doling out fist pounds and shoulder bumps like a politician working the crowd. A few grumbled that was how they saw him, more politico than soldier. But they were hushed down by the reality of a lot of new vacancies having opened up at the top of their clique.

Dred was the undisputed general, their commander-in-chief. His troops would die for their colors, their crew, little more than urban kamikazes. Not caring if they lived or died, they were one-person suicide bombers. All he had to do was rally them, give them vision, promise money, and háve a plan. He could've been a CEO or a politician with his skill set. Instead, he squandered it in blood feuds and magic.

"We ride together, we die together," Dred yelled, calling his meeting to order.

"Look around. See how they do us? They will build new projects to house us and tuck us out of the way so that we ain't inconveniencing anybody by struggling to survive. I don't know about you, but I needs to get mine. I ain't going to be satisfied with hand-outs, told what I can have and when I've had too much. We grew up in this shit. Our cousins, our uncles, our brothers... it's what we do. I'd say our daddies, but fuck 'em. Don't know what they do."

The line got laughs, which was sad to him in some ways. A little too on point.

"So we do this, swim in this shit, every day. Now, some motherfuckers just get to tread water. I ain't about that. We ain't about that. You feel me? If we gonna do this, then we do this for real. Playtime's over. This shit's about to get deep. And ain't no one gonna get in our way. Not the Mexicans. Not the police. Not King."

As King surveyed the area, a faint rustle of leaves behind him warned him. He side-stepped at the last moment, barely avoiding the charge of a shadow wraith.

"Look out!" King yelled.

The creatures sprang up from all around, tendrils of shadow lashing out, creeping along the ground like snakes erupting to wrap around them. The creatures rose out of each person's shadow. Lott punched his shadow self, his blows connecting with something solid. The creature slithered a step back, only then did Lott realize that it emanated from his feet. The creature looped itself around his feet, tripping him up, then poured on him once his legs were taken out from him.

Lady G's eyes widened in surprise then sprinted back the way she came. Another train whistle sounded, drowning out the sound of her footfalls through the brush. Branches slapped her in the face as she veered from the path directly through the copse of trees. She chanced a glance backward. Her shadow elongated, stretched further back like a rubber band caught on something. The line of the woods was only a few more steps away. The train whistle blew again, its rumble vibrating the ground beneath her. When she burst through the tree line, the train rumbled along the track, a slow-moving processional of cars stretching back as far as she could see. The train's engine was almost at the same point where she was, but she thought she might be able to beat the train, crossing the tracks in time to get to the other side.

She broke into a sprint, her eyes fixed on the engine of the train. A warning whistle sounded again, imploring her not to race it. The inexorable grind of the wheels along the track wasn't slowing down for anything. She bolted the rush of air from the train catching up with her. Her arms pumped furiously. Her chest tightened. Only a few more steps and she might be able to make it. Her foot hit a patch of rocks that slipped from under her. Twisting her ankle, she tumbled to the ground, careening toward the tracks, but with slowing momentum. She came to a stop five feet from the tracks. The train cutting her off, she turned in time to see her shadow beast leap upon her.

Tristan slashed at them with her blades, but for every rent shadow, two others sprang up to replace it. Thick fingers gripped Percy's head as if attempting to separate him from his shoulders. The dark wraith hovered over him. Likewise another coiled itself around Wayne like an anaconda squeezing the life out of him. He couldn't work his hands free enough to grip the obsidian creature properly.

King's beast launched itself at him with maniacal fury.

King forced his hands into a defensive position, waiting to swing at the encroaching cast of shadows. He launched himself with reckless abandon, thrown off balance by his own attacks. Dizzy from pain and blood loss. The creature formed a mallet with its fists and pummeled King. Part of him wanted to curl into a ball as Dred's crew gathered around to watch the blood sport for their entertainment. They called for his death. He would show them how he would go out. His hand stretched, reaching out for the hilt of his Caliburn. His fingers scrabbled hungrily for it once they found purchase. He worked the gun into his hand and a renewed vigor filled him. The endless chorus of the poor and the powerless cried for his blood until a tiny voice cut through the din.

"Daddy?"

The crowd fell silent and parted as Dred escorted a little girl forward.

"Nakia?" King asked. Then the darkness overwhelmed him.

Lee parked in the Indianapolis Zoo and waited as he decided whether or not to call for backup. In his patrol car, alone. The situation seemed too large. He didn't know what was out there. What awaited him. The last time he was caught up in a situation like this was with the mad man, Green. Lee still remembered him lumbering toward him, no longer human-looking. A mass of flesh and branches, he carried a human head which it had just severed. It was just him. Scared. Not just fresh-out-of-the-academy scared, but down-to-his-core terrified. He might die tonight. Omarosa all but said she wasn't coming back. So he had to make a choice: to go on being scared (in which case he needed to be off the streets or quit); or to get over his fear (in which case he needed to get out of his car and risk getting his ass handed to him).

Lee picked up the radio. He wanted every available unit.

Like bundled packages, King, Percy, Lady G, and Lott were brought to the center of the Camlann site and deposited.

"You can give me that thousand-yard all day, King. I ain't afraid of nobody's stare. You may want to look around. These boys here, my crew, would just as soon shoot you if you looked at them funny."

"Nakia, you okay, baby?"

"She's fine, King. Just insurance."

"Hiding behind a little girl? That how your crew does it? A bunch of badasses against a little girl."

"You're going to want to keep a civil tongue, King. Or else I'll hand her over to a very special babysitter. You've heard of his handiwork with Lyonessa."

Noles stepped forward, his hair flat on his head and cut with a severity along his forehead. His face meticulously clean-shaven except for the razor-thin goatee around his mouth and the growth of a beard only over his Adam's apple. A dress shirt hung loose on his frame, making him appear skinnier than he was. Only one half of his shirt was tucked into jeans. His eyes studied her in that way. They roamed and lingered.

Noles ran his large hand across the front of her pants while holding her firmly. She screamed, scared and confused, not understanding anything that was happening to her. Noles cried out in imitation of her, a mad howl in a falsetto voice. And laughed.

"Don't do this. It's me you want."

King was powerless to protect his princess. He pulled and jerked with all of his strength but was held firm. Fingers gripped tighter into his arms, nails driving into him. Jolts of fresh pain as they punched him in the side for struggling.

"Daddy!" Nakia screamed, her wide eyes pleading.

King begged for the strength to free himself, to help his little girl. His mind raced for any plan, mad or ingenious. Tears blazed hot trails down his face, his vision blurring. He slumped in his shackles, deflating. Beaten.

"That's enough, Noles. I just wanted King's mind focused so we could have a little chat."

"You know what your problem is?" Dred lowered on his haunches to get level with King. "You give a fuck when no one's paying you to give a fuck. You speak of peace. We aren't men of peace. Neither of us. Don't delude yourself. You earn peace at the point of a gat every bit the same way I do. You want to hit me, go ahead." Dred waved King's Caliburn in front of him. He reached into his dip to retrieve another. He held them both up, allowing the light to reflect from them. "A matching set. The way they were meant to be. You settle conflict the same way I do, except with hypocrisy. You think you're different. You try to be nice, normal. But there's a part of you that will never be that guy. Look at you. You're a façade. Your whole look is designed for everyone else. 'Look, but don't touch. Don't approach. Don't get close.' Like me. So desperate for folks to love you, yet so incapable of feeling love. You are easier to manipulate. You see yourself as their leader. Their pastor. Their shepherd. But at your core, you're still the insecure little boy you always were. Not sure of yourself. Not sure of your decisions. You're weak and that weakness can be exploited."

King's eyes bugged like disjointed marbles. His fists clenched. His chest high as his whole body shook with rage. With a snarl King turned and spat at Dred's feet.

"This is what I wanted," Dred said. "My birthright. The two reunited, the way Luther used to have them. A pair, never meant to be separated."

"Like us?" King asked. "You want me to join you?"

"We both know that would never happen. I'll make this simpler for you. All you have to do is give up and leave. You see, Indianapolis is all I know. Like you, I was born and raised here. These streets pump through my veins. So I can't leave. Nor do I really expect you to. "

King's chest tightened and his body trembled. Fear welled up in the back of his throat, and it had a coppery aftertaste. Grabbed by the forearm, shadow tendrils dragged him to the center of the room. He peered into the creatures' night eyes. He imagined his end might come like this. Surrounded by thugs, some armed with chains or bats or knives but mostly guns. He knew that to take a stand against them might end with his death. Execution.

"The storm is passing," he muttered. The rain fell lightly upon his shadowy form, as if attempting to cleanse him of the darkness of the night. He marveled at how far he had come, how much he'd learned in so short a time. Dred strode with determination and power. The Egbo Society controlled the gangs, the drugs, the money in Indianapolis, served at the pleasure of the Board of Directors and they to the Hierarchy. Not content to remain a lieutenant or a captain, Dred vied to get to the Board. For as long as he could remember, his ambition drove him to get the power and reign as the supreme power in the Egbo Society. Already he was one of the Ndibu, the high order of the Egbo Society. Soon he would have it all. Hands skeletal and gnarled, he uttered an incantation, a low whisper. Shadows danced about like ghostly dark flames. They lit along his body, wisps of black fire. He writhed in pain.

Dred had prepared a sacred place, carved out by his ritual. His pulse quickened. He lit a lone candle, and with its bare luminance, prepared the necessary instruments. Adorning the wall of the incomplete building were a legion of clay statues and wooden figurines, wrapped in twine, of various sizes, depicting personages of an earlier time. Three drums laid in wait next to the sacred vessels. Dred quickly rose and poured the water from the first vessel on his feet and then in a path toward them. He walked the water path to the rear, where he raised a small pot full of ashes. With them, Dred etched symbols along the beams.

Dred lowered his robe to his waist. Two yellow rings circled each breast. Below them, a white ring stamped his middle. Underneath it, two more yellow rings, forming a square on his chest. His back had the same pattern emblazoned on him, with the color scheme reversed. Alternating yellow and white stripes ornamented each arm.

Dred began to speak, his face falling into its shadows. "Ours is the house without walls. We call upon Obassi to guide and protect us. Okum ngbe ommobik ejennum ngimm, akiko ye ajakk nga ka ejenn nyamm."

The creatures' features morphed, becoming ebon sculptures of people he was unable to save or protect. Michelle Davis. Parker Griffin. Tavon. Rellik. Rok. Iz. Baylon. Prez.

Nakia.

No one thought to ask the question "Where's Baylon?" Not Dred. Not King. Not the knights. Not any of Dred's crew. Truth be told, no one cared. Except for one person. Omarosa cared where Baylon was. She cut through the underbrush like a deadly wraith. Snuck around the concrete debris, the spires of discarded rebar, the piles of brick, the mounds of gravel, with the ease of a lioness on the prowl. And she caught his scent, not too difficult to do with him smelling of graveside rot. A spark of interest flickered in Omarosa's eyes. He wouldn't be like any of the usual level of street trash she dealt with. However, his petty magic – parlor tricks, really – while they might have worked against other folks, she was of the fey. Her heightened hearing matched her heightened sight. She glided smoothly over the packed dirt, waiting for a telltale blunder or charge. Wisely, he didn't move. She turned her back. Not only was he upwind, the air thick with his stink of sweat and fear, his jackrabbit heart thundered in her ears.

His jogging suit reduced to a farm of mildew. His hair disheveled, whorls of knots. His complexion ashy, an ashiness that ran down to his soul. He was gone long before Dred had cast his spell which used Baylon's vitality to cure his paralysis, leaving Baylon little more than a shuffling husk. It wasn't the spell which broke him, it was the decision to use him for the spell. The betrayal. They were like brothers, Baylon had told himself. Dred came to him, chose him, found him, and said come do this thing with me. Together, they assembled the crew. Together, they ran things. Then King returned to the scene. It was like Dred forgot about Baylon and became obsessed with King. It wasn't as if Baylon wanted Dred to choose him over King, he just wanted to matter. Not be used and discarded.

"I'm surprised you're not standing with your boy," Omarosa said.

"I'm here. Where I always am. In his shadow. Supporting him as necessary." He continued to watch the ceremony.

"I'll never get you, B. Here Dred does you like he did, and you still here. That's some serious co-dependent shit right there. You're like a faithful puppy that no matter how's he's kicked, he comes right back to nip at his master's heels."

"Even the most faithful dog," Baylon turned to her, "can get kicked one time too many and not return home. Or if he do, it's to tear down the home from the inside to remind the master what all he's capable of doing."

"That's the difference between me and Dred. I got a dog and it comes home and starts chewing up my furniture, I just go ahead and put him down."

Omarosa trained her sawed-off shotgun on him.

"You all about business. I ain't holding, so this must be personal."

"You killed my brother."

"Who?"

"Colvin."

Baylon remembered.

The mad half-fey gestured furiously, his hand danced about. The occasional green gleam sparked, but dissipated as if shorted out. King strode toward him with furious intent. Colvin locked eyes on him, so focused he did not hear the click of a blade springing to life behind him.

Baylon fought for his throat, but Colvin twisted out of the way at the last instant. Not to be denied his opportunity, Baylon arced the blade again and buried the knife up to its hilt into the fey's belly. He turned the blade then drove it up, spilling his insides. Eyes splayed open in shock, his mouth agape as if pain was an entirely new sensation which caught him short, Colvin dropped to his knees.

"So, he was your kin. He needed to be put down."

"I don't argue that. He was of the land and I am of the sea. And I hated him with that special fury reserved for siblings. You understand the betrayal of a brother."

"Me and Dred, we were like brothers."

"But Colvin was still of the fey. He deserved to be taken down by someone worthy of him. Not some lap dog. No offense."

"None taken." Baylon began to move his hand. Omarosa checked him with a nod of the barrel. With a slow and deliberate motion, he reached into his pocket. He withdrew the ring Colvin had given Garlan. "I suppose you'll want this back."

Baylon rushed her. The shock of her recognizing Colvin's ring threw off the timing of her attack. Baylon possessed a speed that belied his condition. Adrenaline and the need for vengeance choked Omarosa, clouding her assassin's instinct. She staggered into his fist. It spun her around and his wizened arms wrapped around her. They pinned her arms to her side with her unable to find purchase. Face to face with him, she stared into his eyes. Cold, dead things without a hint of recognition.

Anticipating that she was about to head butt him, Baylon slammed her into the ground, allowing his full weight to smash into her back when they landed. He shuffled out of the way, landing a fierce kick to her side. A rib cracked. He brought his fist down, a hammer blow to her mouth. Pain wracked her. White-hot tendrils of pain shot up her neck into her skull.

She regained her footing, then entangled his legs with hers. Omarosa clocked Baylon in the face. She crouched with a feline grace, her hands a blur of stiff finger strikes. Baylon deflected some of them, but with his sluggish movements, he appeared to think about each blow, choosing to defend himself only against every third one. She struck several nerve clusters along his arm. His left arm hung at his side, useless. Her leg snapped forward, landing first in his side, then at his head. That was it. Half-kneeling, Baylon was already defeated, even if his body hadn't fully accepted it. Omarosa retrieved her shotgun.

"Dred didn't deserve you," she said.

"That's what was so sad. I knew he didn't and I served him anyway."

The shotgun at the ready, she squeezed the trigger.

"The game doesn't have to be played this way. So many bodies. So many lives ruined. You're destroying our community."

"Acceptable losses. Collateral casualties. You are a weak king making grown-up decisions. Your choices can end lives. You are arrogant and unworthy. You lack the strengths, the will, to use power. You spent a lifetime repressing your emotions, thinking that was the best way to act. All you did was button it all away, let it eat at you from the inside, spilling out in ways you couldn't control. You should give yourself permission to hate. It's cathartic. Freeing. Energizing. It can give your life fuel and passion. You've got enough hate for both of us. I'm just sad. This whole place makes me just... sad."

Dred addressed his assembled crew. He wanted them to witness King's absolute humiliation and know that it came by Dred's hands alone. "The crown is not for dreamers or idealists. Artists nor politicians. But men of steel. Men don't want unity. They want leaders. People who know how to use power. You are a weak king. A weak king knows nothing of power and how to use it. If you want to be king, sometimes you have to be willing to take what's yours."

Dred swung a haymaker right to King's jaw, the blow rattling his head. The rush hit him like a junkie sending a load home. It got his head up. Dred threw another punch, hitting him on the other side of the face. The beating got to feeling good to him. With his right, he hooked King a few times to the kidneys then mirrored the attack with his left. King looked over to Nakia and silently took the beating.

"Do you think you're some hero, King?"

"No, I don't," he whispered.

"You lie. To me, if not to yourself."

"Not anymore. I know what it's like to be caught up in your pain, your hate, your vengeance. It blinds you. Gets in your head so deep you can't think straight. You lose track of who you are."

"Damn you, King." Dred punched him in the eye. This wasn't how it was supposed to go. He never expected King to switch sides and run with him as his second. Nor did he think King would rollover and leave Indianapolis to him. He did, however, want King broken. To have him plead for his life, beg Dred to stop. To turn over his crown before his people and Dred's. Let them all see who the bigger man was. But each blow King took only haggled Dred's nerves.

"What do you think you're showing your people, your daughter right now?"

"That I won't always be here to fight their battles for them. That they have to be willing to fight them for themselves."

The shrill peal of laughter froze everyone to their spots. Dred craned about, trying to determine where the sound came from. Heavy footfalls encroached from the tree line ringing the site. In her full war paint, La Payasa was the first to step out of the dense foliage.

"Smile now, cry later," she cried out.

With a simple application of makeup, she was transformed from an introverted, depressed, lonely, suicidal young girl into La Payasa: an extroverted, quick-witted and funny, sought out, welcomed figure who was powerful, both listened to and respected. The blood rushed to her skin as she led her shirtless cholos into battle. The entire scene devolved into utter chaos. The addition of the cholos added to the pandemonia. Those few with guns couldn't shoot: between the night and the close press of bodies, there were no clear shots.

They weren't alone.

Pastor Winburn led a dozen of the Breton Court residents into the fray. Barbers, delivery men, teachers, they rallied behind Pastor Winburn and represent for their community. They weren't there to fight, but they were there to stand tall and let people know they weren't going to be packed out of their own neighborhood.

Wayne held a man in a headlock, trying to keep him from hurting anyone. All he could think about was how he had officially entered a gray area when it came to client interaction and dreaded the idea of having to do the paperwork at Outreach Inc. on this encounter.

Lott evaded the initial volley of punches. Noles' fist struck like a warhammer. Through a dew of sweat, Lott gripped his bat with two hands against the downward stroke. The force of the collision reverberated through the handle. Lott kicked him in his undefended mid-section, then spun the handle about, connecting with the man's jaw. He made sure he stayed down before he moved on. A breathless love threatened to sweep him up in its intensity and bent him into fury.

Tristan, La Payasa, and Percy dove into the rest of the crew. Punching at the air, swinging just to be swinging, hoping to clock someone. Spinning his arms, kind of keeping his guard up, ready to jab at any near target. A cloud of dust was caught in the moonlight, like ground fog, kicked up as they skirmished. Bringing a fist down, but having left his feet to deliver the blow, there was no power to it. Jerked out of the way of the wide arc of the bat's swing. Heavy thwack to his body as he was hit with a bat when he connected the next time.

Tristan followed through with a slashing movement, driving several of her attackers to La Payasa. Planting her heel to the back of his knee, she dropped him. She reeled backward, dodging the jabs of another boy, her slight figure dancing about, easily evading him before wandering back within range to lay him out with a couple of punches.

Lady G gagged on the taste of soot. Gasping for breath, she woke to the smell of smoke. Fire ate through walls. Flames blazed up around her. She grabbed handfuls of air, fought the urge to drift into it, to drop her hands and run into it. The layers of clothes with which she wrapped herself: a T-shirt featuring a panther wrapped by a cobra under a grimy, faded blue hoodie, under a jacket that had seen better days. No matter the temperature, she carefully selected her wardrobe in order to hide her shape. She hooded her eyes. Lady G made her way to Nakia. Pepper spray in one hand, the other clutched after the girl.

"You're safe, baby. I won't let anyone hurt you."

"Are you a friend of my dad's?" Nakia asked.

"I am," Lady G said.

"You're pretty."

Police sirens wailed. Dred's crew scattered, running wild through the mini-woods. The copse of trees offered few hiding places as uniformed officers swooped in. A police helicopter circled above them. Cantrell and Lee, trailed by a film crew, led the officers into the melee.

As soon as the chaos erupted, King threw himself into Dred. The Caliburns flew free. King quickly scrambled for the nearest one. Dred slammed into a girder then hunted for the other gun. King whirred and began blasting at the shadow creatures. His bullets tore through them, a stream of light trailing in their trajectory. With a grotesque twist of their mouths, the wispy substance dissipated like fog in the morning sun against the cleaving magic of the Caliburn. The ebon vapor tendrils faded into nothingness. Dred's face contorted into a mask of hatred and madness, though his eyes remained those of a little boy lost. He spied the Caliburn and dove after it, finding cover behind a pallet of bricks.

"Like I said before, for all your talk, in the end, you settle things the same way we do: with guns and fists," Dred said.

"I know. Most I can hope for is that when the cause is just, God will give me a pass."

"I'm afraid not, King. Luther's blood runs in both of us, my brother. There is a birthright to be claimed. We are Cain and Abel."

Brothers. Things began to make sense to King, but he didn't have time to digest the implications. He pushed the revelation to the side and rushed toward Dred, too close for him to get a clear shot. King used his Caliburn to close in on Dred's wrist, deflecting Dred's shot. The momentum threw him off balance, his gun drawn low.

Grappling in close quarters, Dred raised his leg with the hopes of throwing off King's aim, though King wasn't trying to shoot him. Dred straightened from his crouch after ducking a wild swing from King and slashed his weapon toward King's shoulder. King shifted to the side, blocking the pistol whip, and punched Dred. Twisting aside, bent at the waist, Dred's arms pinwheeled in a pendulum slice, crashing his gun-weighted hand into King's nose. Capitalizing on the lucky blow, Dred threw an uppercut which snapped King's neck backward. King sprawled on his back, dazed but still holding on to his Caliburn. When his eyes focused, Dred had drawn down on him.

"And so it ends."

"It doesn't have to be this way. We can find another way."

"King, the story ends the way all stories end: in pain and death."

"Please, Dred."

The sound of Dred's Caliburn firing caused King to fire.

Lady G screamed. King managed to squeeze off three shots as the bullet punched through his shoulder and took a chunk of flesh out his back. Every action movie he'd ever seen had folks take bullets in the shoulder yet keep moving like they barely nicked themselves shaving. His arm refused to move, his fingers dancing off the edge of his hand to their own accord. Took a while to realize they throbbed to the pulse of his heartbeat. The pain exploded in his brain and all his body could do was drop where he once stood.

The next bullet tore through his belly. He collapsed next to Dred, clutching his belly with his good arm. Dred's eyes stared at him, vacant and glassy, accusatory to the end.

Lady G ran to King. She stopped short when she saw how much blood there was. His mouth opened and closed. She dropped beside him, testing his hand in her lap. She held his hand, slick with blood, to his stomach, pressing to staunch the blood loss. He seemed so small in her arms. Dirty. Bruised. Not believing she deserved to mourn him, she let her tears run down her cheeks.

Pulling his hand from hers, he brushed her hair from her face. A blood smear scored where he touched her.

"I got you right here." She put their hands on her heart. "I love you. You can believe that."

He knew it was too late for himself. He'd finished what

he'd set out to do. He swallowed blood. His breath came in rapid flurries.

"I'm so tired."

He kissed her hand. "I understand something now. I wish I could start over and do everything right."

"I know. And you will always be in my heart."

A silence settled over the scene. Lott and Wayne wept in their own ways, to themselves. Percy sobbed uncontrollably. Pastor Winburn lowered his head. Omarosa slipped in and out of the scene to retrieve the Caliburns. Lott watched as she disappeared into the waters of the White River with them. She would find her way back to the lake. Paramedics pushed them aside to go through the motions of resuscitation, but it was too late.

King was gone.

EPILOGUE

Stories are made up by people who make them up. The ones that work, endure. It was a time of bloody battles. A time of dark brutality, when life was short. Chivalry. Honor. Courtly love. Loyalty. Courage. Humility. Ideals of an earlier age were not entirely lost.

At first blush, nothing much had changed about Breton Court. The neighborhood waited out the evil, let it run its course like a boxer punching himself out. They survived it. Once again, it survived the city's threat to raze it. The owners of many of the condos within, under pressure from the city and local ministers, sold many of the condos to local residents. There would be no slumlords here. Wayne walked to Big Momma's place to meet Lady G. The dedication was today. The laughter of children filled the air. Percy's little brothers and sisters played on the Slip 'n Slide as Big Momma hustled them indoors in order to get ready.

The Boars walked through the neighborhood with a lawnmower. It was probably stolen, but it was the start of him attempting to make an honest living. Wayne measured progress in baby steps. Sometimes a client smoking weed instead of crack counted as improvement. And cutting lawns definitely was better than working a corner.

"I know you made it to church," Rhianna said.

"I didn't see you," Wayne said.

"Yeah. I'm on sabbatical."

"That's what you call it now."

"Yeah, we'll be back next week. Up in the pulpit."

"You may want to ease into it first. Maybe make it to a pew."

"You know, some people running around here saying King ain't dead..."

"Come on now, he ain't Tupac." Though the thought warmed Wayne. "What do you think he's doing?"

"You need a unicorn that body surfs on rainbows. Along with a mule sidekick that is the keeper of all of the secrets of the universe. We need an enchanted castle with a moat full of Skittles because that's what the rainbow turns into once the unicorn gets home." Rhianna gestured wildly as if painting the picture in the air. "Picture it: King rides the unicorn after consulting with the mule on exactly where he needs to go and what mission to pursue. And no one can eat the Skittles except for the three of them, because everyone else who tries spontaneously combusts."

"Are you high?"

"It's been months and I've done nothing but talk to a one year-old. It's okay to learn to smile again eventually." Rhianna studied the sidewalk. "And I just miss Merle, too."

"Yeah."

"Girl, where you been?"

"Around. Got my GED. Plus I got a little one to look after. Can't be running the streets with you all. I heard you and Lott took over Youth Solidarity."

"Seemed like the right thing to do. The place looks nice. Got some government grant money and everything."

"You and Lott look happy."

"Yeah. Got our own place."

"He'd be happy for you both."

"You think?"

"Well, eventually. Man was still human."

"Yeah."

"Hard to believe it's all over."

"It's never over."

"They got Noles on the Lyonessa thing. Then they started pinning bodies on him. Fool took credit for all kinds of mess including Rok, Prez, and Fathead 'cause the cameras were rolling. You know those detectives thought they hit the lottery."

"Makes sense though. If he going away for doing the little girl, he's gonna want some bodies on him."

"You hear about Tristan? She up, too. Wanted to take the full weight for Mulysa. Walked up and confessed to the police. I told her I would walk beside her through this as much as I could. I spoke on her behalf at the hearing. Special circumstances and all. Asked for leniency, for the system to not give up on her."

"What the judge say?"

"Judge Rolfingsmeyer still gave her five. Three suspended. Plea with a self-defense angle. She almost got off entirely, except most ladies don't defend themselves with Riddick blades."

In a lot of ways, Tristan reminded Wayne of La Payasa. The last thing she said to him was "Don't worry about me. I get by." She never asked for anything. She earned it or did without.

They gathered at King's final resting place at Avalon Cemetery. At the top of a large rolling hill, steep like a green pyramid in the heart of the cemetery. One of the highest natural points in Indianapolis, it was crowned by a lonely mausoleum reminiscent of a ruined abbey. Beside it stood a tower. They called it the Isle of Apples. The image of a tree etched into the glass on the tower was Lott's idea. An eternal flame burned in its heart.

The chairs were reserved for family. Nakia and her mother. Big Momma. Lott. Wayne and Esther. Lady G. Percy. Had. Most of the neighborhood turned out. Folks from the barbershop. The Boars. Even members of the police.

"I was invited to say a few words because I knew King from when he was little. He was like a son to me. A fine boy who grew into a fine young man taken from us too soon." Pastor Winburn's black suit rippled in the slight breeze. He had performed dozens of funerals in his years. None were easy. This dedication was even more difficult for him. He paused and put his fist to his lips. A chorus of "come on now" broke out among the crowd, which strengthened him to continue. "King, like all of us, was called to a royal priesthood. He was an everyday pastor in ritual and routine. A prophet interrupted, who shook up the spiritual lives of all those he came in contact with.

"He wasn't a perfect man, but who among us is? We could all pray 'Lord help me to discover the self-deceived and self-persuaded Pharisee within myself.' Iffen we feel the need to sit in judgment. But I'll tell you what he did right. He took this command seriously: 'whatever you did for one of the least of these brothers and sisters of mine, you did for me.' He walked what he believed. No one was invisible to him. Every life meant something to him. And no one, not even himself, was beyond redemption.

"We believe in an author behind the story. We believe in life everlasting. We believe that relationships are forever. We believe in resurrection. We believe in hope eternal.

"Here lies our once and future King."

There was a young boy in an old man's body and an old woman in a young girl's body who sat in the twilight, locked away in a cave of their own making. No one would ever find them, for they had imprisoned one another. She believed she had him trapped, not realizing she was bound to him. Forever intertwined. They regaled each other with stories, of kings and queens, knights and quests, monsters and fairies. There were adventures and nobility and sadness and death. But that was the point of stories.

"It is finished," Nine said.

"I know."

"The age is almost over."

"The Wheel of Fortuna turns again."

During twilight, the veil between the worlds grew thinnest and they could watch as if sitting on a lattice window gazing out into the world. From their perch they could spy into the world of man or into the world of fairy. A grand vista churned away in silence, with all of the delicate colors of life on resplendent display. In time they would be forgotten. Only the best stories endured. The sun was nearly set and it was time for mysterious creatures to scamper about.

"You're sad."

"Endings always make me sad. The end is goodbye."

The lovely Nine pursed her lips. Not wanting her good mood spoiled, she snapped her fingers. An elf returned with a golden chalice. Sprites handed Merle a chalice. "We have mead, but rather than drink that, a duke of this age gave me a delightful bottle of 1787 Chateau Lafite, which was once the property of Thomas Jefferson."

"You are delightfully full of random," Merle smirked.

"I propose a toast. To family, even in their absence."

A brown and black squirrel, with a gray streak along its back, darted up a tree with drooping branches overlooking King's grave. Resting on its haunches, its head turned left and right on the watch for predatory eyes. It sniffed the air once, twice, then fiddled with an acorn.

And waited.

ACKNOWLEDGMENTS

Writing comes at a cost.

The cost of creation is usually time, as one has to squirrel themselves away in an office, a locked room, a basement in order to get into that mental space, undisturbed, to perform the tasks of their craft. The ones who pay that price first and foremost are the artist and their families. With that in mind, I thank Sally Broaddus, Reese Broaddus, and Malcolm Broaddus, for dinners missed, television not watched together, and balls not tossed. I thank them for their patience, their love, and their understanding.

Because writing comes at a cost, it's important to have friends who support you in such an endeavor.

The ones who understand what you are going through, the stress, the frustration, the solitary and singular madness that comes with nursing at the bosom of one's muse. And they encourage you to carry on. The Indiana Horror Writers, Brian Keene, Wrath James White, Gary Braunbeck, Lucy Snyder, Daniel and Trista Robichaud.

Writing can be a spiritual endeavor. As one, created in God's image, joins with the Creator in order to likewise create. So I thank those who remind me of the spiritual journey I take, my church family at the Crossing; the pastors of Loving Accurately Ministry; and the tireless, selfless workers of Outreach Inc.

Writing can be fun. And it's important to have folks who share those fun times with. Jason Sizemore and Jerry Gordon.

And Chesya Burke. Lord knows, where there's a will, there's a Chesya.

To my family, and my friends (who are the family that I choose), I thank you so much and love you from the bottom of my heart.

ABOUT THE AUTHOR

Maurice Broaddus is a notorious egotist whose sole goal is to be a big enough name to be able to snub people at conventions. In anticipation of such a successful writing career, he is practicing speaking of himself in the third person. The "House of M" includes the lovely Sally Jo ("Mommy") and two boys: Maurice Gerald Broaddus II (thus, he gets to retroactively declare himself "Maurice the Great") and Malcolm Xavier Broaddus. Visit his site so he can bore you with details of all things him and most importantly, read his blog. He loves that. A lot.

Maurice holds a Bachelor of Science degree from Purdue University in Biology. Scientist, writer, and hack theologian, he's about the pursuit of Truth because all truth is God's truth. His dark fiction can be found in numerous magazine, anthologies and novellas.

www.mauricebroaddus.com

MAURICE BROADDUS

KING MAKER
THE KNIGHTS OF BRETON COURT

"THE BRILLIANCE WE'VE ALL BEEN WAITING FOR —
BROADDUS DELIVERS IN A VOICE THAT CANNOT BE
IGNORED." ~ GARY A. BRAUNBECK

The
Dragon
is
Rising

MAURICE BROADDUS

KING'S JUSTICE
THE KNIGHTS OF BRETON COURT II

"A TRIUMPH. BROADDUS HAS CREATED A MASTERPIECE
OF ORIGINAL, COMPELLING AND THOUGHT-PROVOKING
DRAMA, IRRESISTIBLE AND UNFORGETTABLE."
~ SF & FANTASY UK

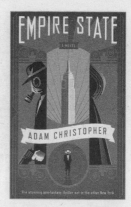

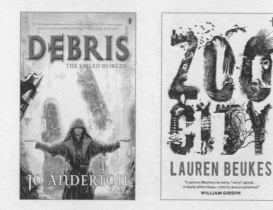

Let's go.

Twitter @angryrobotbooks

ANGRY
ROBOT

THE ONE WITH THE MOST "STUFF" WINS!

Snare the whole Angry Robot catalogue

DAN ABNETT
- [ ] Embedded
- [ ] Triumff: Her Majesty's Hero

GUY ADAMS
- [ ] The World House
- [ ] Restoration

JO ANDERTON
- [ ] Debris

LAUREN BEUKES
- [ ] Moxyland
- [ ] Zoo City

**THOMAS BLACKTHORNE
(aka John Meaney)**
- [ ] Edge
- [ ] Point

MAURICE BROADDUS
- [ ] King Maker
- [ ] King's Justice

PETER CROWTHER
- [ ] Darkness Falling

ALIETTE DE BODARD
- [ ] Servant of the Underworld
- [ ] Harbinger of the Storm
- [ ] Master of the House of Darts

MATT FORBECK
- [ ] Amortals
- [ ] Vegas Knights

JUSTIN GUSTAINIS
- [ ] Hard Spell

GUY HALEY
- [ ] Reality 36

COLIN HARVEY
- [ ] Damage Time
- [ ] Winter Song

MATTHEW HUGHES
- [ ] The Damned Busters

TRENT JAMIESON
- [ ] Roil

K W JETER
- [ ] Infernal Devices
- [ ] Morlock Night

J ROBERT KING
- [ ] Angel of Death
- [ ] Death's Disciples

GARY McMAHON
- [ ] Pretty Little Dead Things
- [ ] Dead Bad Things

ANDY REMIC
- [ ] Kell's Legend
- [ ] Soul Stealers
- [ ] Vampire Warlords

CHRIS ROBERSON
- [ ] Book of Secrets

MIKE SHEVDON
- [ ] Sixty-One Nails
- [ ] The Road to Bedlam

GAV THORPE
- [ ] The Crown of the Blood
- [ ] The Crown of the Conqueror

LAVIE TIDHAR
- [ ] The Bookman
- [ ] Camera Obscura

TIM WAGGONER
- [ ] Nekropolis
- [ ] Dead Streets
- [ ] Dark War

KAARON WARREN
- [ ] Mistification
- [ ] Slights
- [ ] Walking the Tree

IAN WHATES
- [ ] City of Dreams & Nightmare
- [ ] City of Hope & Despair